SPIRIT SERVICE

ALSO BY SARENA AND SASHA NANUA

Sisters of the Snake

Daughters of the Dawn

SPIRIT SERVICE

Sarena and Sasha Nanua

Simon & Schuster Books for Young Readers
NEW YORK   AMSTERDAM/ANTWERP   LONDON
TORONTO   SYDNEY/MELBOURNE   NEW DELHI

SIMON & SCHUSTER BOOKS FOR YOUNG READERS
An imprint of Simon & Schuster Children's Publishing Division
1230 Avenue of the Americas, New York, New York 10020
For more than 100 years, Simon & Schuster has championed authors and the stories they create. By respecting the copyright of an author's intellectual property, you enable Simon & Schuster and the author to continue publishing exceptional books for years to come. We thank you for supporting the author's copyright by purchasing an authorized edition of this book. No amount of this book may be reproduced or stored in any format, nor may it be uploaded to any website, database, language-learning model, or other repository, retrieval, or artificial intelligence system without express permission. All rights reserved. Inquiries may be directed to Simon & Schuster, 1230 Avenue of the Americas, New York, NY 10020
or permissions@simonandschuster.com.
This book is a work of fiction. Any references to historical events, real people, or real places are used fictitiously. Other names, characters, places, and events are products of the author's imagination, and any resemblance to actual events or places or persons, living or dead, is entirely coincidental.
Text © 2025 by Sarena Nanua and Sasha Nanua
Jacket illustration and interior map © 2025 by Liz Parkes
Jacket design by Sarah Creech
All rights reserved, including the right of reproduction in whole or in part in any form.
SIMON & SCHUSTER BOOKS FOR YOUNG READERS
and related marks are trademarks of Simon & Schuster, LLC.
For information about special discounts for bulk purchases, please contact Simon & Schuster Special Sales at 1-866-506-1949 or business@simonandschuster.com.
Simon & Schuster strongly believes in freedom of expression and stands against censorship in all its forms. For more information, visit BooksBelong.com.
The Simon & Schuster Speakers Bureau can bring authors to your live event.
For more information or to book an event, contact the Simon & Schuster Speakers Bureau at 1-866-248-3049 or visit our website at www.simonspeakers.com.
Interior design by Hilary Zarycky
The text for this book was set in New Spirit.
Manufactured in the United States of America
0325 BVG
First Edition
2 4 6 8 10 9 7 5 3 1
Library of Congress Cataloging-in-Publication Data
Names: Nanua, Sarena, author. | Nanua, Sasha, author.
Title: Spirit service / Sarena and Sasha Nanua.
Description: First edition. | New York : Simon & Schuster Books for Young Readers, 2025. | Audience term: Preteens | Audience: Ages 8-12. | Audience: Grades 4-6. | Summary: "A group of twelve-year-old girls start a small business helping their local neighborhood spirits pass on to the other side."— Provided by publisher.
Identifiers: LCCN 2024033698 (print) | LCCN 2024033699 (ebook) |
ISBN 9781665955171 (hardcover) | ISBN 9781665955195 (ebook)
Subjects: CYAC: Moneymaking projects—Fiction. | Spirits—Ficton. | Friendship—Fiction. | City and town life—Fiction.
Classification: LCC PZ7.1.N3615 Sp 2025 (print) | LCC PZ7.1.N3615 (ebook) |
DDC [Fic]—dc23
LC record available at https://lccn.loc.gov/2024033698
LC ebook record available at https://lccn.loc.gov/2024033699

*To Georgie Uncle—
your spirit, memory, joy, and laughter
will always live within our hearts*

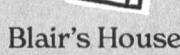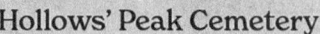

ONE

Ring, Ring, Ring, Your Doom Is Calling!

"It isn't fair."

Those were my three magic words. They weren't really magic; after all, magic didn't exist except in books and movies. But in the real world, magic was something else entirely. It was the itch in my nose when I needed to sneeze but stopped right before I could. It was the dream that vanished as soon as I woke up, like a stream of autumn leaves snatched by the wind.

Magic wasn't real. But according to my mom, I'd need a whole heaping spoonful of it if I wanted a cell phone before winter break ended and school began. Which was *tomorrow*.

Maybe I didn't need magic. I needed a miracle.

"Nothing's fair in life, Raveena," Mama countered, her rose-pink lips twisting into a frown as she skimmed a parenting magazine in Yoon's Antiques. Did she just get that line from her current reading material? Or maybe from her collection of Indian bridal magazines, which each started with a wannabe fortune cookie quote? (I might have snuck a glance at the latest issue. Plain saris are so last season, and don't get me started on accessories!)

"But Lillian always uses her phone to call her pops." That's what my BFF called her dad. "You know, to make sure he knows where she *is* for *safety purposes*." How could Mama reject my carefully worded counterargument now?

Truly unfazeable, Mama said, "You'll get your phone when eighth grade starts, like we agreed."

I faced The Boss one more time with my arms crossed. According to Lillian, every video game has a boss—someone to defeat if you ever want to win the game. Guess real life wasn't so different. Except this boss was my mother. And at this point, undefeated. Even my puppy-dog eyes (by now, I was almost Pomeranian) weren't working. I needed someone who would listen.

I needed Grandmama.

My heart squeezed. Mama never spoke so sternly to me when my nani was around. Once upon another time, Mama would've slipped her fingers through my hair playfully, wrecking my carefully parted bangs. But she hadn't done that since BGL.

Before Grandmama left.

I had to up the ante—convince Mama I needed a phone *now*, just like most of the other kids in my grade.

"Phones are more than just two-way talking devices, you know. You could track my every move! You could send me funny memes and check on me at lunch!"

"Not the memes argument again," Mama muttered, swapping the parenting magazine for the town newspaper. Splashed on the front page was a grand photo of City Hall. The headline read:

> ONE HUNDRED YEARS OF HOLLOWS' PEAK
> FESTIVAL ON THE HORIZON!

Before I could stop myself, I blurted out, "Grandmama would've let me get a cell phone. She wouldn't have even thought twice."

Mama froze. Her face darkened as she shuttered the *Hollows' Herald* closed and placed it back on the newsstand.

Striiiiike one! the imaginary umpire boomed in my head.

Instinctively, my mom reached for her pocket, where she once kept Grandmama's medicine. Now her pockets were cold and empty.

I caught her doing that often, reaching for something that was no longer there. The place setting for Grandmama at the kitchen table, the handheld radio she used to listen to the news. But it wasn't always something physical. Anytime I brought her up, Mama's eyes glazed over and her mind drifted, like she was reaching for warm memories that had gone stale. You know how cinnamon buns taste best when they're fresh and warm and slightly pillowy in the center? That's exactly what my memories of Grandmama were, and they were just as sweet. Yet the empty look on Mama's face, recalling her memories wasn't sweet but sour.

Before either of us could say anything, Mr. Yoon waddled out from his knee-high pile of flyers behind the cash register.

"I have your reserved box of items in the back!" the owner of Yoon's Antiques called out, his kind eyes smiling at Mama, rimmed by half-moon glasses. "Are you looking for anything else today, Ms. Gill?"

Mama nodded before drawing out an old No Frills receipt from her jacket pocket, giving me a look that said, *We'll finish this conversation later.* On the back of the receipt, she'd written a whole slew of strange things. Polka-dot shoelaces. Steel-toed boots. Fireproof oven mitts. (Maybe that one wasn't so strange; who would design oven mitts that could catch fire?)

My mom rattled off the list to Mr. Yoon as I snuck away to the back of the store. Yoon's Antiques was the beating heart of Hollows' Peak—or at least the best place to get a buy-one-get-two-and-a-half deal around here. If someone from out of town visited Hollows' Peak, they'd use the *W* word. *Weird.* But in my hometown, where we celebrated reverse birthdays and gave cats belly rubs, there was nothing really off-limits.

I dashed around a series of wonky bookshelves, filled with everything from joke books to prehistoric encyclopedias, before reaching the back of the store. My besties were already waiting for me, as predicted.

Correction: they were making googly eyes at the store's resident pet fish. Yoon's Antiques had a wide tank with a single puffer fish inside, who always gave me a blank look. Jenna Yoon, who I babysat last summer and was already nearing the size of her family's full-grown husky, aptly called him Pufflepants and even doted on him like she did their dog. But Pufflepants and I weren't on speaking terms just yet.

"Is Pufflepants badmouthing me again?" I joked.

Aiko spun, her brilliant rainbow-dyed hair as colorful as the camp bracelets on her wrist. "There you are! If you were another second late, he *definitely* would've started talking."

"I think he already is," Blair said, leaning close to the glass and pretending to hold a mic up to Pufflepants's mouth. "He's telling me . . . we should hurry up and get boba like we planned!"

Lillian chuckled. "Blair Ricci, fish whisperer and investigative reporter in training."

"Following in your mother's footsteps," I added.

Blair's brown eyes sparkled. "Yeah, except for the fish part."

We all burst into a fit of giggles as Mrs. Yoon came around the bend.

"Is that the Fierce Four I hear?" She pinned a flyer to the wall that read 20% OFF WHEN YOU SPEND $50 OR MORE BEFORE TAXES, COUPONS, AND REVERSE BIRTHDAY CERTIFICATES. "Are you girls excited to go back to school tomorrow?"

There was a reason Mrs. Yoon, our school's music teacher, had dubbed us the Fierce Four last year. We did almost everything together: Our science project on rising sea levels won first place at the Hollows' Peak Middle School fair. Our French presentation on the negative impact of settlers on Indigenous soil got us an A+ and a *fantastique* from Madame Bower. Even though Blair and Lillian were in a different homeroom from me and Aiko this year, we vowed to remain fierce friends.

"Yep!" Lillian nodded excitedly at Mrs. Yoon, her tight coils bouncing in two Princess Leia–style buns. She was always changing up her style according to the latest K-pop trends. "I just wish I could go back to playing in school." She made a motion with her hands as if she were practicing the fingering to an alto saxophone. She could play the chromatic scale like it was nobody's business.

"Me too, girls. Raveena, I hope you're also practicing your flute?" Mrs. Yoon smiled, though it was pretty clear she was hiding sadness beneath it. This school year wasn't the same as the last—and not just because Grandmama was gone.

I mimed playing the flute with my fingers. "I remember all my keys." What I *didn't* want to remember was what Lillian and I had dubbed the Day of Doom four months ago, when Principal Hanover had called the whole school into the gym for a big announcement.

"This year will look different, students," he'd begun with a sallow face. *"Unfortunately, this year, we have no room in the budget for the arts program...."*

I didn't hear the rest of his sentence. My ears felt like they were dunked underwater. Based on Mrs. Yoon's eye bags, it wasn't hard to decipher what was going on.

They were cutting the arts program at school. Not just a portion of it—the whole enchilada.

What's the big deal? I heard some kids snickering. Sports kids, jocks with rich parents. Meanwhile, my heart was shriveling like a stale raisin. (Raisins are gross, stale or not.) Apparently the price of laptops and electronic textbooks were on the rise. Even with government funding, Mrs. Yoon had told me that the school's arts program would likely not recover.

Cue disastrous, world-ending music.

"I'm glad to hear it," said Mrs. Yoon, pinning another flyer to the wall. Her short black bob brushed her chin as she added over her shoulder, "You've always been driven students, girls. Music class or not."

Yeah, driven enough to move my butt all the way to computer science. Not that I had a choice. Most music students, including me and Lillian, were dropped into foreign territory—also known as comp-sci. Lillian told me she kept her saxophone by the front door, as if any day Principal Hanover and the school board might change their minds. I'd be lying if I said I didn't do the same thing with my flute. It was Grandmama who had pushed me into music, after all, just as she had with my mom.

I could almost feel Grandmama's fingers hovering over mine as she helped me read my sheet music. Her favorite piece was "Canon in D," and so was mine, because it felt like a warm, velvety hug when winter breathed a chill into the air. Although I wasn't skilled enough to handle the major parts on my own, Grandmama always made it seem easy. A deep breath from my diaphragm to fix my posture, a nudge of my elbow to adjust my positioning. She grew up with music in every corner of her house, from harmoniums to pianos to tablas, and wanted the same for her daughter and granddaughter.

"Oh!" Mrs. Yoon's eyes lit up. "I almost forgot to ask—how's fundraising going? The school business competition is really heating up, I hear." Using a price tag gun, she slid a reduced-price label onto the base of a snow globe. "The group of girls in eighth grade looking to start an after-school baking program are close to first place. No pun intended, but they might just . . . take the cake!"

Mrs. Yoon was always trying to get a laugh out of us. But in reality, I was too busy mulling over who might actually be in first—a team with a boy-who-must-not-be-named. I'd been refreshing the school website all break for any updates, but nada.

"Our . . . *business model* kind of needs work," Aiko admitted, toying with her bracelets.

Not long after the Day of Doom, Principal Hanover announced a schoolwide competition to help teach kids about business endeavors. Something about the youth of today being our tomorrow, or maybe I'd just read that on the underside of a soda bottle cap. Any group that entered could start a small business and raise money in the town. The group that made the most money by the end of the school year would get to use all the funds toward whatever school activity they wanted, like getting a new computer lab or an extra set of vending machines, or, in the Fierce Four's case, bringing back the arts program.

But we were collecting chump change compared to the other competitors. Our business title wasn't too hot, either. Get Everything Done! was our way of giving back to the community. Need your driveway shoveled? Aiko had your back. Bake sale? Blair was on it. Playing the sax at the Hollows' Peak Retirement Home? Lillian was your girl. Still, it never quite seemed like we were close enough to reaching our fundraising goal. It didn't help that most adults—you know, the people with actual *money* and who made actual *decisions*—wouldn't take our business goal to save the arts program seriously.

The arts made us who we were, so why couldn't adults value it the way we did?

"Raveena, hon? Let's get going to Benny's Boba," Mama called from the front of the store.

"There are my marching orders," I deadpanned, but truthfully, my mouth was watering at the thought of my go-to order: taro milk tea with lychee popping boba. Yum!

I waved goodbye to Mrs. Yoon, who said she was leaving for her lunch break, and left the others to say their fishy-faced farewells to Pufflepants. Mama, now standing before the register, was handing Mr. Yoon a wad of cash. I lifted the heavy, half-broken box off the front counter. Some might call what lay within treasure; others, junk. I'd been watching enough *Storage Wars* with Mama to know the difference, and right now it was the latter.

"Before I forget," Mr. Yoon said as he closed the register, "we just got a matching glassware set in the back. I know you love the Martha Stewart Collection!"

"Martha, you say?" Mama pretended to think it over. "David, you know I can't resist a good deal."

"Who the heck is Martha Stewart?" I mumbled to myself as Mama disappeared around the corner. So much for *Let's get going to Benny's Boba!* Were grownups always so easily distracted by home goods?

The truth was, Mama couldn't turn down a good antique. Leave it to old, dusty piles of *stuff* to get my mom excited. Sometimes I wondered if she loved antiquing because it reminded her of a forgotten era with Grandmama. I always caught her staring at the dishware my grandmother had brought over from India back in the seventies. Pieces of history that had been collected and displayed like precious memories of the past.

I took two steps toward the front door as Mama and Mr. Yoon became engrossed in the glassware out back. "Hey, guys," I called out, pretending to step through the exit, "last one here gets warm boba!"

Lillian, Blair, and Aiko arrived at the front of the shop in record time, likely already rehearsing their orders. Aiko hunched over, catching her breath, like the thought of room-temperature boba was blasphemy. A second later, Lillian glanced in horror at the broken box in my arms, shifting a few items around. "What on earth is *that*?"

"It looks . . . ancient!" Blair shuddered out.

"Terrible," Aiko added. "Terribly *beautiful*. I like it."

I set the box down on the floor, curiosity overheating my body. Were they talking about those polka-dot shoelaces? They couldn't be that bad. I investigated what my friends were staring at, and my eyes landed on a big, blocky remnant of the past.

A *corded phone.*

The phone was a soft baby pink with a vintage slim handset, the cord all tangled up in knots. Its delicate shiny buttons, which rotated in a circle, looked like they were about to pop out any minute now. Where the paint was chipping off, brownish-black marks revealed themselves underneath, like burnt spots on toast.

Aiko gaped in awe. "OMG. This is giving me major *The Goonies* treasure-hunting vibes. You just don't see these kinds of rotary phones anymore!"

Of course Aiko would go gaga over old tech. Her mother had been a classic movie buff, and Aiko had eighties movie aficionado genes in her blood. Mama Tanaka passed away when Aiko was nine, but we all still felt her presence.

The phone's buttons shone like pearls, drawing me in. And I wasn't the only one stepping closer. The other girls were too, each of us craning our necks as if the object were hypnotizing us.

Together, each of us reached out a hand, the phone practically begging us to touch it. . . .

Zap!

"Ouch!" I pulled back my hand. What was that? I stared at my tingling fingers, then at Blair, Lillian, and Aiko. Each of them was gazing at her own hands in fright. Blair looked the most terrified of all, watching as tiny white sparks flushed down her skin and disappeared.

"You all felt that, right?" I asked, just to make sure I wasn't imagining it.

"The phone," Blair began timidly. "It . . ."

"Nearly zapped our fingers off?" Aiko finished.

Lillian's brown skin flushed pale. "What *was* that?"

We all stared back down at the phone. Lillian reached into the box with an inquisitive hand, but I held her back with an arm.

"Lillian, you could get zapped again!"

"I *have* to test my hypothesis," she argued. For Lillian, science was always at the root of everything. Instead of enjoying the magic of a beautiful sunset, she preferred to explain the way light scattered in the atmosphere to form different colors.

"By getting electrocuted?" said Blair.

Lillian ignored us as she blew out a breath and grabbed the phone. I squeezed one eye shut, preparing for another electrical charge as she set the phone on the front counter.

Nothing happened.

"That was some static shock, huh?" I joked. Because what else could it have been?

Blair wiped her brow with relief; Aiko slumped with disappointment.

That was when things got weird.

Lights flickered overhead. The ground momentarily rumbled beneath the soles of my sneakers, making my knees quiver. Even the paperwork on Mr. Yoon's counter fluttered from an unseen breeze.

Blair shrank back. "What's going on?"

Lillian stared up at the lights. "Maybe a power surge? Or an issue with the air vents?"

Just as she finished speaking, a light bulb exploded nearby. We all yelped in unison. Every light source fizzled out one by one, plunging the store into darkness.

No—a dewy silver light was now streaming out of the phone like mist escaping Niagara Falls, filling the air with an otherworldly glow.

The aura from the phone was unlike anything I'd ever seen. White light escaped every hole and button, like smoke escaping a chimney.

And at that exact moment, the phone rang.

TWO

Spirits Say What?

The phone kept on ringing. And ringing. And ringing.

"Okay, this is officially creepy." Blair clung to her long brown braid as her gaze volleyed from the broken light bulb to the glowing phone.

Even Lillian's usual bravado disappeared in the consuming darkness. "Is anyone going to pick that up?"

Baffled, I asked, "How can it ring if it's not plugged in?"

"Guys . . ." Concern pinched Aiko's features, and her lips wrinkled like a sealed drawstring bag as she pulled the coiled cord forward and held it up.

The end was frayed and broken.

My fingers tingled hot and cold, cold and hot. I tugged the phone closer until it was teetering on the edge of the counter.

Brrrrrrrrrring. Brrrrrrrrrring. The phone vibrated, and I cautiously closed a hand over the handset, reminding myself there was nothing weird about an old phone ringing in an antique shop.

Except that it was broken. And it had zapped us. And it was *definitely* glowing.

I glanced around at each of the other girls before lifting the receiver to my ear. "H-hello?"

At first, silence. Then a shaky breath echoed from the other side. It was loud enough that I had to shrink back from the handset. Lillian, Aiko, and Blair leaned in to listen, mouths agape.

"Grand ... daughter ..."

I froze. The voice was frail, like a collection of broken glass fragments cupped in my palms. My mind immediately shot back to when Grandmama and I would call each other using our matching Barbie cell phones and make reservations for high tea with my stuffed animals.

"I'd like a table for two, please," Grandmama would say with a wink. *"I prefer English breakfast tea and not to be seated next to Mr. Fuzzies."* My teddy bear was not one for sharing.

Now I kept the phones together in my desk drawer, like a pair of twins that could never be separated. They weren't broken, but somehow, it felt like they were.

I almost said Grandmama's name aloud into the rotary phone. My hands were shaking so hard that Aiko reached out to steady the handset. "Who's there?" she asked gently.

"*Mija* ...," the voice continued.

Mija? That wasn't what Grandmama had called me. She'd called me *beti*.

I would recognize her voice anywhere. And this one definitely wasn't hers.

Disappointment weighed me down like a rock

sinking to the ocean floor. This wasn't another day playing phones with my fearless grandmother. She wasn't going to answer the call, just like she never answered with our Barbie phones after she left.

"*I need Marisol...*," continued the voice cryptically. It sounded like something ancient, something old as hidden treasure... like someone who'd grown up in the *1900s*.

"Marisol?" echoed Blair. "As in... Marisol *Pérez*? The-boy-who-must-not-be-named's younger sister?"

My eyebrows slashed downward at the thought of my ex-best friend. "Maybe this old lady is talking about a *different* Marisol," I assumed. "Right, Miss...?"

Static crackled from the other side. "*Gabriela Pérez...*"

Aiko covered the receiver to muffle our voices. "So it *is* Marisol's grandmother?"

"I thought she was..." Blair's voice grew small as she made a not-so-savory motion across her neck.

"Don't say it. It's just a disembodied voice," Lillian reasoned, "not a phone call from beyond the grave. Besides, who knows if this is *the* grandma who died? Gabriela could realistically be from her stepmom's side." Leave it to Lillian to turn to deductive reasoning.

The voice became more insistent. "*I need your help. I need Marisol's...*" She trailed off.

"Marisol's what?" Aiko said into the phone. "What do you need of hers?"

The voice let out a breathy sigh before a beeping

dial tone filled the air. The phone call was over. The lights flickered back on, the electrical issue seemingly fixed.

I held up the frayed end of the power cord while Lillian and Blair exchanged worried looks.

"Do you think that was a prank?" I asked, although that old lady's voice sounded serious. Did it truly belong to Marisol's grandmother?

"I don't think so," Lillian said, scratching her shoulder. She always did that when she was nervous. Aiko replaced the phone in its cradle with a satisfying *click*, and the glowing ceased.

Definitely. Super. Strange.

"It had to be," I said firmly. "Because if it wasn't . . ."

Aiko's eyes widened. "There can only be one explanation." She paused for dramatic effect. "Aliens."

"Not again," Blair muttered.

"Come on!" Aiko threw her hands up. "*E.T. phone home.* It's a classic! Maybe that person on the line wasn't a person at all—"

The bell over the front door to Yoon's Antiques rang overhead. Mr. Yoon called out. "I'll be right with you!"

"Quick, get in front of the phone," I told the others. We all lined up not-so-suspiciously in front of it as a boy wearing paint-splattered canvas sneakers, beige trousers, and a designer down-filled jacket swaggered inside. My skin flamed at the sight of him—and not just because of that weird phone call. I would recognize that mess of brown curls anywhere.

Mateo Pérez.

"Well, that's not freaky at all," Lillian whispered as she glanced at the phone behind us and then at Mateo.

Mateo's hazel eyes landed on each of the other girls before finding mine. I caught sight of my reflection in a nearby antique mirror. Heat climbed my cheeks, turning my skin so red I might as well have been a tomato in a Campbell's soup commercial. My straight black hair was frizzy, matching my midnight eyes. There was a small bump along the bridge of my nose that Mama told me I'd inherited from my father. I couldn't remember what he looked like, nor what his surname was. Mama kept her maiden name.

"Hi, guys. Hey, Raveena," Mateo said coolly, freckles dancing along his sun-warmed cheeks. His seashell necklace glinted in the store lights.

"Mateo," I responded, injecting as much venom into the three syllables as humanly possible. Tension crackled in the air like thunder. Or maybe it was just the leftover energy from the phone zapping us.

"I saw you through the window," he said, pointing backward while still looking at me. "I mean, all of you. How's winter break been?"

Hold up—Mateo was paying attention to *me*? A weird sort of smile crept onto my face that I'm sure put the *It* clown to shame. Someone must have replaced Mateo with a kind-smiling robot version of him, 'cause this was *so* not the boy I knew. Wait, maybe he was putting on a phony—pardon the pun—voice to appear nice.

My smile instantly deflated. I could see right through that charade!

"Fine," I clipped just as Lillian enthusiastically replied, "Great!"

I nudged Lillian in the ribs. *"Ouch,"* she muttered.

"Cool." Mateo Pérez shifted his favorite basketball from hand to hand as he glanced me up and down. *Me, Raveena Gill, his classmate for the past several years and, more recently, semi-nemesis.* Not that he knew that. I pretended like everything was cordial—a fancy term for *just fine, thanks*—after he abandoned our breakdance practice for the talent show last year, joining a group of popular seventh graders and leaving me in the dust like tumbleweed. Mateo never apologized for it. Not yet, anyway.

I wasn't going to be the first one to break the ice. Until he apologized to *me*, I planned to keep up my carefully crafted charade: calm, casual, and noncommittal. I didn't want him to know how badly his actions stung me, especially when it seemed like he didn't remember what happened.

Mateo smiled, showing off his irritatingly pearly teeth. "My little sis is having her reverse birthday party in an hour. You should all come! We're going to the local roller rink. It's backward-only day; no skating forward, or you owe me a soda."

Of course it was. Everyone in this town celebrated their birthday not on the day of, but the day before. Legend had it that a town mayor almost choked on his loose front tooth during his fortieth birthday party after he wrestled with a piece of corn on the cob and deemed birthdays a not-so-auspicious day. For whatever reason, the tradition of celebrating the day prior stuck.

"Sorry, Mateo. We have to work on something *actually* important." There. Let him fester in *that*.

He shrugged, catching no malice in my voice. "Okay. What are you all working on?" Mateo's eyes lit up. "It's the business competition, isn't it? What's your business name again?"

"*GetEffreythingDone*," mumbled Blair.

"Hmm?" Mateo leaned in as if he genuinely misheard.

"We're . . . working on a new name. Right, girls?" I said through gritted teeth. No need to air our dirty laundry in front of the seventh-grade class president.

Aiko nodded awkwardly next to me. Lillian whistled while avoiding eye contact. Blair looked like she wanted to crawl into a hole, which, to be fair, was how she looked 99 percent of the time.

"I'm sure it'll be great," Mateo assured us, but I could tell he meant, *Not as great as mine.* "After all, you are the Fierce Four."

Practically the entire school knew we were all tight—especially after Mrs. Yoon gave us our group name—but back in third grade I was only besties with Aiko. That year, we'd become friends after working together on so many projects. *And* we were learning Japanese together during recess. We were inseparable!

Then, the following year, everything changed.

There was no reason for me and Aiko to sit at Blair's lunch table that fateful day, but something compelled us to approach her. Nine-year-old Blair Ricci, who probably said a total of three words in class all year, was giving me major passive-aggressive side-eye and asking if I came to taste test her latest batch of jack-o'-lantern milk chocolate cookies. Turned out her stink eye was her version of a painfully shy *Hey, I have extra. Want some?*

"Yeah, can I try one? They look so good," I'd said brightly. Blair's demeanor totally shifted after that, and from the first bite I started calling her Blair, Baker Extraordinaire. She introduced me to her bestie and neighbor Lillian Baxter, who was listening to some K-pop tunes through her earbuds and scribbling down lyrics in the shape of scientific equations.

It made sense that we had our own little cliques before becoming besties. We were two halves of a broken painting, and only when we all came together could you see the bigger, beautiful picture.

"Maybe I'll catch you guys at the party?" Mateo's eyes were glued to mine as he awaited my response. Something about that look made all my confidence burrow away like a bear in the winter.

"M-maybe," I said shakily. I would gladly join Blair in that hole now. And right when I thought I could return to school as "Cool Raveena!" You know, the kind of girl who changes so much over the break you hardly recognize her—either from a trip to Paris, or a new makeup palette, or from a three-day volunteer session with homeless pups.

Nope. I was still me, and I had to deal with it.

Just as Mateo was about to exit the store, Aiko piped up: "We're so sorry for your loss!"

Mateo halted, tucking his basketball under his arm. "Oh." He spun around. "You mean my grandma. Thanks for your condolences. It's been a tough few months without her." His gaze caught mine, as if he was thinking about my losing Grandmama, too. I'd never spoken to him directly about it.

"Was her name, by chance... *Gabriela*?" Aiko raised a brow.

"Yeah. How'd you know?" Mateo cocked his head to the side.

Blair went into panic mode. "We must have seen it in the newspaper obituary section! RIP, Gabriela!"

"... Right." Mateo turned to me, his eyes softening. "See ya." He gave us a salute and exited the store.

Aiko spun to us. "Did you just *hear* that?" She giddily jumped up and down. "Mateo—"

Blair cleared her throat.

"I mean, *the-boy-who-must-not-be-named* just invited us to his little sister's birthday party! I don't think he's spoken this many words to us since sixth grade."

"*And* whoever was calling us on the phone wanted to talk to Marisol," said Lillian. "Sorry, Aiko, but I don't think your alien theory is cutting it."

"Agreed," I added. "Isn't this all a little strange?"

Aiko glanced at the old rotary phone. "It would be strange . . . if I weren't an avid watcher of *Short Island Medium* and already a certified Ghost Girlie."

Blair groaned. "Here we go again." On top of being an eighties movie aficionado, Aiko Tanaka was the world's biggest ghost-hunting-television-show fanatic.

"What?" Aiko placed her hands akimbo. "Do *you* guys have another explanation?"

"A *ghost* called the phone?" I scoffed.

Aiko blew a colorful strand of hair out of her eyes. "Listen, I'm not Lillian Einstein over here. I don't know how this phone works. But what if this phone is, like, ghost-adjacent?" Aiko always got jittery with excitement when it came to anything remotely paranormal. She also liked to use fancy-pants words like *adjacent*, which we just learned in Language Arts for a vocab test. "If a ghost called the phone, then that means the phone can connect us . . . to the other side!"

Blair shook her head. "Nonono. I don't do well with horror. You guys know that!"

"And the presence of spirits has been debunked by tons of scientists," argued Lillian.

I had to agree with Lillian on this one—this was a stretch—but how else could we explain a *dead person* calling a *broken* phone?

Aiko carried on. "C'mon, fierce fam! The fact that Gabriela is dead should be enough to convince you!"

"I guess it didn't *seem* like a prank call," Blair agreed reluctantly.

I suppose there was *some* proof ghosts were real, especially in our snug little town. The town's namesake came from its founders—the Hollows. In 1925, Rose Hollow settled into a newly forming Toronto neighborhood and served on the mayoral committee after departing from her ancestral home in New Orleans. She wasn't wealthy by any means, but she *was* determined to make a name for herself. Turns out she made a name for her whole family when she revealed that she had an eye for the world beyond "the veil." She claimed to be a medium—someone who could talk to and see *ghosts*. Her whole family had a knack for it. Her daughter, Carmela, had a gift for seeing child spirits who made mischief all over town. Her son, Elijah, was a spirit magnet, drawing any ghost from within thirty miles to his family's humble abode with just a snap of his fingers.

But imagining *real* ghosts wasn't exactly lifting my "spirits." Because if ghosts existed, wouldn't Grandmama have visited me by now?

Anyway, there still was no explanation for how this phone worked. Most likely, Blair and Aiko were wrong, and this *was* a prank call. Who knew—maybe Mateo was behind this whole thing. He *had* stopped into the store today just to speak to me, which was very un-Mateo-like. Maybe I finally got under his skin the way he did mine? And this phone trick was some elaborate plan to shake me up?

Ha, I showed him!

Footsteps echoed from the back of the store. Mr. Yoon and Mama appeared in sight, and I quickly stuffed the phone back into the box before either of them could notice.

"Hmm," Mr. Yoon said. "Looks like the customer is gone. And what happened to that light bulb? I knew I should've replaced it last week," he grumbled. "Well, at least you've got some new china to add to your collection, huh, Ms. Gill?"

"And a thinning wallet," Mama joked.

I turned to Mr. Yoon. "You guys didn't see anything strange back there? No flickering lights?"

"Or a well-timed earthquake?" Blair squeaked out.

Mama shook her head. "You girls and your imaginations. Why don't you go grab your boba? I'll meet you there." Mama's eyes flashed with a misty memory when her eyes landed on mine—clearly she hadn't forgotten about how I'd brought up Grandmama during our cell phone debate.

I nodded quickly and escaped Yoon's Antiques unscathed. Mama would have a stern talk with me later, but that wasn't important right now.

"We should go to that birthday party and figure out what's up. Phone included," I told Aiko, Blair, and Lillian as we stood in the frigid cold outside Yoon's Antiques.

Blair's breath came out in puffs. "What happened to *We're working on something* actually *important*?"

Lillian wrung her fingers together. "I know Mateo hasn't been the same since he started hanging out with older kids, but maybe we should give him another chance?"

"Well, I need boba, or I'll melt into a puddle like the Wicked Witch of the West!" said Aiko.

"Boba first," I agreed—seriously, someone should plaster that on a T-shirt—"but after that, we need answers. And there's only one way to find them." I squared my shoulders. "We're going to the roller rink."

THREE

I Face an Angry Grandma with Killer Hockey Moves

Peter's Roller Palace, named after the establishment's owner (and not Peter Rabbit like I thought as a child), hadn't changed a bit. It even had the same distinct odor of melted cheese, guacamole, and rubber. The floors were carpeted in a flashy disco pattern, the wooden tables and chairs still creaked at the slightest movements, and the giant statue of roller skates at the front hadn't been rid of its graffiti.

But the reverse birthday party brought *some* new life to the place—including the screams of ten eight-year-olds playing Simon Says.

"I said *Marisol* says that time!" shouted a girl gleefully. She tapped her freckled nose and then pointed at a small boy in front of her. She shook free her crown full of curls, topped with a glittering tiara. "You're out!"

"But you're Marisol, and you said to touch your toes!" the boy complained.

"I'm not Simon, but you still do what I say. *That* doesn't make any sense, does it?" Marisol countered. The group of kids looked around in confusion. Before they could launch into a debate on the logistics of a children's game, a man arrived with two boxes of pizza, sending the kids into a tizzy over pepperoni and cheese heaven.

"Your mom dropped us off just in time," Lillian said after sucking up the last of her iced pineapple-passion-fruit tea.

"Yeah. Anyone see Mateo?" I didn't know why facing down Mateo brought an avalanche of sweat to my underarms when we'd just seen him an hour ago. Maybe it was the sugar from all that boba. I gripped the bulky phone tighter. "He's got to be around here somewhere."

"Maybe he's already on the rink," offered Blair, still slurping on her mango slush. She'd barely drunk any of it on the way to Peter's Roller Palace, too caught up in the thought that we'd spoken to a *literal dead person*. If that was true. *Anyone* could have called the phone and called themselves Gabriela. And I had a sneaking suspicion that that person was Mateo.

The four of us closed in on the wide oval-shaped, shiny wood-floored rink, but Mateo was nowhere to be found.

"Let's split up," I decided.

We each scoured the roller rink like we were detectives in an Agatha Christie novel. Mama devoured her books when I was younger, but she didn't have much time for reading lately. Raising me alone, and especially without Grandmama, was tougher on her than she would admit. Maybe I'd inherited some of her stubbornness. And a love of whodunnits.

"You came," a familiar voice announced from behind me.

I whirled. Bingo.

Mateo's eyes homed in on the phone in my hands. "What's that? You didn't need to bring a gift."

"It's not a gift," I huffed, then pasted on a nonchalant smile. "You called me on it. You wanted to prank me and my friends, so tell me why."

Mateo frowned. "I don't know what you're talking about, Gill."

Ugh, he'd pulled the last name card. I hadn't called him Pérez since sixth grade (pre-talent show fiasco), when we regularly hung out at his moms' taqueria. My mouth watered as I thought of El Grillo's homemade street corn tacos with cotija cheese and spicy salsa verde. I hadn't eaten one of those in a long time. "Mateo, tell me the *real* reason you called me."

"What?" Mateo rubbed the back of his neck. "Seriously, I didn't call you. I thought you didn't have a phone."

"I don't. I . . ." Why did Mateo know that about me? "I don't know how you did it, but making this rotary phone glow and ring—that's another level of *weird*." Mateo was nearby Yoon's Antiques when the phone first glowed, *and* we'd gotten a call about his little sister. *Coincidence? I think not.*

He must have been the reason behind all this . . . *otherworldliness*. "Admit it. You wanted me to come here."

"Okay," Mateo said blandly. "I wanted you to come here."

"Why? For another prank?" My voice pitched higher, a sure sign that my temper was rising. So much for calm, casual, and noncommittal.

"Just . . . because. And I swear, I never called you. Now can we get to roller-skating? You can grab your size over there at the counter." Mateo nodded at the shoe guy, who I recognized was the same guy who brought out the pizzas when we came in. Must've been a staffing shortage. Or an unfortunate job posting.

"I don't roller-skate." I crossed my arms. "I mean . . . I can't."

"Then I'll save you a lesson," Mateo said smugly. Where was this boast of confidence and bravado earlier? Boys. They were just a box of puzzle pieces without a guide, impossible to put together and understand.

"I'll think about it." (I wasn't going to think about it.)

Because Mateo and I were more than just sixth-grade talent show partners. We had been good friends once— *best* friends since the first grade. We raced each other on our bikes and pretended we were knights in a joust. We visited each other's homes every month, with our moms being good friends, and traded Pokémon cards like they were rare jewels. We even used to bake horchata cookies together. It was strange how easily all of that went away. Mama got busy with work and stopped meeting Mia, one of Mateo's moms, after Grandmama's passing. And after the talent show last year, all I felt between me and Mateo was a cold block of ice.

I wasn't all Elsa-mode, though. When Mateo's grandmother died a few months ago, Mama cooked up batches of soup and butter chicken to give to them, like neighbors welcoming each other to the street. Except this wasn't a welcome thing at all. Months earlier, I'd learned exactly how it felt to lose a grandparent, as if someone had drilled a screw into my heart. Was he feeling the same way about his grandmother? I couldn't know for sure, because we weren't talking. Not like we used to.

Before Mateo could return to backward skating, a group of his friends rolled up in their gear, sporting icy blue elbow and knee pads. Eighth graders.

"Mateo! Come on, let's roll!"

"Coming," he said, but just as he turned away, one of his friends—Jaiden DeVoss—grabbed on to his shoulder and pointed at me.

"Is this the girl trying to save the arts program?" His jaw hung open. I looked around, but I was the only person in the area.

"Y-yes, that's me." I cleared my throat. An eighth grader actually recognized *me*! This was my first big celebrity moment, and I wasn't about to mess it up. "Autographs—"

Jaiden snickered. "That's so dumb. Keepin' It One Hunnid is making money for the Hollows' Peak Haunts." That was the name of our school's basketball team, which Jaiden and Mateo happened to be a part of, topped to a tee with a mascot of a ghost. We liked being on the nose around here, in case you didn't know.

Their business name was also pretty eye-roll worthy.

All they did was plaster the red *100* emoji on anything you wanted. T-shirts? Sneakers? Backpacks? Babies? Okay . . . maybe not that last one, but apparently their "merch" was worn by every eighth grader in Hollows' Peak, and then some. It also helped that Jaiden's parents owned a clothing line and were currently expanding into the ever-lucrative key chain business.

"Our team's pump is fried, and our jerseys are so old-school." Jaiden skated closer to me. "Don't you think *your* team should be making money for something important too?"

Now I was the one trying not to let my jaw fall open. "Excuse me?"

All the eighth graders, chuckling and high-fiving their ringleader, went back to the rink. Mateo's mouth opened and closed like a fish, as if he were unsure what to say. Finally, he landed on, "Maybe Jaiden's right. Get Everything Done! isn't exactly working wonders." He looked back at the group of eighth graders, who were hollering for him to come over. "I'm sure you'll come up with something. And thanks for coming. I'll see you around?"

He didn't wait for me to answer. Instead, he rolled away, and my vision turned red. Why was he acting so different from when he was around just me and my besties? He went out of his way to invite me to his sister's party and then treated me like a total stranger? Years of friendship, gone. And worse, he didn't even stand up for our arts program.

He didn't stand up for *me*.

Little did he know why our business meant so much to me. It wasn't just about bringing the arts back to our school. It was about fulfilling Grandmama's final wishes.

To keep pursuing my art. My passion.

Only six months had gone by since Grandmama's passing, but it still felt like a fresh wound unable to be stitched closed. Mateo's friends making fun of Get Everything Done! was the last straw. It wasn't just making fun of me or my friends. It was about Grandmama.

"At least I don't rely on my parents to get pity money!" I shouted at his back.

Mateo looked over his shoulder, his skin flushing red. I didn't even know it could *do* that.

Oh, pickles.

Well, I wasn't totally wrong, though. There was a big rumor going around that the eighth graders, Jaiden included, had gotten most of their funds from wealthy family members. Totally *not* cool.

But yelling at Mateo's back wasn't cool, either.

I couldn't take back what I said, but I also didn't want to give Mateo the satisfaction of an apology when *he* couldn't even offer me one to begin with. So I stormed away, my face leaping from one emotion to the next. I wasn't sure if I should be enraged at Mateo and his friends or embarrassed by my outburst. But I knew one thing: I wasn't about to get upset the day before school started, not over silly eighth graders—and *especially* not over Mateo Pérez.

The arts mattered just as much as a pump or a jersey. I just needed to prove it.

"Raveena, over here!" Blair called. I spotted her near Marisol's friends, although Marisol was nowhere in sight. The kids were currently entangled in a game of pin the tail on the ghost. (Donkeys are overrated.)

I caught up with Blair, who looked like she was out of breath from corralling the children. "I need help getting away from the kids. Where are the chaperones at this party?"

I shook my head. I hadn't seen Mateo's parents at all, either. "I think Mateo's in charge or something." Not that he seemed to care, too busy hanging with his "cool" friends. I wrinkled my nose at the thought.

"You spoke to him again?" Blair arched a brow before one of the kids tugged on her hand, ready to blindfold her.

"Yeah. I don't think he was the mystery caller."

"So, bust?" Blair said, fighting against another kid pulling her leg toward the ghost board, which had a tail on just about everywhere but its behind.

Lillian stumbled over to us, hair buns lopsided. "Not necessarily," she huffed, out of breath. "Marisol might be able to get us some answers."

Lillian moved aside to reveal Marisol. She strolled toward us, sporting glittery fairy wings on her back and matching fuchsia sneakers.

"Hey, there you are, Marisol! Cool party!" Blair had finally freed herself of the last child, who'd forgotten about her in favor of the Timbits and doughnuts from Tim Hortons.

Marisol gave her a look like, *Who are you again?*

Lillian bent down so she and Marisol were at eye level. "Do you mind telling us about your grandma? Did she call you mija?"

I could tell what Lillian *really* wanted to ask: *Can you please explain why we got a phone call from your deceased grandmother asking for you?*

Marisol nodded. "I just came from the bathroom, where I saw my abuelita."

I exchanged a loaded glance with Lillian and Blair. Did she say *abuelita*? As in her *grandmother*?

"But . . . ," Marisol continued.

"Yes?" Blair tapped a pink Converse sneaker furiously on the carpeted floor. She hated not getting answers out of people—a consequence of her mom's reporter job on Channel 13 News.

"She wanted this." Marisol pointed at the hair bow in her curls. "It belonged to her mamá. But I told her it completes my fairy outfit! She didn't seem happy about that answer. I dunno where she went," she said before skipping off. All the guests were now skating off the roller rink and meeting up in the party room for cake cutting. Even the people running the roller palace were nowhere in sight. Looked like Mateo's family booked the whole place for Marisol's birthday, which was pretty cool of them, but it also meant that we were the only ones left in the space.

35

"So she *saw* her dead grandma?" Lillian asked.

"Can today get any spookier?" Blair shivered.

"We've got to find Aiko." Surely my movie-buff-bestie could make sense of this.

Right on cue, Aiko came running up to us. She skidded to a stop just a foot away from me, her rainbow hair fluttering over her shoulders. Panic crept into her voice. "Uh, guys? We have a situation."

Aiko's eyes fastened on the rotary phone in my hands. Her supernatural spidey-senses must've been tingling. "I think something happened when we answered it, because . . ."

Aiko pointed at the roller rink. Something was slowly swirling in the middle of it, a vortex of bright light and swirling particles. The wind picked up, and I had to shield my eyes against the vortex's glow—the same glow I'd seen when the phone rang.

We braced for impact as the vortex of light touched down. The ground shook stronger than it had back at Yoon's Antiques, like a garbage truck was rolling through the arena. Roller skates lining the cabinets trembled along the walls before soaring toward the rink, pulled in by the wrath of the bright funnel. I had only seconds to set the phone on the nearest table and cover my head from the onslaught of abandoned streamers and party hats sailing past us. The funnel continued sucking anything in its path, including an empty pizza box, which nearly clipped my ear.

Blair's face contorted with terror. "TAKE COVER!"

We all hid beneath the nearest table. Lillian's voice broke through the din. "I told you climate change was coming for us!"

After she spoke, the whistling wind stopped, and the chill in the air died down. We each peered over the table. Inside the party room, people chanted, "Are you one, are you two . . . ?"

"Is it over?" I asked, but I had spoken too soon. The spooky factor had cranked up from a light simmer to a raging boil, because I was *so* not ready to face what came next.

I watched in utter horror as the vortex broke apart. Those glittering particles took the shape of an elderly woman made of wisps of white light. A grandma, by the looks of her, with curly gray hair that was tucked under a . . . *hockey helmet?*

My eyes didn't register it right away, but the woman was dressed in a large New York Rangers jersey, gripping a hockey stick in her hands. She tapped the stick on the rink as if there were ice beneath her, eyes narrowed. She let out a growl as her eyes hardened on mine.

Major gulp.

Hockey Grandma slammed her stick forward and made a direct hit with an abandoned pair of roller skates, causing the shoes to soar. . . .

Straight toward us.

"Duck!" I cried, dragging the others under the table. My heart rampaged in my chest. I forced myself to breathe deeply like Grandmama taught me and assessed the facts:

Fact #1: I was assuming the fetal position in a roller rink.

Fact #2: There was an elderly woman-hologram-spirit-*thing* who looked like she wanted to body-check me.

Squeezing my eyes shut, I chanted under my breath, "This isn't real. This isn't real. . . ."

Another pair of roller skates soared over the table. Okay, so maybe this was a *little* real. I glanced through a part in the tablecloth, mouth agape as I stared at the glowing figure. I blinked twice and did everything I could to rid myself of this hallucination. But when I opened my eyes, that otherworldly nimbus of light still shone bright. This wasn't a hallucination. Hockey Grandma, somehow, some way, was real.

A final pair of roller skates swooped overhead and landed in an empty shoe rental basket. Hockey Grandma shouted, *"HAT TRICK!"* She waved her stick in the air and whooped.

"You can all see her, right?" asked Blair, peeking through her hands as each of the girls poked their heads out of the tablecloth next to me. "I'm not just dreaming this up? Because my mom said that if I ate too many chips before bed . . ."

"You're not dreaming," Aiko said, eyes wide with fright or delight—I wasn't sure there was a difference in her supernatural-obsessed mind. "Don't you see what's happening? This is *Gabriela*. We've officially made contact with the spirit world!"

"As in *Gabriela* Gabriela? The dead grandma?" Lillian smacked a hand over her face. "Why couldn't it just be global warming?"

"That's a sentence I've never heard Lillian say." Aiko laughed.

Blair trembled. "So it wasn't a prank? We really got a phone call from Marisol's grandma? She's a real live *spirit*?"

"'Real live spirit' is a bit of an oxymoron, don't you think?" Aiko said. "I knew it! I knew something supernatural was going on with the phone!"

"Well, whatever's going on, I don't think she'll make many friends with *that* jersey. She'll be booted out of this place in no time," Lillian commented.

"Forget the jersey—we need holy water, stat!" shrilled Blair.

I panicked. "Guys, now's not the time. We're in danger!"

The outline of Hockey Grandma grew stronger as she drifted closer to us. Her incandescent eyes flamed with fury.

"I . . . need . . . that . . . bow!" Gabriela raised her hockey stick in the air and slammed it down on her knee, breaking it with a growl. Anger scrawled across the rivers of veins that poked out of her weathered brown skin.

"I think she's stuck," Aiko said, stepping out from under the table to face Hockey Grandma head-on. "On *Short Island Medium*, ghosts can't move on unless they receive help from the living."

"*She understands,*" the spirit-grandma confirmed, looking down at Aiko. "*And until I get what I need to move on, I will wreak havoc on this place!*"

With an undeniably supernatural air, Hockey Grandma soared up and flew around, moaning. If we didn't act fast, this spirit might evolve into a Category 5 hurricane of ire.

"Abuelita?" someone called innocently. Hockey Grandma froze in midair. She slipped off her helmet to get a good look at the source of the voice.

"*Marisol!*" Hockey Grandma's woes slipped away as she floated toward her granddaughter. What was Marisol doing outside her party?

"I noticed the ground shaking, but no one else did, so I said I had to pee." Marisol glanced up at her grandmother. "Do you *really* want my hair bow right now? Mom and Mia are going to take pictures, and I put a lot of effort into looking super cute!"

I wondered briefly if Marisol understood that she was talking to a ghost. Not just any ghost—her dead grandmother's. Even *I* was struggling to wrap my head around it all. Sure, Hollows' Peak was known for its weird charms, but ghosts making calls to old broken phones and playing hockey in roller rinks? I pinched myself to make sure I was really here—ouch! Yep, definitely *not* dreaming.

But Marisol was acting like this was any other day in the Pérez household.

"*My soul needs comforting. I need to move on! Carlos*

is waiting to reunite with me in the afterlife!"

"All my medium shows have trained me for this!" Aiko made a *stay calm* motion, touching all her fingertips together on each hand and lowering them in front of her, and reapproached Gabriela. "O Mighty Spirit, to send you to the afterlife, I will make a sacrifice of great importance!" Aiko closed her eyes, then peeped one open, waiting for us to catch on.

I cleared my throat. Two weeks of acting camp last summer had led me to this moment. I retreated from my hiding spot and said, "O Most Spirited of . . . Spirits!" I didn't know ghosts could give side-eye before I saw the look on Gabriela's face. Clearly my acting lessons weren't cutting it. "We will provide a great sacrifice indeed. . . ." I glanced around, unsure, as Blair and Lillian were still taking cover under the nearest table.

We were either screwed or Aiko Tanaka was about to save us all.

"I will offer my one-of-a-kind, special-edition camp bracelets to you, Marisol, in exchange for the hair bow." Aiko removed the bracelets and proffered them while down on one knee, like she was about to be knighted in a ceremony.

"I only wear *pink*," Marisol said, but she still considered the camp bracelets with sparkling eyes.

"I have a pink scrunchie." Blair cautiously waded out from under the table and tossed it to the birthday girl before scrambling back under the cloth. I joined in, offering a glittery hair clip from my purse—one must never travel without them!—and Lillian gave her a semi-tattered but pink shoelace.

Marisol's eyes lit up. "Best. Birthday. Ever!" She tugged off her hair bow and offered it to me. In an instant, she skipped off with her new belongings and retreated to the party room. "Bye, Abuelita!"

When Marisol disappeared, the spirit exhaled, *"Finally."* I swore the hair on the back of my neck stood on end as Gabriela inched closer to me. I could see now that her eyes weren't flaming with need—they had softened to a light, icy blue of gratitude.

"H-here you go," I said, offering the hair bow. The spirit slipped it into her hands, revealing a clip with initials engraved on the back: S. L.

"Safrina Lopez, my mother. Now that I have this, I am at peace. Thank you, Guardians...."

The spirit of Hockey Grandma shimmered and burst, swirling away on the nonexistent wind, until any trace of her was gone. I blinked twice just to be sure.

"Did we just...?" I trailed off.

"Help a spirit cross the veil?" Aiko wiped a tear from her eye. "Yes, fierce fam! We did it!"

I didn't know how, and I didn't know why, but one thing was for sure: My paranormal-loving bestie was right. We had just done the impossible.

We'd vanquished a *spirit*.

FOUR

Keep Calm and Ghost On

There was nothing quite like a visit from a ghost to shake up your Sunday afternoon.

The reality of the situation crashed down on the Fierce Four like a sudden downpour. Thoughts thundered in my brain, reminding me that this wasn't imaginary.

It was real. We'd all seen Marisol's grandmother's spirit successfully cross out of this world and into the afterlife, or wherever it was that spirits went to party.

A light bulb switched on in my brain. "The phone!"

We dashed back to the table where I had set down the rotary phone. It looked so . . . *plain* now compared to the maelstrom of a spirit we'd just faced. How could such an innocent-looking phone harbor the ability to speak to—to *see*—

"Ghosts," I murmured. After what I'd just seen, there was no denying that the phone was connected to another world . . . one full of things I hadn't even thought could be real hours ago.

I couldn't shake my mind of the realization as partygoers trickled out of the party room and returned their rented roller skates. A bunch of the teenage employees moaned when they came back from their union-mandated break, blaming the strewn party hats and roller skates on messy kids. And a vacuuming situation gone awry, thanks to Aiko's quick thinking.

Disco music played overhead, and the rink returned to a normal level of messiness. Apparently it was half-price skating after six o'clock, and everyone from children to seventy-year-olds came trickling through the front doors. The old folks' home must have been holding a geriatric skaters' night, because there was now a sign plastered by the rental desk that read: WEAR YOUR SHIN PADS AND SKATE CAREFULLY—DON'T LOSE THAT HIP REPLACEMENT NOW!

Outside, Aiko slipped the phone into her *Stranger Things* bag and said, "Those ghost documentaries came in handy, huh?"

"For once," Lillian mumbled under her breath. "We're *sure* that wasn't a bunch of pollen brought to life through some crazy experiment, right?"

Blair swallowed the tremor in her voice. "I don't recall putting *talk to spirits* on our seventh-grade to-do list."

I hugged my arms around my ribs, all my emotions shaken like a can of fizzy soda, ready to bubble over. "We need to talk about what happened back there," I said. "First, the glowing phone and then Gabriela's spirit showing up with a wicked wrist shot? I definitely didn't wake up this morning thinking, *I can't wait to help a hockey-obsessed ghost cross over! But first, cereal!*"

Blair chuckled. "Me neither. Should we head to my house? Mom's making tzatziki pasta again." That was her ultimate comfort food. "I think we're all going to need it after what just happened."

"I can't turn down a Ricci Special," Lillian agreed, to the surprise of no one, since she's been a regular dinner guest at Blair's house since first grade.

Aiko shot off a quick text to her dad that she'd be home a bit late. "We'll get to the bottom of how this phone works, one way or another."

The smell of heavenly al dente pasta wrapped around me like a pleasant hug. Mama Ricci truly did make the best untraditional pasta around. She wanted to blend her and her husband's family traditions by melding Italian favorites with Greek traditional eats. The results were just as warm and inviting as Blair herself, once she gets over her shyness. Her family's food made you want to say *Opa!*

Lo and behold, the Riccis already had guests—Lillian's family, the Baxters.

"Dig in!" chimed Papa Ricci from the dinner table. Blair said grace, twirled her fork in the spaghetti, held it up to mouth level, and took a big hearty gulp. We all followed suit. After all, family dinner at the Riccis' house was a well-mannered affair. Blair's parents always raised her to say her pleases and thank-yous and not misbehave at church. Unlike Blair, Lillian's twin brothers, Chase and Donovan, were always running around like whirling dervishes and apparently enjoyed burping in chorus during sermons.

On the other hand, Lillian's adoptive parents were *cool.* They listened to the latest music, wore trendy sneakers, and even let Lillian play video games and watch television after 8:00 p.m. Mama always shrugged me off whenever I'd mention what Lillian was allowed to do. *Hello, Mama, take a hint!*

The dining table wasn't big enough for all of us, so the Fierce Four sat on barstools at the kitchen island.

"The quicker we eat," I whispered furtively, "the quicker we can go someplace more private. You know, to discuss the *ghost incident.*"

The girls bobbed their heads in agreement, chewing faster.

"How was the reverse birthday party?" Papa Ricci asked after wiping his mouth.

"Frightening," Blair answered honestly before remembering herself. "Frighteningly . . . fun!"

"Because what eight-year-old isn't frightening?" Lillian muttered between bites, eyeing her devilish little brother, Chase.

"What's frightening about being eight? *I'm* eight!" Chase crossed his arms.

"So am I!" Donovan huffed.

Lillian's mom sighed, like, *Not this again.* I recognized the sound well from my own mother.

I eyed Blair as I chewed on my garlic toast. Her mousy brown hair and general hatred for all things horror made her seem timid and squeamish, but behind that scaredy-cat was a girl with a messy, flour-spattered apron and a whole lot of heart. You could see it from the way her parents doted on her at the dinner table.

And by doted, I mean politely *stared her down.*

"Slow down, hon!" said Blair's dad as he sprinkled Parmesan over his dinner plate.

"I can't! Mom, Dad, this food is sooo delicious!" Blair said, horking down her pasta like we were in some sort of eating contest.

Lillian must've gotten the hint, because she scraped her plate clean too. She nearly hiccuped on her last bite. Lillian's pops raised his eyebrows so high, they became hidden behind the brown coils that draped over his forehead.

"Ready for seconds?"

"Oh, I couldn't impose! Let me wash my dish!" Lillian jumped up with Blair, and Aiko and I nodded. Affirmative!

We cleaned our plates and zoomed out of the kitchen, up to Blair's bedroom, which faced Lillian's. Made it very convenient for them to send each other Morse code messages with their phone flashlights. (Sure, they could text, but where was the fun in that?)

"Let's gab ghosts!" said Aiko, plopping on Blair's purple canopied bed while I took a spot next to Lillian on the shaggy rug.

"So . . . ghosts are real?" Blair looked up at the ceiling and pleaded, "Oh, Nonna, please don't visit me from the beyond and make me wear another one of your old puffy-sleeved nightgowns! Nonna's fashion was a *choice*."

"We aren't here to talk about *our* grandmas," I said, carefully pulling out the phone from Aiko's bag before checking the hallway for eavesdroppers. When I was sure no one was near Blair's room, I lowered my voice and added, "We need to figure out how we saw the s-p-i-r-i-t grandma."

Lillian scratched her head. "How do we explain how a spirit contacted a broken telephone? Does it run on electricity? How *could* it run on electricity if it's not plugged in? These are the questions!"

"What if this phone works differently from others?" Aiko tapped her lips. "Think about it—in most movies, spirits can be detected with electromagnetic field detectors, meaning that they radiate a special kind of energy. The phone could operate on its own energy, similar to electricity, but fueled by spirits themselves instead of electrons. Maybe *that's* why a spirit could call the phone!"

"That doesn't explain the phone's glow," Lillian countered.

"Or the zap." Blair lifted her hands in front of her face, staring at them as if the little white currents were still coursing across her fingers.

"Spiritual energy aside," I said, "I think the phone glowed at the antique store for a reason. Mateo and Marisol's grandma called us. And guess who was around when the phone rang?"

"Mateo." Lillian's eyes bulged. "You think a spirit can *sense* if someone's close by, and then the spirit can contact them by calling the phone?"

Aiko nodded. "Marisol's grandma must have sensed Mateo was near—that's why she could call the phone. But she didn't show her spirit-self until she was around *Marisol*, because what she needed to move on was from *her*, not Mateo."

"The hair bow," Blair whispered.

Lillian tapped a finger to her lips. "That *seems* logical. I mean, only if I truly believed in this ghost stuff."

I sensed where Lillian was coming from—I wanted more scientific evidence to explain the phone too. But actually *seeing* a talking spirit today was enough to get me thinking about spirits in a new way.

"But why do these spirits have to call the phone?" I wondered. "What's so special about it? Why can't they just appear?"

"There must be a reason," Aiko deduced. "Maybe they can only call their loved ones? And once they get what they need"—Aiko made a hand-poofy motion—"they move on to the afterlife! Banished forevermore!"

Blair groaned. "The only thing I want to banish is the rising cost of baking soda!"

Ignoring Blair, I stated, "I think we're asking a lot of *what*s and *why*s. We can't figure this out all on our own. We need an *expert*."

"A little dose of help," Aiko agreed. "Like from someone who can see into the great beyond."

I caught on to Aiko's thinking. "Tía Paola."

"*Tía Paola?*" Blair nearly shrieked, slapping her hands against her cheeks and gaping widely, much like that painting we studied in art class called *The Scream.* "I've heard people who walk *into* Paola's Predictions don't walk *out.*"

Lillian nudged Blair in her side. "I'm no psychic believer, but even *I* think we need help from someone with a penchant for fortune-telling. And that's saying something."

Aiko stroked the phone like it was a floofy kitten. "She might be our only hope of figuring out more about ghosts. My family are big believers in spirits. In Japanese folklore, yōkai are intelligent and sometimes mischievous creatures."

"I don't think we're dealing with those," Lillian said. "These are humans. At least, Gabriela was."

"Either way, we need more information on this . . . *phantom phone.*" I could tell Aiko was proud of that alliteration.

From what I knew about Paola, or *Tía Paola* as everyone in town called her, she'd delved into some pretty interesting stuff.

I stuck in my crisscrossed hands in the signature Fierce Four handshake. Lillian quickly followed suit, with Aiko and Blair bringing up the rear.

"Tomorrow after school, we'll enter the psychic's lair."

It was officially time for BTS. No, not the K-pop group. Back to school.

My tie-dye shoelaces were sure to make a statement today, and even though I wore the same old puffer jacket, I didn't mind. Coupled with my laces, my hat would do all the talking. It was a beige winter toque with a label stitched on the front that read, IF YOU CAN READ THIS, YOU'RE STANDING TOO CLOSE. There was a biting chill in the air, the kind you feel when you walk by a cemetery. A chill that crept its way through my skin and into my bones.

Or maybe it was a side effect of vanquishing a spirit yesterday.

The good thing was that Madame Bower didn't go overboard during her afternoon French lesson, meaning we had almost no homework. I finished conjugating all my verbs as soon as the final bell rang and handed in my worksheet. On the way out of school, I waved goodbye to Principal Hanover, who always waited at the entrance to say goodbye to the kids. He was munching on a bag of corn chips, his favorite snack. Which I totally didn't get. Everyone knew sour cream and onion was superior!

Blair, Aiko, and Lillian were already waiting for me outside the school: Blair with her fingernails in her teeth, Lillian looking like she was looking for *anything* rational to explain what happened yesterday, and Aiko seeming a little *too* excited for someone about to go meet the town psychic.

Luckily, we wouldn't have to go through the local cemetery and face any lingering spirits on our way there. We paused at the storefront, a purple-striped awning greeting us.

The exterior of Paola's Predictions belonged on the Strip in Las Vegas. Seriously—a grand, marquee-style sign put Paola's name in violet lights, and the store windows were graced with shelves holding all sorts of knickknacks, from cloudy crystal balls to mystical pens and flashy tarot cards. A motto in the window in big, blocky font read: WHERE THE FUTURE IS NOT TO BE MESSED WITH.

Based on the rumors, neither was Tía.

We approached the store as one, steeling ourselves. I knocked three times.

"Tía?" Blair's voice trembled. "Um . . . Tía Paola? Are you there?"

No one answered. I politely knocked again. It didn't help that Tía's peephole was shaped like a moving eyeball that shook with every knock.

The eye slid down, revealing a very *real* one now. We all leapt back. Sheesh—jump scare warning, anyone?

"Depends on who's asking," wheedled a voice like glass. It was gritty and familiar, and the back of my neck prickled at the sound of it. "If it's my mother-in-law, I'm out of office! This is a recorded voice message!"

"Tía, we know you're there. We need your help," I said, mustering as much courage as I could. "For something *really* important."

Her single eye narrowed.

Tía Paola undid a series of locks before creaking open her front door. Wind chimes echoed in the chill

January air, and the scent of blueberry jam and freshly ripened figs wafted out of the psychic's store.

"Do you have an appointment? I'm on my lunch break."

"No. And isn't it almost dinnertime?" I checked my fitness watch just to be sure.

Paola ignored my latter remark. "No appointment, no Paola. Please book a time with my secretary."

"You don't have a secretary!" Aiko retorted. She looked at us and explained, "I visit her shop, like, every other day."

"Well . . . you might be right about that. My last one quit to become a hand model, but who am I to question job security?" Tía Paola shivered down to her toes. "Come in, girls. You're letting in the cold, and we all know psychics can't handle a drop of ice, snow, hail . . . well, any inclement weather, for that matter."

"They can't? Why? Does it have to do with pressure changes in the air? Does that affect your . . . *readings*?" Lillian tapped her chin. Not that she believed in psychics' abilities to begin with, but one should never let off Lillian without an explanation, unless you wanted her going into full mad scientist mode.

"Too many questions, Ms. Baxter."

Lillian froze. Out of the corner of her mouth, she yelped, "She knows my name!"

"I know everyone's name and everyone's future! For a small fee, of course. Let me read your palms quickly, girl."

Lillian reluctantly held out a hand. Tía Paola clutched her pearls. Literally. She was wearing a thick, double-stranded pearl necklace fit for an antique road show.

She gave a throaty gasp. "Poor, unfortunate souls..."

"What? What do you see?" Aiko's eyes widened. "Did her life just flash before your eyes? Do the lines represent her past, present, and future? Is she doomed to an eternity of back pain? That's what my dad says happens to adults after they turn thirty."

Aiko must've gotten that off the back of a cereal box for psychics. The lines on the hands part—not the back pain. You didn't need a crystal ball to know that much.

"No, Ms. Tanaka. I'm referring to my favorite song from *The Little Mermaid*. Ursula truly deserved better, don't you think?"

We all blinked at the town psychic.

"Never mind. Lillian, your hand is just fine, aside from some typical winter dryness, but I have a vitamin E cream that'll fix that right up. Now, come inside before the cold freezes my tush off!"

No one denied Tía Paola, so we shuffled into the shop and loosened our scarves, ready to face down our destinies.

"Welcome, girls."

FIVE

I Get My Fortune Read by the Scariest Woman in Town

From what I could tell, Paola's Predictions was the kind of shop where people whispered and you could still hear an echo. Every shelf was covered in a fine layer of dust, as if even Tía Paola couldn't bring herself to sweep the place. Shelves were stuffed with psychic relics, and counters were littered with lottery tickets behind plastic panes (BUY TWO IF YOU'RE FEELING LUCKY!). The ceiling above us was painted with thick, frosted clouds like cotton candy, but instead of the blush rays of an oncoming dawn, the painted sky was dark, like my fortune was one of doom.

Those who were brave enough to enter Paola's Predictions came for the small stuff. Would their child win tonight's Little League match? Was the shape of their remaining tea leaves a sign of success or failure at work? The dregs of one's tea weren't to be messed with.

"This way." Paola ushered us toward a pair of velvety curtains that parted the back portion of the shop from the front. As soon as we passed through the curtains, I knew where we were.

Tía Paola's reading room.

Like most towns, Hollows' Peak had a rumor mill that ran 24-7. *Paola's got forty cats. Paola's actually from a witch coven in Salem.* Even for a town that practically fed itself on all things strange, Paola was an outlier.

Not that I believed in any of those rumors the way Blair did.

But stepping into her reading room, I couldn't help thinking there was some truth to them. Okay, maybe not the forty cats bit. But clearly she was practiced in tarot reading and fortune-telling. The table before us was littered with all kinds of lit candles and mirrors, probably to enhance her readings and her "seer" capabilities. Some might call it *aesthetic*. I called it a fire hazard.

"Take a seat," Paola offered, pulling out a plush chaise for each of us. I thanked her as I sat on the edge of the chair, scratching at my shoulder. Great, Lillian's tics had rubbed off on me.

"So, how can I help you girls?" Tía seated herself across from us at the reading table. "I must admit, my customer base isn't usually so young."

"We're not exactly here for a reading, Tía," Aiko said. "We have . . . a school project we need help with."

"Homework right after the break?" Paola sneered. "I swear, the education system is broken! Broken, I tell you!"

"Uh-huh . . ." I needed to stop Tía Paola from going on a full-on rant about public versus private education. Mama had already gotten an earful of it when she bumped into Paola at the grocery store last month.

"Actually, the topic of the project is about spirits. And we figured you were the only person in town who might have valuable information on the subject. Do you think you could help us with that?"

"Is this for a book report?" Paola's eyes narrowed.

"No," I said just as Lillian blurted, "Yup!"

Seriously, the Fierce Four needed to work on our synchronization skills.

"Well, book report or no, I can certainly help you in that department." Tía Paola steepled her fingers. "What might you young ladies like to learn?"

"We're interested in learning more about how people can connect to the spirit world. Have you ever heard of something that can do that? Maybe . . . with a *phone*?" I asked not-so-subtly. I hoped speaking about spirits in Paola's shop wouldn't summon the translucent beings to the store, but there was no beating around the crystal ball with Paola.

The psychic pondered my words. "I'm more practiced in seeing into one's future, but I dabble in studies of spiritual energy, nonetheless. The line between the spirit world and the mortal one is thinner than you think. But it's not like paper, where you can easily rip through. You would require something tangible to create a bridge to the other side. I've heard of phones acting as one such bridge—but that's all just well-trodden gossip. Where exactly did you girls read about these phones again?"

"We didn't." I gulped, reaching for the phone in Aiko's

Stranger Things bag. When I revealed it, Paola fell back in her seat, clutching a hand to her chest.

"Looks like she's not breathing!" Blair whispered out of the side of her mouth, face ashen.

"If we cause the town psychic to have a heart attack, we'll have more than a few ghosts to deal with," Aiko whispered back.

Paola suddenly inhaled a throaty breath, shooting up straight, and we sighed with relief. "Where did you get that phone?" she squealed. "It's so delightfully vintage!"

"Mr. Yoon's antique store," I revealed.

"Girls, girls, girls! You have a mighty find on your hands! Tell me—have you already received a call from the beyond?"

I turned to my fierce fam to get their permission, who all nodded. "Well, it all started yesterday . . ." I spilled the tea—or in this case, the tea dregs—on how we found the phone and got zapped, then received a call from Marisol's grandmother and later helped her move on to the afterlife with a hair bow. Before long, Paola was practically salivating over the phone like a dog in search of a bone.

"Oh my, my! How brilliant! That hair bow must have been an important relic. . . . Yes, yes. You four might just give me a run for my money! Well, you can't predict the future like I can, but, girls—you have a connection to the spirit world! You're practically mediums!"

"What does a medium do again?" Lillian asked.

"Mediums communicate with spirits," Aiko answered matter-of-factly.

"We're not mediums," I told Tía Paola. "We're not channeling any sort of magic or energy. The phone must be. All we did was take the call after the phone started glowing, and later, the spirit appeared."

"That still doesn't answer how we could *see* a spirit," Lillian said. "Aren't they supposed to be invisible or something?" She looked to Aiko for confirmation.

"Of course, spirits can't be seen by non-mediums," Paola said, "but you girls said you got zapped before the phone glowed and rang? Well, there's your answer!"

Lillian looked deep in thought. "You mean the *zap* connected us to the phone somehow . . . and allowed the spirit call to come through?"

Paola nodded, preening like a peacock. "Based on my years of experience working with my medium friends in Rosemary Heights, I can only imagine that when the phone zapped you, it activated its powers from a dormant stage. And since you are not mediums, the zap acted as an activation point so that non-mediums—in other words, you girls—can now use the phone. Which means spirits who call the phone are now able to reveal themselves to you!"

"You mean we've got *powers*?" Blair stared at her hands again. "This is like Spider-Man's origin story."

Aiko jumped in her seat. "Except instead of getting bitten by a radioactive spider, we got zapped by a phone!"

"Slow down there, Peter Parker," Lillian said. She leaned in toward the phone. "What's that?"

She was pointing to a tiny bit of script at the base of the phone. Seriously, you needed a magnifying glass to read that thing.

"Let me see that . . . ," Tía Paola said, pulling the phone toward her. "Aha!"

Tía Paola must have had twenty-thirty vision—she could see the future, after all—because she read aloud, "Property of the Hollows."

Blair shivered down to her toes. Aiko gasped.

So this wasn't any normal phone after all. It once belonged to our town founders. Aiko might've already established the phone's paranormal nature, but for me this was only getting more and more real.

Without warning, Paola jimmied open the bottom compartment of the phone with a mystical pen. There was paper sticking out! But not just a single sheet. The phone had its own small book hidden inside it, with a decades-old leather binding and, in gold foil across the cover, the words "Guidebook for Guardians."

"I've never heard of a book in a phone," Lillian noted.

"But you have heard of a phone book, haven't you?" Paola snickered to herself. What was so funny? What was a *phone book*?

"This generation, I swear," Paola huffed.

As I ran a finger over the foil, a memory flashed in my mind. "Remember what the spirit called us yesterday?"

Aiko gaped. "Guardians."

"This appears to be a guidebook for users of the phone," said Paola sagely. "Guidebooks are essential for mediums and clairvoyants to keep track of their work and findings," she explained. "Just like how I keep a record log of all my customers' purchases in the store. It's mostly for dealing with taxes, but that's a whole different kind of ghost story."

Paola thumbed through the pages. "Ah, here it is. A welcome message." She flipped back to the beginning of the book for us all to read:

> Welcome, Guardians! I hope this phone doesn't cause you too much trouble. I, Rose Hollow, crafted this invention to help my children, and their children after them, to get a handle on the world of the dead. Speaking to spirits is not a simple task and can be mentally draining. In fact, I have been so troubled by my abilities that I would like to ease the process of speaking to spirits ... by infusing my power into something as new and advanced as a telephone. I hope this helps bridge the gap between our world and the afterlife and allows each Guardian to help these troubled spirits to move on, one call at a time.

> *If a spirit calls you, this means they are trapped between our world and the afterlife—a place of in-between. The spirit may only be seen by current Guardians and the loved one the spirit is trying to reach. Be aware that there are different kinds of spirits with varying powers. Based on my experience, there are three levels in which they can be categorized.*

"You're telling me that Rose Hollow, founder of Hollows' Peak, *made* this phone? How wicked cool is that?" Aiko practically danced in her chair. "She's, like, my idol!"

"She also said the spirit can only be seen by a loved one and the current Guardians. Maybe that's why no one noticed the spirit in the rink yesterday except Marisol," I realized.

Paola agreed. "Rose Hollow was a wise woman. Her life wasn't always easy, either. Did you know that the Hollows were once outcasts? Back in the olden days, spirits were considered nasty business and speaking to them even nastier. Witches have been burned at the stake for less! But the Hollows turned that all around when they created a business to help their new neighbors communicate with the realm beyond the living. I had no idea they created and used a phone for their service!"

"A service? Like . . . to call ghosts?" Blair shuddered. "I told you, I don't do well with horror!"

"Goodness, girl, haven't you seen *Casper*? He's a friendly ghost! Most spirits are . . ." Paola trailed off, then shook her head. "Besides, it's like Rose Hollow said. Spirits who haunt this mortal world—what I like to call the physical plane—are merely in need of something to help them move on to the afterlife. Only in that place can they reconvene with other spirits. Without help, they will remain stuck in a place of in-between."

"Not quite our world . . . not quite the next." Aiko leveled a somber look at us.

Paola tapped on the welcome message with a long, clawlike finger.

"Keep reading," she commanded. The other girls and I did as she said, leaning in toward the book.

> Level one spirits can be directed to the world of the afterlife using physical objects that conjure memories of the past.
> Level two spirits can only be satisfied with emotional reasoning.
> Level three spirits require something more powerful, as they are—

The rest of the words had been rubbed away, worn off the paper. I snorted. "How convenient."

As much as I didn't want to admit it, Paola's—and Rose's—words made complete sense. Not to mention this guidebook was laying it all out flat for us, describing the ways in which one could transport a ghost to the afterlife. Marisol's grandmother disappeared to the afterlife pretty quickly after we gave her something tangible—the hair bow, just like the guidebook described.

"So Gabriela was a level one ghost," Aiko realized. "All she needed was something physical to move on."

"What if a level two ghost calls the phone?" Blair quivered.

We flipped through the pages of the guidebook, and Paola slammed her hand down, halting us. "Here's your answer, girls. It appears this guidebook is full of spirit slips!"

"Spirit what now?" I asked.

Paola went on. "The slips mention the names of spirits who have been helped with this phone. Guardians have filled in the pages as they faced more and more spirits. Perhaps you girls could learn a thing or two from past Guardians. Take a look!"

Paola rotated the book so it faced us.

> Guidebook Log, 01/06/55
> Guardian Name: Destiny Hollow, daughter of Elijah Hollow

"Whoa, this is so cool!" Aiko said. "Destiny Hollow was Rose's granddaughter. She must have used this phone back in 1955!"

We continued reading:

Spirit Category: Level two

Spirit Issue: Celia, a former Hollows' Peak librarian, was clinging to her husband because she wasn't emotionally ready to move on to the afterlife without him. She would make books fall from the stacks whenever her husband was near to catch his attention.

How I Aided the Spirit: I offered the specter one of her husband's favorite books, thinking she might be a level one spirit. Instead, she needed emotional help, a certain sign of a level two. All she wanted was for her husband to sing the good night lullaby he'd always sung to her to help her fall fast asleep. When he did, Celia was content, and moved on.

"What about level threes?" Blair shuddered. "Do you think there's a spirit slip in here about how to help one of those?"

Tía Paola shuttered the book closed. "You'll cross that bridge when you get there. Or so my mother-in-law says. She still thinks I don't have my career together!" She shut her eyes and inhaled a deep breath, like those yoga instructors tell you to do when you get anxious. Suddenly she clapped, bringing us all back to her attention. "Well, girls, you've made my whole day! When my clairvoyant friends learn what I've gotten my hands on—"

"No!" I shouted. "You can't tell anyone." What if Mama found out that I'd used the phone? That I'd spoken to a *ghost*? We were barely on semi-good terms after what I'd told her at Yoon's Antiques yesterday. Not to mention I barely spoke to her after our ghostly encounter with Hockey Grandma and dinner at Blair's. What was I supposed to say? *Hey, Mom, I spoke to and aided a ghost today! No biggie. How did you spend your afternoon?*

I couldn't get into any more trouble with her, and certainly not with the idea that I was a Guardian who could speak to the dead.

"But, my dears, why not? You have a gift on your hands, and you have been given the ultimate opportunity to be Guardians! You must use it!"

"How?" Lillian was clearly still on the fence about this whole ghost thing. "The phone seems like it was more than Rose Hollow bargained for—it's not just a medium for mediums to speak to spirits, pardon the pun, but it can now be used by non-mediums too. Sure, the electrical zap explains things, but that doesn't answer why the phone is in such bad shape." Lillian pointed out the burned and frayed end of the cord.

"I certainly don't have all the answers, girls, but I do know two things for sure. One: I will be here whenever you need me. Consider me your Guardian guidance counselor! We can even set up lessons to help you girls stay on the right track, should you keep receiving spirit calls. Oh, I can already see the lesson plans now! I knew I was destined to teach!"

Now Paola was *really* going to rant.

"What's number two?" Lillian asked. Good distraction.

"You said number two." Aiko giggled.

The psychic fiddled with her mystical pen. "Well, you children know how special our town is. I've made a fortune this month telling fortunes!" She snickered to herself. "Some of my clients are *dying*—poor word choice, I'm sorry—to reach out to their loved ones. They would pay big money for it too! We're talking hundreds, girls. Think about it. A century ago, Rose Hollow's services reportedly cost just a few dollars. Talk about inflation!"

We all blinked at Tía Paola. Rewind—did she say ... *hundreds*?!

I stood. "Thanks so much for all your help, Tía, but I should probably get heading home soon. You know, that dreaded homework and all."

Paola hummed in agreement before Lillian added, "Same here. I'm watching a new soap with my parents tonight. *Days of the Glorious*, followed by strict belly button hygiene."

"TMI much?" muttered Blair, nose scrunching.

As we all got up from our seats, I placed the phone back in Aiko's bag, even though I was definitely taking it home tonight. After all this information, how could I not want to dig deeper? I needed to read through that *Guidebook for Guardians* ASAP!

Paola's inquisitive eyes shone. "You four have a great responsibility to uphold. It takes a special kind of person to be chosen for such a thing."

"We're not that special," Lillian said matter-of-factly. "We're just normal humans who've somehow accessed a power that's, well, above the understandable limit. A science we can't yet comprehend. Our brains aren't supposed to process this kind of information."

"*Adult* brains, yes. But children have a deep and wonderful imagination. Perhaps that makes you all great Guardians!"

I slipped on my jacket. "Thanks so much for everything, Tía. You've really illuminated what this phone can do."

"Oh, pishposh . . . but do go on," Tía Paola said, fluttering her long lashes.

My BFFs extended their gratitude before they slipped out of the reading room. On my way out, Tía Paola placed a strong hand on my shoulder. I braced myself. Was I in trouble? Or did Paola really need to get that education rant off her chest?

"Raveena," Tía Paola said, "I'm so sorry about what happened to your grandmother. I never had a chance to offer my condolences to you."

"That's okay, Tía," I said. Truth was, I had hardly ever bumped into her, aside from short trips to the hairdresser, where Paola got her signature blowout.

"Let me offer you a card reading, on the house." I had a feeling she wasn't asking. She expected people to be groveling for her psychic services, so I didn't argue with the town's reigning scary lady. And I could use some help in the what-does-my-future-hold department anyway.

I returned to my seat as Paola shuffled her cards. She placed three in front of me.

"Pick one."

With quick hands, I chose the one in the middle.

She turned the thick violet-and-gold card over. The front was decorated with a beautiful series of stars, all aligned above a woman holding her arms out as if to summon the wind and sky, which swirled above her.

I read the bold writing on the bottom. MOTHER NATURE.

"What does it mean? I always recycle."

A dark shadow crossed Paola's face. "I don't believe it has to do with the environment, dear," Paola said vaguely. "Are you experiencing any turmoil with maternal figures in your life?"

I nodded, mostly because I didn't want to get into my whole situation with Mama right now. But I didn't need a tarot card to tell me what I already knew.

I got up from my seat, but Paola wasn't finished. "I would be careful, Ms. Gill. This card only appears when a mother, or a maternal figure, is about to cause upheaval. Kind of like my mother-in-law. I just stopped answering her calls."

"Right . . ." I had spent way too much time with Paola for the day. With the quickest goodbye I could muster, I circled on my scarf and found my friends outside.

But I couldn't help wondering—was the Mother Nature card talking about Mama . . . or my grandmother?

SIX
Cemetery Tours and Fishy Business

Remember that part about not going through the local cemetery?

I lied.

There was something on my mind ever since Tía Paola brought up how Rose Hollow was the owner and creator of the phantom phone. Last year in history class, we learned all about Rose and how her grave remained in a mausoleum at the back of the cemetery. Lucky for me—ahem, *us*—our houses were just a hop, skip, and jump across from the cemetery, which gave me the perfect excuse to pop in for a look before dinner.

"Do we REALLY have to do this?" Blair tightened her knuckles around her backpack straps. "Like, wasn't seeing Tía Paola enough torture for the day?"

"Totally," Lillian said, nodding along with Blair. "She said my hands were as dry as a bone!" She hugged her hands to her chest. "Maybe I really have been focusing too much on belly button hygiene...."

"Let's talk innies and outies later," said Aiko. "Paola aside, Raveena's right! We've *got* to do some investigative work on Rose. Figure out more about the phone. Isn't your mom a reporter, Blair?"

Blair grumbled about how her mom had "gently pushed" her into joining the Journalists of Tomorrow Club—AKA the school newspaper—this year.

"Then?" Aiko pointed to the gates and said with an overexaggerated flourish of her hand, "To the cemetery!"

My boots crunched through the packed snow as we crossed the threshold into Hollows' Peak Cemetery. The local graveyard was just as creepy as you would imagine. From the outside in, iron gates stood sentry over countless headstones, moss crept along the ground and over the names of the deceased, and bare trees shivered among the presence of so many who had moved on from this world.

Hopefully.

An unbidden thought rose to mind. Grandmama, calling me her precious beti and telling me to play "Canon in D" on the flute as she shut her eyes to immerse herself in the music. While she died half a year ago and we'd already spread her ashes over her favorite ravine, the cemetery brought back reminders of death twofold. It was a weird thing, to remember the dead. To feel haunted by them. But what if we're not always haunted by ghosts or apparitions? What if we're more haunted by their absence?

Absence of life. Absence of love.

Blair's teeth chattered, breaking my reverie, and it wasn't just because we had a lot of snowfall after the freezing rainstorm last night.

"Doesn't the s-snow look like f-fluffy whipped cream?" Blair's eyes raked over the snow-covered headstones. "If you squint just right, the h-headstones look like c-cupcakes."

"Blair, if you're scared, we can turn around," I reassured her.

"No way!" Blair shook her head. "I'll just think happy baking thoughts. Preheat the oven to three fifty. . . ."

We headed deeper into the cemetery, where one of our town's signature cemetery tours was currently being conducted. I snuck to the back of the crowd, and my friends quickly followed suit. Only thing was, I couldn't exactly see over anyone's shoulders, and their long puffy jackets didn't help either. I crawled toward a better vantage point to see what was going on.

"And over here we have the founder of Hollows' Peak, Rose Hollow, buried in this very mausoleum. . . . Notice the engraved roses decorating the stones. . . ."

The tour guide, a pimply teenager who was probably getting much-needed volunteer hours out of this, sounded extremely bored for a speech about the very influential, very important Rose Hollow. "Rose is buried in this very building, with the headstones of her children, Elijah and Carmela, situated right in front."

For someone telling a creepy-crawly story, the tour guide sounded like he wanted to be anywhere else but here. "Take it all in. No flash photography, please."

Someone snapped a blindingly bright picture

with their camera. The teenager blinked mindlessly.

"Mooooving on," he said, ushering the group to the next destination.

"Now," I whispered to Lillian, Blair, and Aiko.

We closed in on the mausoleum. I reached out to brush off some dirt on Elijah Hollow's headstone, which read BELOVED SON AND BROTHER. A chill peppered the air, more haunting than cold, as we all peered deeper into the mausoleum.

"Mrs. Hollow? Are you in there?" Aiko whispered, her breath freezing over in a small cloud of fog. She pulled out the phone from her bag. "If you or your family needs help moving on, maybe give us a ring? It's toll-free!" she added enthusiastically.

"Aiko, don't tell me you're trying to summon a ghost!" Blair said after crossing herself. "Wasn't dealing with Marisol's abuelita enough?"

"Well, we are Guardians. I thought that might mean we have a connection to the phone's creator, that Rose might give us a call." Aiko peered inside the mausoleum, careful not to step inside, but nothing stirred except for a few fallen leaves. The phone remained silent. "What if we go inside? There could be something important there about Rose. Or the phone!"

"I'm so not going in there," Blair said.

"It'll be quick," Aiko reasoned. "You and Lillian can wait outside to keep watch. Right, Raveena?"

I'd never stepped foot inside a mausoleum before—

heck, I wasn't even sure it was *legal*. But I had to get answers. "Yep."

Aiko and I inched closer to the mausoleum. A cold breeze trickled out of the site, slipping into my boots and wrapping around my ankles. That breeze locked around me like steel cuffs, freezing me mid-step.

"AHHH!" Aiko tripped and fell forward, dirt now caking her face. "Help!"

Blair and Lillian rushed over, helping her up. I broke free of my frozen state and leapt toward my friend, breath fogging the air. "Aiko!"

"I—I'm okay." Aiko rose with Blair and Lillian's help. Together, we found the culprit—a vine curled around Aiko's foot.

"Was that vine always there?" Aiko brushed stray crumbs of dirt from her face. Even my paranormal-loving bestie appeared to be spooked.

"I don't think so," Blair shrilled. "I think this is Rose's way of telling us our idea is no bueno. I'm out!"

"Good idea. I think we've had enough scares for the day," Lillian declared. Even I didn't want a repeat of whatever had seized hold of me. It took "frozen with fear" to a whole new level.

Just as we turned to leave, a sound came from behind us.

Snap.

I froze. "Did you hear that?"

"Hide!" Blair whisper-yelled.

We scattered like marbles. Aiko and I hid behind a

nearby grave—I would have to drop apology flowers later—and Lillian and Blair sought out a safe haven behind a willow tree.

"Do you think anyone saw us?" My breath was coming out in puffs, so I held it, hoping no one would find us. What was the penalty for sneaking into a dead person's living quarters?

A voice harped, "What are you girls doing there?"

I gasped with fright as I spun around. It was our school librarian, Mrs. Nkosi!

"Didn't mean to scare you!" the librarian added with a well-mannered chuckle, her ebony skin glowing in the oncoming moonlight. "I was just taking my nightly walk and thought I saw someone. It's usually quite lonely out here in the evenings."

Mrs. Nkosi peered down at me through her clear-framed glasses attached to a delicate gold chain. It was like there was some unspoken law that librarians needed to have glasses to get the job.

I relaxed, brushing mud off my jeans. "Hi, Mrs. Nkosi. We were just—well, we, um . . ."

"Were working on our school business project for Get Everything Done!" Aiko ventured with a grimace. "Today's job: cleaning gravestones!" She flicked a piece of dirt off the nearest one. "See? Spick and span."

"Hmm," Mrs. Nkosi said, as if in deep thought. "And how is your business going, if I might ask? I recall you girls want to get the arts program back up and running."

"Getting there," I answered. Then, with more honesty: "We're kind of . . . stuck."

"Physically? Or mentally?" Mrs. Nkosi was also a part-time guidance counselor.

"Both. The business is going kind of *blah*, and we're not raising enough funds," Aiko said, though I caught her hand drifting toward her ankle. She was still thinking about the stray vine.

"We need to rework our business plan," I agreed, trying to get her mind off it.

"Ah, the dreaded business plan." Mrs. Nkosi leaned in and stage-whispered, "That's why I went into library sciences."

"You need to study science to become a librarian?" Blair asked, emerging from behind the tree.

"No, but you *do* need to study everything from cataloging to archiving to book preservation! Isn't that neat? Now, girls, if you need any help, don't hesitate to give me a visit at school."

The Fierce Four practically *lived* in the school library thanks to Mrs. Nkosi. She let us have first dibs on new books and helped us put early holds on the newest *Ms. Marvel* comics.

"We'll keep that in mind. But maybe you could help us *now*." I pointed at the mausoleum. "You've done tons of research on Rose Hollow, right?"

Mrs. Nkosi's eyes sparked with excitement. "Of course! Rose Hollow was one of the preeminent historical figures of this town. We often don't speak about historic women enough in our history books, but thankfully, our school doesn't have that problem," she added with a wink. "Still, people don't know just how powerful Rose Hollow was. Even before she founded Hollows' Peak, she was a strong medium. Did you know that she, along with her husband and children, led an army of spirits against a horde of wayward specters and even won a battle back in New Orleans?" She looked like she was about to go on when her fitness watch beeped. "Oh, there it goes again. Time to get walking!"

And with that, the librarian waved goodbye and disappeared with phantom footsteps. Even outside the library, librarians had to follow their own rules.

I glanced at the sky. "It's getting dark. We should head home."

Worry melted off Blair's face. "Good. Not just because I'm afraid of ghosts, but because logically, if I'm not home in time for supper, I'll be grounded. Like, *deeper than six feet in the ground* grounded."

We hurried toward the exit. Fog spilled across the cemetery, brewing like a cauldron. Either someone forgot to shut off their fog machine, or this place truly was haunted.

Before we departed, I paused, blinking, as fog swirled from afar. In the fog I made out letters, made up of those water vapor wisps, spelling out a term of endearment.

A name only one person had ever called me.

BETI.

. . .

All night, I tossed in bed. Because the one person who ever called me beti wasn't alive anymore.

Grandmama.

Was it possible I was just seeing things? A side effect of becoming a sort-of-medium, sort-of-Guardian who sometimes saw ghosts?

One grandmother had shown up by calling the phone. Could another?

At school, I thought I saw the letters in my alphabet soup rearrange to spell the same thing. Then, during French class, Madame Bower wrote *beti* on the board. Except she didn't. After I shook my head and blinked three times, I saw she'd only written *bonbons*. Seriously, what was up with me today?

Maybe it was all because of the crazy idea I came up with last night—the one I was about to reveal to my besties.

After muddling through school, I gathered with the rest of the Fierce Four for tacos at our usual after-school haunt. Pun totally intended.

The local taqueria, El Grillo, was decorated with traditional Mexican flair. Papel picado, or colorful, perforated paper decorations, were strewn above the windows and tables, and the wooden tables and the smell of freshly made masa gave the whole restaurant an air of warmth and coziness—and maybe a touch of salivation.

"Table for four," I told the waiter. On instinct, my eyes sought out Mateo's moms, the owners of the taqueria. El Grillo was named after Mateo, their little cricket. Mateo always acted embarrassed by the name whenever we ate El Grillo's signature spicy enchiladas, but I knew he secretly liked it.

That is, back when we were close. Now I felt like I barely knew anything about him anymore.

Once we were seated with cups of ice water, Aiko asked, "So what's up, Raveena? What's this *wild idea* you told us about at lunchtime?"

"Yeah, the one you said had to wait till after school?" Blair said, too busy eyeing the menu to sound impatient.

Lillian clinked the ice around in her glass. "We all know Raveena's idea of wild is staying up past ten."

"*My* idea of wild is baking cookies past ten!" Blair chuckled.

"Well, my idea *is* wild. Because I got it from Tía Paola yesterday. And you're all going to need a whole bowl of chips and guac if you want to stomach it." I knew I was going to need them too.

"Avocados *are* good for digestion. . . ." Blair became lost in Foodie-Landia as Lillian pulled out her signature black glittery pen and washi tapes.

"You said the idea is about Get Everything Done!, right?" she asked.

I nodded. "It's just not working."

"I hear you on that. I've already shoveled Mr. Dao's driveway three times. If I keep going back, he'll expect me to salt the pavement too!" Aiko cried.

"And my neighbors can only handle so many of my cookies," bemoaned Blair. "Turns out they're soy-free one week, gluten-free the next! I can't keep up!"

"Which is why I came up with something . . . *else.*" I paused for dramatic effect. Or maybe just to make sure what I was about to say wasn't totally out of my mind. "Remember what Tía Paola said about Rose Hollow's business? How she helped people communicate with deceased loved ones using the phone?"

"All I remember is *We're talking hundreds, girls!*" Lillian mimicked while clasping a nonexistent necklace. It was a pretty spot-on impersonation, which made the Fierce Four giggle.

"Exactly. *Hundreds.* Imagine *us* making that kind of money for the business competition and beating Mateo and those eighth graders."

"*And* raising funds for the arts program," Aiko reminded me.

"Right. That too. So . . . are you all thinking what I'm thinking?"

"That when life gives you lemons, you should actually make lemon squares?" Blair said. She glanced around the table to find blank stares. "Okay, you *clearly* don't watch enough Food Network."

"I'm thinking . . ." I bit my lip. I didn't usually speak so irrationally, so *excitedly.* But after everything we discovered, it was like someone had melted down Skittles and injected them into my veins. "I'm thinking I just figured out how to win the business competition."

The girls leaned forward, expectant.

"We use the phantom phone."

SEVEN

Ghost Girlies? Phantom Fighters? Energy Evaporators?

"Oh?" Aiko quirked a brow. "You're saying we make a paranormal spirit business and help other people connect with their loved ones?" She chortled, but the rest of us were silent.

My eyes lit up. I fished out my notebook from my backpack, flipping it open to where I'd scribbled down ideas last night. Now that I looked at it in broad daylight, it seemed like I was some kind of mathematician working out equations. The key one, however, was this:

Spirits + Moving On + Helping Loved Ones = $$$!!

A terrible, preposterous late-night idea. Or a brilliant one.

I'd only just learned spirits existed, but in all honesty, it wasn't that unbelievable from all the other weird and horrible things going on in the world. So why not go for something totally wild if it meant it would benefit the rest of us?

"I know the idea sounds a bit out there," I said

through a strained voice. "But this is Hollows' Peak! Most of the adults in this town would go for it."

"Wait a minute." Blair shook her bangs out of her eyes. "Are you suggesting we face down another killer spirit with a hockey stick? Because I almost *died*."

"That's a bit of an exaggeration, B," Lillian declared. She turned to face me. "How would that even work anyway? The phone called *us*. You know, somehow. Scientifically." Then, in a quieter voice: "Still trying to figure that part out."

"Because we kept the phone near people with lost loved ones," I urged. "Think about it. All of us have lost someone. Haven't we?"

I hadn't meant to bite down on a harsh topic, but Blair suddenly looked down, cheeks beet-red.

"Fluffy was a good cat," Blair said, crossing herself. "Rest in peace, Fluffster."

Aiko and Lillian fidgeted uncomfortably. Aiko lost her mother just a few short years ago. Lillian's family wasn't gone—she had her younger brothers and parents—but when her family moved here in first grade, she'd had to leave behind most of her extended relatives in New Orleans.

"So why hasn't one of our family's spirits called us?" Aiko asked, her voice just barely rising above the din of the taqueria.

"I'm not sure. But you saw what we did for Gabriela. We could help so many more people . . . people whose loved ones haven't moved on. This could be huge for our community." *And me*, I thought. I hadn't ruled myself out of this equation.

Because as soon as I'd learned what this phone could really do, another idea came to mind like a tender flame growing from a candle's wick. If that phone could *truly* contact spirits, and if I saw Mateo's grandma . . .

Who was to say I couldn't see my own?

Grandmama's health had suddenly declined, even after doctors promised she was on the mend from her illness. What would I say if I had just one more chance to speak to her?

This phone might be my chance to reconnect with Grandmama. After all, I did see those letters in the fog. That had to mean my grandmother was stuck in the in-between place, trying to make contact!

Even though Mama and I had dealt with enough grief, maybe, just maybe, she could reconnect with Grandmama one final time too and heal from the pain of the last six months.

My throat swelled up. Now I knew why they called it a frog in your throat, because I croaked out my next words. "These spirits are more real than I ever imagined. And they need our help."

Lillian tapped her gel nails together. "We *did* summon those . . . *spirits*. It appears that proximity has something to do with when the energies can call."

"Energies?" Blair echoed.

"Yeah. Spirits must be a collection of energy," Lillian explained. She must've done a lot of thinking on this last night too. "If someone wants to speak to a loved one, theoretically, they just have to be near the phone. And if their loved one needs help moving on, the phone will ring."

"So you're in?" I asked Lillian, feet shaking on the ground.

Lillian nodded. "Only because I can't turn down a scientific opportunity like this! I'll be researching all the scientific sources I can. In fact, we should all conduct our own research to learn more about the phone." She steeled herself, taking a deep breath. "Plus . . . you're one of my best friends, and I trust you."

I squeezed Lillian's hand. "Thanks, bestie."

"I was half joking about the business thing, but now that you've put it out there, you already know I'm on board." Aiko added, "And I'll definitely be doing some paranormal research of my own. Watching ghost-hunting TV shows counts!"

I chimed in, "I'll read through the guidebook to see what else I can find."

We all turned expectantly to Blair, who was avoiding eye contact and messing around with her butterfly-shaped cell phone charms. She finally exhaled her words. "Fine. I'll put on my mom's investigative hat and ask around the neighborhood if there have been any . . . *ghostly* encounters. See what we're dealing with. But we're stopping this when the business competition is over, agreed?"

"Agreed," we said in unison.

And to think, just a few days ago I hadn't believed in

spirits at all. However any of this was possible, I didn't care. My friends and I finally had a way to fulfill our goal for the arts program. I *had* to believe in it.

"Let's say we take on a few clients a week." I pointed at the schedule I'd scribbled in my notebook. "Blair can be in charge of making appointments. We can provide her cell number and create an email address for our posters and social media ads. But we have to keep ourselves anonymous. If my mom finds out we're using that phone..."

I trailed off. Honestly, I didn't really know *what* she would do. But with no cell phone in sight, I didn't want to take any chances, like, *Hey, Mom, I'm making a business with my friends and we're going to help spirits go to the great beyond!* If I said that, I'd be the one kicked straight into the "great beyond" before I had a chance to even *start* eighth grade.

"If our parents ever have questions, we can pretend we're still doing Get Everything Done!" Aiko assured me. "For the posters, we'll keep our identities a secret to attract our initial customers. Some people might be put off by twelve-year-olds handling their ghostly dilemmas—but like Paola said, some people are dying to speak to their loved ones again."

"Perfect." This was all starting to come together!

Just when I was starting to feel lighter than a ghost, a new waiter came to take our order. And not just anyone.

"M-Mateo?" Lillian gasped.

I choked on my water. Aiko sniggered, and I skewered her with a look.

"That's the name. Don't wear it out," Mateo said with a glinting smile. Oh, how I hated that infuriating smile. It was gentle enough to say, *What's up?* but still bared enough teeth to mean, *Yeah, I ditched you at the roller rink, so what?*

While Mateo hadn't exactly ditched me, that was what it felt like. Sixth-grade talent show all over again, except now the emotions rose twofold.

"So, can I get you gals a starter? The nacho trays are going fast," Mateo said slickly. He was good at selling food to customers, that much was obvious.

"No," I answered. Something about seeing Mateo made my appetite disappear. I took a gulp of water instead, pretending—and failing—that I was eating one of those delicious-looking nacho trays at table four. A group of kids were ravenously snacking, queso dripping from their mouths.

Blair asked, "Can I have an elote cup?"

Mateo took the other girls' orders and tucked the notepad into his apron pocket. The dark blue apron was inscribed with El Grillo's logo: two hands gently holding a stuffed hard-shell taco.

"On a serious note, now that you're all here . . . I want to apologize."

I sucked in a breath. Was Mateo about to drop the Biggest Apology of All Time? The one I'd been waiting for for over half a year?

"I want to apologize for my sister," Mateo continued, and the balloon in my chest deflated in an instant. "She mentioned something about seeing our grandma at her reverse birthday party with you guys. I know, weird, right? She gets pretty over-imaginative, especially since my abuelita's recent passing. My moms said they'll have a talk with Marisol—you know, to make sure she understands that she's gone."

So he *didn't* know we actually saw Gabriela's ghost. Phew. At least Mateo had blamed Marisol's confrontation with his deceased grandmother on the imaginative rants of an eight-year-old.

"Of course," Aiko said. "No need to apologize. We've all been there."

Mateo nodded. Were his eyes shining? I couldn't tell, because the next moment he twisted away and headed to the back of the restaurant.

I never really thought about what Mateo went through after his grandma passed away. At that point, he'd already ditched me and we barely spoke all summer. But just because he had his new friends and seemed A-OK at school didn't mean I didn't want him to secretly confide in me. Then again, I had lost Grandmama not long before he lost his, and I hadn't spoken to him much about it either.

It didn't matter anymore. He'd chosen his crowd. The popular kids always bounced back with easy, confident smiles. But me? After Grandmama passed away, I was a blubbering mess. Didn't exactly make me the best person to hang out with anyway.

"That's *two* Mateo conversations in three days," Aiko remarked. "I think we've hit a new record."

"We should get back to business if we want to *beat* Mateo instead of talk to him." I opened my notebook to a fresh page. "We need a business name. Any ideas?"

"Ghost Girlies?" suggested Aiko.

"Phantom Fighters?" Blair blurted.

"Energy Evaporators?" Lillian proposed.

"I like the short titles, but they're just not grabbing me," I admitted. We needed something punchier.

An idea sparked in my brain. "Remember what Paola said about Rose Hollow's business?"

Aiko sifted through her memory before nodding. "A service for calling ghosts." Aiko had an awesome memory. She could recite just about any actor's classic movie lines, from Will Ferrell's *"Buddy the Elf, what's your favorite color?"* to Arnold Schwarzenegger's *"I'll be back!"*

"Exactly!" I jumped up and down, making the customers at a nearby table twist their heads. "We're providing a service. A *spirit* service."

"Spirit Service. It's got a ring to it," Lillian admitted.

"Let's do it," Aiko said, then hummed to herself. "We should make a Spirit Service slogan!"

"Something catchy," I agreed, taking my seat. "Lillian, any ideas?"

"How about *who you gonna call?* Sounds good, right?"

"Already taken," Aiko droned. "*Ghostbusters*, 1984, supernatural comedy film directed and produced by—"

"Thanks, Aiko," I said with a stiff smile. "Any other ideas? Blair?"

"Hmm . . . we call, you bawl?" Blair suggested. We all stared her down. "What? *Someone's* bound to react that way."

"Which is why we need to have rules for these interactions. We've only just gotten to know how the phone works. We need to be careful about this. Our focus should be on allowing people to recover from their grief while giving them an opportunity to heal by helping their loved ones."

"So . . . like . . . no calling our favorite dead celebrities?" Aiko asked, glancing at our faces for a reaction that didn't come. "Right. That was rhetorical."

"We don't even know how to *call* anyone on the phone," I said. Though with the way my body buzzed like a hive of bees, I knew that one day, in the near future, I would have to learn how, if Grandmama didn't reach out to me first. "Right now let's just focus on helping these spirits."

"And our potential customers!" Blair added.

"Our loyal client base," Aiko corrected with a smile.

I nodded. "Speaking of clients," I continued, even though we didn't have any customers (yet) to begin with, "we'll need a place to meet them in private. Then, once we help the spirit, we get our set fee." I pointed at the dollar amount I'd written down. One hundred dollars would be our base price. At the start of the business competition, we all agreed on a total fundraising goal of five hundred dollars, which would be much more achievable with our new rate.

"We should space out our fees based on the level of spirit we're dealing with. We can increase by fifty-dollar increments between levels one, two, and three," Lillian suggested. Some of her parents' bank knowledge must've seeped into her brain. Most people knew Lillian as just a plain old brainiac, but she always said, *We contain multitudes!*

"Let's hope we won't have to deal with any level threes. I'll research what they might need to move on, just in case," Aiko noted, which probably meant she'd be watching a lot of TV tonight. Then she gasped, nearly salivating like a Pavlovian dog, when our food arrived. When Lillian offered to share her chips and guac with me, I gave in. How could mashed avocado and seasoning taste so *good*?

With Lillian's glitter pens and washi tape, we decided upon a simple but effective poster design, making the ends of the S in "Spirit Service" a coiled cord like the one connected to the rotary phone.

"Aiko, you're brilliant!" I said as she finished sketching out the design.

She shrugged nonchalantly and said, "In another life, I'd be Picasso. But without the misogyny."

We all giggled. "When do you think we should start posting online?"

"That's the thing," Aiko said. "While we should use social media to spread the word, a lot of Hollows' Peak townspeople are, well, *offline*. They might not even see our posts."

"You're right, Aiko," Blair said, tapping her temple. "Always thinking."

"Then do you think we can transfer this digitally and print some posters at the school library? The community center has a bulletin board where we can post them," Lillian suggested.

"Sure. I can have this done and printed by next week," Aiko estimated.

"Great. There's one more thing." I pointed at a spot on the poster where we'd written *insert slogan here*. We needed something to draw clients' attention.

"How about: *Here to help you move on?*" Blair suggested.

"I love it!" We were helping spirits move on, but in turn, we were helping loved ones work through their grief too.

"We can set up business hours after school. If they do call during school hours, they can leave a voice message," I reasoned. "And we still need a place to meet up with the customers. Somewhere private." Ideally a no-parent zone, which meant none of our houses. School wasn't exactly the best place for our business, either. Spirits running amok in the stinky gym? A recipe for disaster.

Just as I spoke, Mateo walked by to clean up a now-empty table splattered with queso. Behind him, I spotted a glass shed through the window. The enclosed herb garden was used to harvest fresh herbs year-round, but it also held storage for chairs and tables that Mateo's moms set up outside in the summer. "Patio dining" was the hot thing, apparently.

"The shed!" Blair suggested, following my line of vision.

I spent so much time there two summers ago, and adults never came inside. Mateo had mostly tended to the herbs while the Fierce Four recorded videos for sketches that we vowed would never be uploaded to TikTok. I shook away the memory. "No way. I am *not* staying within a ten-meter radius of *Mateo*."

"Did someone call me?" Mateo asked, approaching our table. Pickles. Did I say that aloud?

"Raveena did," Lillian said sweetly. I narrowed my eyes at her. Oh, I was so getting her back for that!

"Do you need the bill? Because the starters are on me," Mateo said.

"We don't. I mean, we do. I mean—" My brain fizzled like soda. Why was I like this? Why was *Mateo* like this, giving us food for free when his friends insulted me to my face?

"We need your garden shed." Aiko latched on to my sentence and ran with it. "For fundraiser meetings. Our homes aren't cutting it."

"What about school?" Mateo asked, tossing a rag over his shoulder.

"Well . . ." I made up an excuse on a whim. "School cramps our style."

Mateo pursed his lips in confusion. "Oooookay. I would need to get Mom and Mia's permission first, though."

Mateo's mother had gotten remarried to Mia after her husband left. Much like me, Mateo never knew his father firsthand.

He quickly refilled our waters before returning to the back of the house. I slapped my hand to my face. Cramping our style? Who even said that?

"Relax, Raveena," Lillian said. "I'll send you my K-pop playlist. When you get home tonight, you can chill, soak your feet in a bubble bath, and hit play."

I let the calming image run over me, but Mateo returned to the table with a wide smile on his face.

Moment ruined.

"My moms say it's fine, since they know you," he said, staring at the table more than me. "Just let us know when you're going in and out, and we'll give you the key."

"Perfect," said Blair, polishing off her elote cup. "Now, what's for dessert?"

EIGHT
Open for Business!

The week passed in a blur of French quizzes, Mateo avoiding, and lunchtime poster making with the rest of the Fierce Four.

Now my besties and I were heading toward the warmth of the Hollows' Peak Community Center. Our neighborhood's iconic bell tower, located in Hollow Square right next to City Hall, rose behind it like a fist brushing the clouds.

"Friiiiiiiiday!" cheered Aiko. "*Finally*. I was afraid this week was never going to end. Kind of like that 1989 movie *This Week Is Never Going to End*."

"Let me guess—it never ended?" Lillian quipped.

"Spoiler alert," Blair said after popping her bubble gum. "You guys know I watch movies in the background while I bake!"

Shivering from the lower-than-zero-degree weather, my friends and I hurried into the community center. We beelined straight for the bulletin board, which was studded with all sorts of posters. TAKE A NUMBER FOR DUCT CLEANING. BABYSITTERS AVAILABLE FOR HIRE. LOST PUPPY, PLEASE RETURN TO THE REYNOLDS BEFORE OUR TRIP TO ALASKA.

I took the pins Aiko bought from the dollar store and put our poster up. In big purple font, it read, SPIRIT SERVICE: HERE TO HELP YOU MOVE ON. Just an hour earlier, I'd set up an official Instagram account just in case the odd local spirit enthusiast happened upon our business page. Blair turned to us and flipped her ringer on.

"We're really doing this," I said. The sound of melodic laughter and splashing water caught my attention. I turned, my eyes landing on the tall glass wall separating the hallway from the swimming pool. My feet subconsciously stepped toward a familiar figure in the water—Marisol, her hair done up in pigtails as she bounced in Mia's arms. The scene made me smile. Was that how me and Grandmama looked during our swim lessons? Tears rushed to my eyes.

"Raveena, are you okay?" Lillian placed a hand on my shoulder.

My besties had seen me get emotional before, but for some reason I didn't want to get into this right now. "Uh, yeah." I sniffled. "The chlorine makes my sinuses act up."

I could tell Lillian wasn't buying it; thankfully, Aiko interjected, still admiring the poster. "There's a world of spirits who need to contact *us*. We have a big responsibility on our shoulders."

Blair's eyes widened. "I just had a terrifying thought. What happens if we *can't* help a spirit move on?"

Aiko shrugged. "That's what the guidebook is there for. I've already given it a skim; it'll take forever to read the whole thing."

I nodded. I'd been flipping through it as well during my spare time this week, and it felt like it was never-ending. At least Mama hadn't noticed the phone was missing from its box. With her new work schedule, she was so busy, she came home late every other night.

"Plus, Tía Paola promised to give us lessons," Lillian noted.

"Why doesn't that make me feel any better?" Blair moaned.

"Just think of the end goal," I reminded her. The phantom phone was more than our ticket to bringing back the arts. It was our beacon of hope. Our connection to the afterlife. Maybe, even, to my grandma.

This is for you, Grandmama.

Each of the Fierce Four put in a hand, and we shook on it with our secret handshake.

We all cheered, "Spirit Service is now open for business!"

Business was *not* going well.

Friday evening crawled by. Then Saturday. All weekend, Blair's phone didn't ring. Well, except for one crummy scam voice message she received while she was preoccupied with a batch of burnt cookies. *Your bank account is currently empty! Call us ASAP to get your hard-earned money back!*

Ugh. If you're gonna scam someone, at least have the decency to say *hello, good day,* or *bonjour, comment ça va?* before you go taking people's funds!

(Do not take people's funds, kids. Signed, a tween with no bank account.)

On Sunday evening, just when I thought things couldn't get any worse, Mama told me she and I would have to clean out the basement. Yeah, the *basement*. It is a truth universally acknowledged that basements are cluttered and creepy. But at least I knew there weren't any ghosts down there.

Mama would have been proud of my Jane Austen reference, even though she forbade me from reading her copy of *Pride and Prejudice* until I turned thirteen. But last summer the library had closed for repairs for *two whole days* and I had no choice but to dive into my mom's book collection. That Darcy guy could've used a few gummy worms to chill out. Or maybe a stern talking-to from someone like Hockey Grandma.

Now I was standing in the Land of Lost Things, our basement, where Mama attempted to "organize" piles of *stuff* for donation, sale, or just plain hoarding. Who knew Mama kept things like vintage bookends, scraps of fabric for the quilting project she swore she would get around to but never did, and even an unkempt applehead doll that should never see the light of day? I packed away the doll but hung on to some of the fabric. It had belonged to Grandmama.

Letting things go was tough. Letting *people* go was even tougher.

And helping a spirit go into the afterlife was the most mind-boggling of all.

I still couldn't get over how Marisol had spoken to her grandmother as if she'd never, you know, *passed on*. It was strange, the way only the four of us and Marisol seemed to notice the spirit's presence. I guessed Mama was a bit like Marisol: stuck in a place of in-between, refusing to acknowledge—or remember—the past.

I caught sight of a box in the corner of the basement, with Mama's violin sticking out of it. Mama slowly stopped playing before Grandmama's passing.

I wished she would pick up the violin again, that we could play together like old times. But as soon as Grandmama left this earth, music left Mama's heart.

I dug through a box, hitting a pile of strange photo albums I'd never seen before. Some of them sported velvet-wrapped covers and frilly lace all around them, like they firmly wanted to stay in the 1980s. I heaved one of the big books open, coughing at the sprinkling of dust it tossed in the air.

"Is that . . . Grandmama?"

I pointed at a black-and-white photo of my grandma in her twenties, dressed in a black sari and holding a coconut-shaped purse as she smiled at the camera softly.

"Where'd Grandmama get that from?" I pointed at the purse. Mama, who was previously engrossed in opening the packer's tape with much difficulty, paused. She turned to the photo album with a gleam in her eye. I thought it might've been a tear, but she blinked it away too fast for me to notice.

"The Philippines," Mama said, like she was reminiscing on an old home video. "She used to live there before she and your grandfather moved to Canada."

Mama had told me the story once, but I'd begged her to tell me more. Grandmama didn't like reminiscing too much about her childhood. It wasn't the easiest, she'd told me. She'd had to drop out of school after contracting a now-eradicated disease. In her early twenties, she'd gotten married and moved to Canada. My grandfather passed away before I was born. I didn't know too much else. Now, seeing her in this photograph, so young and full of life—it made her feel like she was really here again.

Like her spirit was here, in this very room.

Then again, I'd seen a *real* spirit now, and its wrathful funnel would've turned this place upside down. If it weren't *already* upside down, that is.

I blurted out, "Mama, do you believe in ghosts?"

"Ghosts?" Mama perked a brow. "Where is this coming from?"

"N-nowhere," I stuttered, clutching the velvety book to my chest, like all the photos of my ancestors might clear my spirit-addled brain. Or give me a runny nose. The dust was making my nostrils tingle.

"We should keep these photos upstairs, don't you think?" I asked.

Wrong move.

Mama snapped the book shut. She placed the photo album back in the box and sealed it closed, using her teeth to rip off the tape.

Striiiiike two! I was on thin ice since last weekend's cell phone fiasco at Yoon's Antiques, but now the ice had a large, jagged crack.

I knew bringing up Grandmama was a tender subject. There was still a maw in my chest, a gaping hole that would never be filled with her musical laughter again. But didn't Mama feel the same way? Couldn't she talk to me about it?

"Sorry, sweetheart. It's hard to think about that right now. Let's finish this up, and I'll make dinner," Mama said, using the excuse she often gave me. "How's meat loaf?"

"It's . . ." Repulsive? Slimy? A compound word that should've never been invented? "Fine. That's fine, Mama."

Nothing was fine, but Mama liked to pretend it was. And eventually, so would I.

When Blair's cell phone finally *did* ring on Monday morning before school, the Fierce Four galloped over to her locker to see what was going on. Blair's eyes lit up like she'd just perfected her cinnamon-dusted croffle recipe. It's a cross between a waffle and a croissant and totally *chef's kiss* worthy!

"Thank you for calling Spirit Service! How can we help you—"

"Move on?" Aiko finished into the speaker phone, jittering. Someone remember not to give her extra maple syrup at breakfast.

A chorus of identical voices chanted back:

"We require your services for our poor lost soul!"

"We'll pay any price, within reason!"

"Paola says your service comes highly recommended . . . by her, of course!"

Blair mouthed, *Oh my gourd!* Despite the seasonal reference, Blair was a pumpkin enthusiast year-round. Summerween is a real thing—look it up.

Blair cooled herself with an exhale before leveling the phone speaker with her mouth. "Of course we can help with that! But first I'll need to take down some information." Blair motioned for a pen and paper. Lillian was at the ready, collecting the client's details and setting up a meeting time at HQ, short for Spirit Service Headquarters—AKA El Grillo's herb garden shed.

"Thank you so much for calling." Blair hung up. "Did that just happen? We secured our first client?"

We all eyed each other silently before we let out one long, matching *squeeeeee!*

"I don't know how I'm going to focus on conjugating verbs after this," I admitted. My favorite French verbs were a tie between *pouvoir* and *comprendre*. But right now I *could* not *comprehend* anything besides the fact that after school we were going to handle our next spirit call.

See what I did there? (A bit of French wordplay for you. Madame Bower would be proud!)

Thankfully, the school day flew by, because the next thing we knew, we were outside El Grillo, holding a shiny key in our hands. Mia had gladly offered it to us—with the caveat that we all taste test her newest recipe, an appetizer composed of burrito bites accompanied by salsa roja. It was delicious, of course; Mia had one of the best palettes out there, aside from Blair. We said as much and were rewarded with the key and an extra plate of burrito bites.

Now, with the key in the lock, Aiko pushed the door open and announced, "Voilà!"

The shed at El Grillo was exactly as I remembered it. Warmly lit with barn lighting (#HGTV vibes) and some fairy light strings, the shed smelled of freshly watered herbs and peonies. *Pee-uh-knees*—Mama's favorite flower. She used to buy a whole vase of them fresh from the farmers market before Grandmama died.

"Our customer will be here any minute now," I told the rest of the Fierce Four. "And if they're anything like Tía Paola, we need to be prepared."

"Should we have dressed this place up with velvet curtains and crystal balls?" Blair raised a brow.

"No need. I was actually thinking we should assign roles. It'll help us organize our business."

"I'll be the secretary," Blair offered. "I'm taking phone calls anyway. I'll log our customer meetups and be sure to communicate them with you guys. I can make a shared online calendar and even color-code it!"

"My parents teach me a lot about money, so I'd say I'm a good fit for treasurer," Lillian added.

Aiko nodded. "I'll be the promoter, since I made all those posters."

I tapped my chin. "I guess that makes me . . ."

"President?" Blair offered. "You did come up with Spirit Service."

Lillian and Aiko agreed. "You can be in charge of keeping the phone safe at all times," Lillian said. "After all, it was *your* mom who bought the phone."

"Well, I was originally thinking we could all rotate the phone?" Aiko glanced around for support, but Blair and Lillian didn't look like they wanted to be within two feet of the phone longer than necessary. "No, you're right. Raveena can keep it," she finished with a slight crack in her voice, looking down at her hands.

Blair looked out the window. "I wonder what's taking our customer so long. Maybe we should wait outside so they know where we are."

Blair and Lillian headed out the door, chatting all the while. I turned to Aiko, motioning for us to have a seat on the bench by the door.

"Listen, Aiko, there's something I want to tell you. Remember that day in the cemetery? When we left . . . I saw something. The fog was spelling out the word 'beti.'"

The hairs on Aiko's arms stood up. "Whoa. Isn't that what your grandma called you?"

"Exactly," I told her, drawing out the word. "You know what that means, right?"

"Sentient fog exists?" Aiko said with a completely serious look.

"No—" I huffed. "I think Grandmama was trying to get my attention. Maybe she's stuck in the in-between place Rose Hollow was talking about? Is that too much of a leap?"

"Not at all. If it really is her, that's *big*. Have you told Blair or Lillian?"

I shook my head. There were certain things I only confided in Aiko, not because I didn't trust Lillian or Blair, but because I never held things back from Aiko. It was the way our friendship had always been. "I didn't want to until I was *absolutely* sure."

"Well, we're pretty new to being Guardians, but I hope she contacts us." Aiko steadied my hands in hers. "Thanks for telling me."

Three knocks came at the shed door. My body tensed with anticipation. Aiko and I shared a charged look, eyes sparkling.

Our first client was *here*!

NINE

Ghosts Can Play Fetch Too

"Come in!" Aiko called out.

Behind Lillian and Blair, a trio of identical women in their late thirties entered the shed, each of them dressed up as if they'd come straight out of the seventies. They even wore matching royal-blue lipstick, shade Bodacious Blueberry from Mrs. Wang's hair salon (which also sold the best lip glosses, sticks, and liners around). She'd tested the shade on me last summer, and let's just say blue is *not* my color.

"Hello, dears!" the trio of bell-bottoms and tie-dye cried out together.

"Welcome!" we all chanted back. *Our first customer!* Or rather, customers. That explained the chorus of voices on the phone this morning.

"We love to support local," one of them said, wearing a shirt that read, GHOSTS ARE TOTALLY GROOVY.

"I'm Wisteria Jones," the tallest of them said.

"I'm Dahlia Jones," greeted another, pushing up her bifocals.

"And I'm Iris Jones!" the shortest of the bunch said.

They each had matching tattoos on their forearms,

but I couldn't make out what it was. A wolf, maybe?

"We own a shop in Rosemary Heights called Blossoms and Specters," the tall one, Wisteria, explained. "For each ghost we communicate with, we offer a flower arrangement to the receiving customer!"

"Flowers are necessary for those grieving," Dahlia said. "Especially roses."

"Black ones are an extra three fifty a stem," Iris added with a wink.

It took me a moment to realize they were *triplets*. I always found twins and triplets spooky, but triplets who spoke to ghosts? That took it to another level.

"That's . . . actually brilliant," Blair said. "But if you're already *mediums,* how can we help you?"

I set the phone on the table in the middle of the shed as Lillian courteously pulled out chairs for each of the triplets. Iris began, "We can communicate with the deceased, but not with anyone related to us—or anyone who's *lived* with us."

"Meaning . . . ?" Aiko asked.

"It's our boy," Wisteria blubbered. She held back the waterworks as she said, "He passed away a few months ago, and we can just *feel* that his spirit hasn't moved on!"

"When we heard about your service, we thought it might be our only hope," Dahlia said.

"Our last hurrah!" Iris confirmed.

I turned to my fierce fam and nodded. As the newly instated president of the agency—I felt so fancy saying that—I needed to take charge.

"Before we begin," I started, "we ask that you spread the word about our service to your friends—but please refrain from revealing our identities. We prefer anonymity for ourselves and our clients!"

"No problem! We'll pass on the message to the busybodies at our monthly mahjong tournament," Dahlia agreed.

"Great. Let's begin. Please approach the phone as one," I told the triplets.

Dahlia, Wisteria, and Iris held their breath collectively as they eased forward. I turned to my fierce fam with an apprehensive look. Blair shrank back from the phone, while Lillian glared at it as if still questioning the logistical scientific properties behind a ghost phone.

Is this going to work? Or was this whole business idea a total flop?

"What now?" I asked Aiko. Our resident promoter—and paranormal enthusiast—offered me a reassuring gaze.

My colorful friend spread her arms wide, like a magician about to start a show. I could see the velvet curtains parting now.

"Spirit Boy from the Great Beyond, please bless us with your ghostly presence! Or . . . just give us a little phone call, pretty please!"

If the triplets found our business practices odd, they didn't say anything. After all, they all had spoken to ghosts before, so they didn't carry any of the nervousness we did. They were *ready* for this.

But what if the spirit that approached wasn't as easy to help as Gabriela? Or worse—what if it enjoyed hockey just as much and knocked a puck right through the glass shed?

That wouldn't be easy to clean up. And it'd cost a fortune.

"When is the phone going to ring?" Doubt crept onto Wisteria's features. "Paola promised us we would get to see our boy and give him a belly rub!"

"And a slobbery kiss!" Dahlia proclaimed. Whoever this boy was, I wasn't sure he wanted Bodacious Blueberry lipstick all over his cheeks.

Thankfully, the glow of the phantom phone put my mind at ease. It sparkled a brilliant white, its aura pulsing just like it did in Yoon's Antiques. A *brrrrrrring* rang through the shed, clear as the peal of a bell.

It worked!

"Who should answer it?" Blair rubbed her knuckles together. The rings echoed again and again.

Wisteria huffed. Dahlia fiddled with her bifocals. Iris tapped her Converse All Stars on the concrete. I could see the triplets were getting impatient. After all, if we didn't answer, we'd just ruined their chance at communicating with their boy, whoever it was.

"How about we do it together? On three," I told the girls. "One—"

"Three!" Wisteria, clearly the oldest and most wizened of the bunch, egged us on with a scowl.

We answered the phone.

"H-hello?" Blair asked tentatively.

No answer. Instead, the spirit revealed itself in an instant, materializing out of thin air. Thankfully, no vortex accompanied it like the last time. This spirit was much calmer—it was short and scampered around so fast that, for a second, I could hardly make it out clearly. When it stopped, Wisteria jumped for joy, trying to collect the spirit in her arms but failing.

"There he is, our boy Ruffles!" Wisteria exclaimed.

"Ahh." Now the belly rub and slobbery kiss made a whole lot more sense. Ruffles was a Labrador dog with the sweetest smile and a long, drooping tongue. He panted and wagged his tail as he wove between the legs of his former owners—the Rosemary Heights triplets. So *that* was their matching tattoo—their deceased dog!

Iris cried, "Oh my! Ruffles, you came back!"

Dahlia declared, "He needs our help moving on! Tell us what we must do!"

The dog yipped longingly. The Fierce Four almost leapt back—we didn't know we could communicate with ghosts a little over a week ago, let alone ones who were *animals*.

"I think he's trying to tell us something," Blair noted. Now that we knew the spirit was a dog, she looked much less afraid. She even reached out to pet the scruff under his neck, but her fingers went right through him. It appeared that trying to touch spirits was impossible, like trying to capture air. But apparently spirits could still interact with the physical world if they wanted to. Howling ghost dogs included.

Exhibit A: A pot of basil tipped over and cracked as Ruffles found his target. We were *so* getting in trouble for that.

"Look! He's digging!"

Ruffles was indeed pawing his way through the dirt of the former basil plant. When he didn't find what he wanted, he scoured his way past the triplets and out of the shed.

"Ruffles, wait!" Iris called out, nearly tripping over her long bell-bottoms on her way out the door.

Outside, the ghost dog kept digging small holes across the patchy grass, like he was making small plots for a flower garden. He turned back to us with a quizzical look on his face.

Then it hit me. The dog wasn't just digging for something. . . . He was *looking* for something he'd lost.

"Guardians," I said with as much confidence as I could muster, "we've got a level one on our hands."

"How do you know that?" Lillian asked, flipping through the guidebook.

"Can't you see? Ruffles is looking for something buried. Wisteria, do you know what Ruffles might be looking for? Something he might have buried before he died?"

"He had a beloved chew toy that he often played with outside. . . ." She tapped her chin. "In fact, he would chew it right over there while we grabbed a mojito and carne asada fries!"

"You're right, sis!" Iris said, scampering over to Ruffles. "Is what you want over here, boy? Go fetch!"

Ruffles followed Iris and started barking. Success!

He dug like no ghost dog had ever dug before. In a matter of seconds, he revealed the chew toy he couldn't dare part with—a squeaker toy shaped like a bone with tassels on the ends. The names of the triplets had been engraved on it, making it extra special. This must have been the physical relic he was looking for—just like the hair bow for Gabriela.

See? I'd been paying attention to Paola.

Ruffles scampered to each girl to give them a kiss. Or rather, a slobbery lick. The triplets appeared to be tickled, which meant they felt whatever Ruffles wanted them to feel—his love.

"I miss you so much, Ruffles!" Wisteria swiped away tears.

"I hope you're taking your vitamins in doggy heaven!" Dahlia said as Iris made baby-cooing sounds.

The ghost dog let out a howl in farewell. His spirit vanished into thin air, leaving no trace of him behind except the sparkle of its ghostly white glow.

"I don't think I'll ever get used to that," Blair said, mouth agape.

"Me neither." Lillian reached out toward the disappearing sparkle, as if she wanted to capture some of it and test it under a microscope.

Wisteria smiled tearfully. "Thank you, girls! Your service has inspired me to be a better medium."

"And a better mother to our hamster, Hammy," Iris said with absolutely no sarcasm. I supposed talking to a ghost dog might inspire one to be a better pet mom, but how would I know?

Wisteria fished for the cash fee in her purse and plopped it down on the table inside the shed. Lillian, treasurer extraordinaire, counted it up before the triplets left, content.

"A hundred and fifty bucks in the till! That includes a tip!"

"Fifty dollars is a tip?" Aiko's jaw hung wide open.

"Maybe in Rosemary Heights it is." Tía Paola wasn't kidding—people *were* willing to pay big money to communicate with spirits. Lillian made sure to tuck away the money in her new money box—we had to hand in our profits every week to Principal Hanover's office, where it would be kept safe before the end of the business competition.

I glanced out the shed's circular window, where the sky was beginning to turn a dusty rose—it was almost time for dinner. I tucked the phone and guidebook into my backpack. "I'd say that was a successful first customer! Let's hope for more to come. See you guys tomorrow?"

"Yep!" Blair zipped up her North Face jacket. "I'll get the key back to Mia. Secretary on duty!"

"Paola could use one of those," Aiko said, and everyone snickered. "Well, after helping that good boy,

I'm sleeping like a dog in a new doggy bed tonight!"

Knowing what I did about spirits, I wasn't sure I'd be getting much rest at all.

The following day after school, in the incense-heavy reading room at Paola's Predictions, Tía Paola dropped a plate of ingredients on the table.

"For our first official lesson, we're going to get hands-on." Paola grinned at us, her brown skin wrinkling around the corners of her eyes.

"You mean . . . we're going to learn more about the connection between the mortal world and the spirit world?" Aiko said. "Using crystal balls and other relics?"

"Not today," Paola intoned. "No, Aiko, I think *you* of all people know what we're doing today." She winked.

"Oh." Aiko chuckled. "Right." She turned to us and said, "Today, we'll be making . . . mochi!"

"I'm sorry, but what does mochi have to do with learning about spirits?" Lillian asked, peering at the ingredients.

"Today's lesson isn't about spirits," Tía Paola revealed. "It's about teamwork! Teamwork is essential for Guardians. If you don't know how to work together, a spirit—or human—could cause serious harm. I asked Aiko during one of her spontaneous visits last week to bring an activity that could put the Fierce Four's *fierceness* to the test."

"And mochi-making sounded perfect! Plus, I make it all the time."

"If cooking or baking is involved, I'm on board," Blair said.

"I don't know how this is going to help us guide spirits into the afterlife, but . . . okay?" I pulled the tray of ingredients toward me. Inside was a whole slew of ingredients like rice flour, green tea powder, and some kind of paste.

"That's red bean paste," Aiko explained. We all huddled around the table as Tía Paola watched over us with keen silver eyes that peered down like a hawk's. "I already froze it. That was the first step."

"What's the second?" I asked, genuinely curious. I didn't often get in the kitchen except when Mama asked me to prepare dinner when she came home late from shift work at the local grocer. Which was becoming more and more often.

Aiko took us through the process step by step—thankfully, Paola's Predictions had a microwave in the back (Paola had to heat up her lunch during busy workdays somehow!) for the dough balls we made from rice flour and green tea powder.

I brought the warm dough back to the work surface Tía Paola usually did her readings on, which was covered with a tablecloth splattered with flour. Blair not-so-surreptitiously dug her fingers into some rice flour and pitched it at Lillian's face with her fingers.

Lillian gawked. "Oh, we're going there?"

"Yup!" Aiko flicked her flour-covered fingers at my cheeks. "Food fight!"

We all giggled and ducked each other's attempts at spattering flour on each other. I flung green tea powder at Lillian, messing up her velvet headband, and veered to my right just as Blair tossed a frozen piece of red bean paste at me. It soared over my head, landing right on . . .

Welp.

We turned around to find a stern-looking Tía Paola, red bean paste globbed onto her forehead. A frown bracketed her lips as she said, "Girls . . ."

"Are we in trouble?" Blair squeaked out.

Paola's frown flipped upside down. "Of course not—this is exactly what I was talking about! Teamwork!"

"You mean making a mess?" Lillian giggled through flour-dusted lips.

"I mean, you four are clearly great at working together. Rolling dough takes patience, just as guiding a spirit and listening to their problems takes composure. Creating the perfect consistency of the cornstarch and flour takes calculated thinking. Measuring out ingredients is much like measuring the level of spirit you're facing—and, in the psychic world, very similar to reading one's palm with accuracy. You wouldn't want to give someone an incorrect reading—or not be able to solve what a spirit needs—would you?"

"I never thought about it that way," I realized. Maybe Tía Paola really was teaching us a lesson on spirits after all! And not all of it had to do with the supernatural realm.

My fierce fam and I finished making the mochi by placing the frozen red bean paste into the dough balls and closing them tightly into a circular shape. Once we cut the mochi down into bite-size pieces, we tumbled butt-first into our seats and dug into the deliciously sweet and savory dessert.

"I've never tasted anything like this!" Blair said. "And I bake. A lot."

"Thanks for sharing your recipe with us, Aiko," Lillian added.

A cloud passed over Aiko's face. "It's not my recipe actually—it was my mom's. I never told you guys this, but when she was alive, I made mochi with her every year. I kept up the tradition with my dad, though. It helps me feel more connected to her. Pays tribute to her memory."

"That's beautiful, Aiko," Tía Paola said, giving her a hug. Our Guardian guidance counselor, giving someone a *hug*? Now I knew we were on Paola's good side!

As we all shuffled out of the room, I hung back. "Paola," I called out, "I know this doesn't have to do with today's lesson, but I'm eager to know—can Guardians *choose* a spirit to contact? Like . . . a dead relative?"

Paola listed her head. "I'm afraid I don't know the answer to that, young one. But I can certainly ask my friends in Rosemary Heights. Gold star for thinking ahead!"

I chuckled awkwardly. "Thinking ahead. Right."

What Paola didn't know was that my grandma was

trying to reach out to me. I just needed to take initiative, figure out the next steps.

Paola might not have known the answer . . . but what if a past Guardian did?

TEN

A Peek into Hollows' Peak

I stayed up half the night reading the *Guidebook for Guardians.*

It started with the evergreen *just one more chapter* spiel. One chapter turned to two, turned to three, and unraveled into an accidental reading spree.

With my flashlight under the covers, I thumbed through page after page, in awe of all the spirits who had been aided thanks to former Guardians. No one appeared to have helped level threes. Did level threes even *exist*? Or worse...

Was no Guardian alive to tell the tale of vanquishing a level three because they *died*?

I shook my head. I was going into scaredy Blair territory. For all we knew, level threes were just a combination of ones and twos. See? Not scary at all.

There must be something in this book that could shine more light on how I might contact Grandmama. Was there an account of someone who wished to contact a loved one instead of waiting for them to call? Someone who, like me, needed to hear their grandmother's voice one last time?

Back when Grandmama was alive, she volunteered at

pop-up markets in Hollows' Peak, lobbied for more safety at crosswalks, and even hot-glued fake diamonds to her cane. She would shoo away bees when I would run screaming. She flipped rotis with her bare hands over a hot-as-fire stove. She even bought me my first flute off eBay.

She was the definition of a superhero—except instead of capes, she wore saris and salwars.

If she could do all those things, the least I could do was try to reach her.

I was about to flip the page when a phantom wind shivered through me. I glanced around my room. When did it get so cold in here?

Flip. Flip. Flip.

That sound made me freeze—if I wasn't cold enough already. Stiffly, I looked back down at the book to find the pages were turning . . . by themselves.

What was happening? I watched in shock as page after page of the guidebook zipped by until it landed on one in particular.

> WARNING: What I've written below is for experienced Guardians alone. Take caution.

I gulped. The top of the page confirmed that this was written by Elijah Hollow, Rose's son.

> Mother built an amazing invention.
> I've met so many more spirits than I

> would have with my own natural Gift, which offers me the ability to call upon hordes of spirits at my whim. Sometimes the spirits are still blissfully asleep—or horridly, mid-bath—when I snap my fingers. Those ones are much grumpier than usual.

I imagined an old, wrinkly spirit yelling, *I was just about to finish the daily crossword!* and shaking a cane.

> I never told Mother this, but I took the phone to my chambers and attempted to make my own phone call. I wished to see Father again. Wouldn't it be so glorious to speak to him and tell him that his effort in the war wasn't for nought? Every day I stared at his gravestone in the cemetery. But the day I took the phone to my chambers, I was hoping to see more. I placed his treasured chronograph next to the phone, hoping an heirloom from his past would summon him to me. And oh, did it ever work! Father's ghostly form appeared as if he had never left, albeit with a slightly luminous glow. Finally, I could tell him the farewell I had never given to him when he was lost to the battlefield.

I gaped, my mind churning as I skimmed the rest of Elijah's account. All I could focus on was how he'd *summoned* someone using the phone—his own father!—using a special heirloom.

Which meant I'd need an heirloom of my own if I ever wanted to see Grandmama again.

"Good afternoon, class," my history teacher, Mr. Bisson, greeted us the next day. His voice echoed in the computer lab we were currently sitting in for today's lesson. "Today marks the start of your midyear project! Any guesses on the topic?"

A kid in my class named Rudy raised his hand. "The Hollows' Day Festival?"

I thought back to the copy of the *Hollows' Herald* Mama had been holding in Yoon's Antiques. The headline read ONE HUNDRED YEARS OF HOLLOWS' PEAK FESTIVAL ON THE HORIZON! The information on the whiteboard behind Mr. Bisson was almost the same, word for word.

"Very good, Rudy," Mr. Bisson said. Under his breath he grumbled, "At least I know he can read something other than text messages." His smile brightened. "Indeed! This year marks one hundred years since our township was founded. At the upcoming festival, Mayor Clayton will be opening a time capsule that was buried fifty years ago. Does anyone know what a time capsule is?"

I raised my hand. "Kind of like a buried treasure

chest, but for old stuff, so people years and years in the future can open it and discover what it was like living back then."

"Exactly! Thank you, Raveena. And to commemorate this festival, I have an assignment for you all. You'll each have to research, write, and present on one aspect of the town's history. In other words, let's take a *peek* into Hollows' Peak!"

When no one laughed, Mr. Bisson mumbled, "I knew I should've gone to comedy school." Our homeroom teacher was only funny by accident. For example, at recess, he liked to pop spearmint gum bubbles when he thought no one was looking. Lillian and I cackled so hard, our stomachs hurt for the whole afternoon.

"This is a big project, since you'll each be presenting your displays at the festival." Mr. Bisson went on about the due dates as he handed out slips of paper with our assigned research topics. Mine read: *History of City Hall*. Aiko got *The Great Parrot Migration of '96*. Why was my topic so *boring*?

I turned my attention to my computer as the buzz of students' voices built around me. I knew I should be focusing on the assignment, but first things first:

Heirloom, I typed into the search bar. A bunch of results turned up. Heirloom tomatoes—yummy, but not what I was looking for. Aha! There—heirlooms were defined as something valuable that's passed down from generation to generation. So for Elijah, that was his father's chronograph. Another quick search showed me that that was an old kind of wristwatch.

But what heirloom did I have from Grandmama? Mama had some of her things from India, but would those work? Those coconut purses from the Philippines were nowhere to be found. I would need to dig into Grandmama's old things, but Mama and I had *just* cleaned out the basement.

"Talk about bad luck," I mumbled.

"I prefer the term 'misfortune,'" Aiko said from beside me without turning. A word she learned from her second-favorite TV series—*Mayhem, Misfortune, and Miniature Ponies*. She paused her typing to fix me with a look. "What's up, Raveena? You seem frazzled."

"I do?" I fixed my bed hair, which I'd forgotten to brush in the morning. But even if my hair was neatly straightened, Aiko would *still* know something was amiss. We just had a connection like that. "I was up late reading," I revealed.

"The *Guidebook for Guardians*? What did you find?"

"Just some old logs and musty paper," I said with a *no big deal* shrug, but my inner self couldn't help babbling more. "And . . . something Elijah Hollow wrote about contacting his deceased father."

"*Oh. Em. Gee!*" Aiko stage-whispered. "You mean it's possible to make contact with a family member? You don't have to wait for them to call?"

"I'm still figuring it all out," I admitted. "But yeah, I think so. Elijah used something called an heirloom.

A watch that belonged to his dad. Imagine if I found something of Grandmama's!"

"Imagine that," Aiko said, but her eyes looked far away. "What else did Elijah say?"

"Not much." I didn't want to confess *all* my secrets just yet. "Besides, as Spirit Service's president, it's my duty to conduct as much research about the book as possible, you know, to keep our business afloat...."

It took me a moment to realize Aiko wasn't listening to me. I snapped her out of her trance. "Earth to Aiko?"

Aiko blinked twice. "Sorry, back from my space mission," she joked before hammering away at her keyboard. I sensed something off about her but didn't voice my concerns aloud. Mama taught me some people just need their space.

I turned my attention back to my topic and started searching. Last week, Mrs. Nkosi taught us students how to narrow down our searches using keywords. I fiddled around with a few different searches before I found an article on City Hall that caught my eye. It was a timeline, all the way from its construction in 1925 until now.

I stopped at 1975. "Bell tower struck by lightning . . . nearby City Hall burns down in Hollow Square . . ." The article mentioned a freak lightning storm that hit the bell tower in the square. Twenty-odd residents in the next-door City Hall died that night in an electrical fire.

"That sounds *awful*," Aiko said. I didn't even realize I'd been reading the headline aloud. "My topic on parrot migration in the nineties doesn't hold a candle to an actual *fire*." She pointed at the article she found on the *Hollows' Herald* website with a picture of a parakeet.

"You can read old editions of the paper online?"

Aiko nodded. "Blair's totally into that stuff. Her mom says *vintage* is coming back."

"Debatable." I searched up the *Hollows' Herald* website. It only went back forty years—apparently you needed special permission to access older articles. Otherwise, there was only one place where you could find old records.

It was time for a quick trip to City Hall.

"Hey, fierce fam!" I greeted my friends after school. Aiko, Lillian, and Blair waved at me while munching on Blair's latest stress-bake creation—caramel-glazed profiteroles, a fancy word for cream puffs.

"I needed choux dough to get my mind off the fact that we haven't gotten another phone call or email," Blair explained as I dug into my puff. City Hall was just a few blocks away from school, and I told my besties-slash-business-partners that we needed to go there for *research* purposes. Not just for my assignment, but also to go over what each of us learned about the world of the paranormal over the weekend. We didn't have time to chitchat in between helping Ruffles and our lesson with Paola.

"I'm sure all businesses start off a bit slow," I told Blair. As president, I needed to keep team morale up!

"Let's just focus on our assigned research roles. Lillian," I said as we crossed the threshold into City Hall, a grand domed building with a magnificent marble ceiling. "What have you learned from your scientific sources?"

Lillian dropped her backpack onto a circular leather couch with just enough cushions for the Fierce Four. We all plopped down and examined the marble statue at the head of City Hall, a handcrafted model of Rose Hollow herself with her two kids, Elijah and Carmela. Rose had a halo of hair tied up in a high bun. At her side, her child Elijah wore a sneaky smile. Carmela, slightly shorter than Elijah, wore pigtails and a vintage dress with puffed sleeves. Imagine those making a comeback. I shuddered.

Rose's husband had already passed by the time she moved to what is now known as Hollows' Peak. I thought again of what Elijah said—that he was able to summon the spirit of his father to him. If that was possible, then nothing was off-limits.

"A *lot*," Lillian said, turning my attention away from the statues. She snacked on another profiterole, making us all wait in anticipation, before she continued. "I found articles from accredited sources that describe ghosts as collections of 'energies' or electrical forces."

"Like what you said at El Grillo," I recalled. "What happened to 'the presence of spirits has been debunked by tons of scientists'?"

"Here's my line of thinking. Since the phone is an electrical item and zapped us, that confirms that ghosts and spiritual energies aren't so different from electricity and science itself."

"Go on," I said.

"Remember that unit we had on electricity? For electrical currents to get from point A to point B, they have to have a conductor, like a wire. What if the phone is like a conductor of sorts, using spirits—or rather, their electrical force—as a current to power it?"

Aiko gasped. "Lillian, are you saying you believe in *ghosts*?" She fake wiped a tear from her eye. "My girl is growing up!"

"I'm two months older than you," Lillian remarked. "And *maybe*. Ghost grandma and dog aside, my cross-referencing has me starting to believe that the spirit world isn't so far-fetched. But like any good experiment, more research needs to be conducted."

"I knew you'd come around!" Aiko threw her arms around Lillian with glee, who was obviously trying hard not to smile.

"And you, Aiko? What did you learn during your TV marathons?" Secretary Blair was currently taking minutes—detailed notes from our meeting—in a fresh notepad.

"Well, you know me. I can't just do one thing at a time. I have to go all-out!"

We all glanced around. "Like?" Blair finally asked when Aiko didn't elaborate.

Aiko huffed. She dug for something in her bag, sort of like how Ruffles dug for his chew toy, and reappeared, triumphant, with her prize. It was a small but mighty collage of construction paper, printed articles, and lots of glitter, washi tape, and colorful markings. The middle of it all read: GHOSTS ARE FRIENDS, AND GUARDIANS THEIR HELPERS.

"Check it out—it's a spirit board! I'm keeping all my ideas and research about ghosts, including questions I have about them, right here on this board. I also may have watched more reruns of *Short Island Medium* over the weekend. I'm thinking I've figured out what a level three spirit could be."

"Really?" My eyes widened.

Aiko flipped her hair over her shoulder, like, *Did you ever doubt me?*

"I think level three spirits are made up of more . . . *chaotic* energy. In other words, they don't *want* to move on."

"Then what *do* they want to do?" Blair wondered. "Do you think Rose Hollow wrote about level threes in the guidebook?"

I shook my head. "I read through a bunch of the book last night. No info on level threes—nor does Rose Hollow explain what they mean."

"Great," Lillian moaned. "Maybe this is some kind of rite of passage for new Guardians. Figure out the level threes, and win a free pass to Chucky's BBQ all summer long!"

"I think I still have a stomachache from when I ate Chucky's rib special in third grade," Blair said. She may have been a foodie fanatic, but she also had her foodie "aversions." AKA food she stayed *far away* from just because of one bad experience.

"Chucky's rib special *aside*," Aiko said, "maybe Rose never actually got to face a level three, and that's why there's no information on them."

"Possibly," I said, adding that to my list of theories for level threes. "Blair, have you started your snooping? I mean, investigating!"

"Kinda," Blair admitted. "I spoke to a few neighbors, including Mrs. Fitz. Apparently, she communicates with her dead husband every day using potato chips. Don't get me started on how."

"That probably leaves a lot of crumbs on the table," Lillian chided. On top of belly button hygiene, and soap operas, the Baxters also prized tidiness.

Blair continued. "Mrs. Fitz told me she's never actually *seen* his spirit. But if his spirit is still able to communicate with her, then imagine how many other spiritual happenings are going on in town?"

I thought of those words in the fog spelling out "beti." Grandmama, reaching out to me...

"Who knows," Blair added, knifing into my thoughts. "Maybe Mrs. Fitz will even book an appointment with Spirit Service!"

"You sound pretty chipper," noted Lillian. "Are you sure you're not still afraid of ghosts?"

"Am not!" Blair huffed. "Okay, cute ghost doggie aside, spirits are still pretty scary. But if Mom's reporter skills have taught me anything, it's that looking into things from an objective lens can help anyone overcome their fears."

"So you won't scream the next time a spirit pops up after the phone rings?" Lillian smirked.

"No promises!"

I giggled. Honestly, it made me happy to see Blair making progress with her fear, little by little.

"What did you discover, Raveena?" Lillian asked.

Aiko looked at me as if expecting me to tell the others about the cemetery fog. For some reason, I kept my lips sealed. I wasn't sure if I should bring up the whole Elijah-speaking-to-his-father thing I read about in the guidebook, either.

"Nothing much," I said nonchalantly. Aiko touched the base of her neck, as though confused by my response.

"Maybe we should book a lesson with Tía Paola soon?" Lillian suggested. That seemed to cheer Aiko up.

"I visit her shop, like, all the time," Aiko said animatedly. "You never know when you'll need a new psychic relic! A lot of the stuff she sells is rooted deep in Hollows' Peak history."

I twisted in my chair. "Speaking of Hollows' Peak, I'm doing some research for a town history assignment. I'm focusing on the town fire in 1975. Do you guys know anything about it? Apparently, City Hall burned down."

Lillian nodded. "It was reconstructed not long after.

Actually, a lot of Hollow Square had to be rebuilt. Pops told me there was a bank there back then, but it eventually moved to Main Street."

"Really? When I looked online, it also mentioned the bell tower was struck by lightning."

"Did I hear you girls mention the bell tower?" Mrs. Nkosi drifted in from my peripheral vision. She *really* needed to stop spooking us like that. And what was she doing here, wearing blue medical gloves? She was a librarian, not a surgeon!

"Yeah," I said. "I'm looking for information on the night lightning struck the bell tower. It's for a school assignment."

The librarian adjusted her glasses. "Well, lucky for you, I volunteer here after school hours in the Archive Room."

"An Archive Room? As in, a place that houses old files and newspapers? Could you take us there?" That would be perfect for my assignment!

"Of course!" Mrs. Nkosi led us across the lobby, which was full of workers buzzing around like bees in a hive, and up a set of polished marble steps. We passed a single-person staff bathroom, which required a key to get in, and to the right of that was a room labeled MAYOR CLAYTON'S OFFICE. The door was open, and I spotted the mayor inside.

Mayor Clayton waved to us. "Hey, girls," he said, his Afro forming a crown of curls. We waved back. He came to our school pretty often, since he was tight with Principal Hanover.

At our destination, the librarian used one of the keys on her lanyard to open the frosted glass door and said, "Welcome to the Archive Room!"

I don't know what I was expecting—maybe an Indiana Jones type of treasure room—but it was mostly cardboard boxes and a flashy microscope, probably for reading all that fine print.

Mrs. Nkosi set to work, ruffling through the boxes labeled by decade. She drifted over to the seventies and tapped her nose. "Got it!"

"What are your gloves for?" Blair asked Mrs. Nkosi.

"Can't ruin the original papers," she said. "It's a part of the archival process, keeping everything intact and in its original form. Oil from my fingers could stain the fragile state of these older newspapers. See here? This paper is from 1975. The day after the electrical fire."

"May I?" I asked.

"Certainly." The librarian handed me a matching pair of blue gloves and let me hold the paper. This was awesome! I was holding a piece of the town's history right in my gloved hands. Mrs. Nkosi was right; the paper was delicate and fragile, slightly yellowed around the edges.

"There's a before and after picture," I said, pointing out what City Hall looked like before it burned down. Based on how it looked now, the restoration process was pretty smooth.

But when I looked closely at the before picture, I could see three people standing in front of City Hall with big smiles on their faces. One of them in particular, a woman with a long black braid and a sweet grin, jumped out at me.

"Is that . . . ?" I stopped in shock. *Grandmama?*

ELEVEN

Coincidence? I Think Not!

Three names captioned under the photo leapt off the page: Hanbin, Georgia, and . . . Avneet.

That was Grandmama's name. Was this a sheer coincidence? I glanced again, but I wasn't so sure. I'd never seen this photograph before in any of our photo albums.

Then again, Mama was so dead set on scrubbing away Grandmama from our home—from hiding those photo albums to stashing all our old stuff in boxes in the basement—that maybe we *did* have this picture, and I just never saw it before.

"Mrs. Nkosi," I began, "that's my grandma in this picture. Do you think you could make me a copy of it? I'd really appreciate it."

"Of course. What a delightful bit of serendipity!" the librarian said, leaving the Archive Room.

"Or plain old destiny," Aiko said. "It's like we were *meant* to come here today for our meeting!"

Destiny . . . that word tickled the back of my brain. Destiny, as in Destiny Hollow. Elijah's daughter. Elijah had mentioned a warning—that trying to summon someone with the phone required caution. *And it* required an experienced Guardian. But we'd only just become the phone's Guardians. Was it really so wrong to try something new, despite his warning?

To try summoning Grandmama?

I hadn't *told* Aiko that I was dead serious about contacting my grandma, but my BFF had encouraged me—even told me she wished Grandmama might reach out. Aiko would understand. Aiko would get it.

Besides, if I waited around for Grandmama to call, she might never do it. I couldn't take any chances. I had to summon Grandmama soon, just like Elijah did for his soldier father.

"Hey, Raveena?" Aiko pulled me aside so we were standing at the lip of the doorway. "Do you think I could take the phone home tonight? I'd really like to look into the *Guidebook for Guardians* too, since you had a chance to read it already."

"Oh." That would put a dent in my plans to call Grandmama. "Sorry, Aiko. I'm actually not done reading the book yet, and like Lillian and Blair said, I'm president, so I think I should keep an eye on the phone outside of business hours. For now, of course!"

Aiko nodded. "Sure. Totally." Did I imagine the dejectedness in her voice?

"Besides, I left the phone at home," I told her. "We shouldn't bring it to school unnecessarily. Who knows if it'll start ringing, right?"

When the librarian returned with a printed copy of the photograph, I was all smiles. Aiko could wait another night longer—I *had* to do this soon. I didn't have an heirloom of my grandmother's, but maybe I could find one if I looked hard enough.

I needed to go home to find out. Mama couldn't say no to this innocent face, could she?

"No," Mama said at the kitchen table that night.

Ughhhh. All I'd asked was if I could scour Mama's closet for some of Grandmama's old clothes and jewelry. You know, *precious heirlooms* of the past. Those three magic words rose up my throat again.

"It's not fair!" Impatience boiled in my blood. "You're always avoiding talking about Grandmama. Isn't it better to remember her instead of hiding her away?"

"Excuse me?" my mom retorted.

Striiiiike three! You're out!

I didn't care if I'd hit three strikes. Mama always curbed my attempts at talking about Grandmama, and my pent-up frustration was threatening to spill out.

"Don't you find it ironic how much you love antiquing—how much you love the past? But you don't even bother talking about *your* past, or about Grandmama. Why? What did Grandmama do to make you so, so—" I let out an exasperated snarl.

Mama snapped her eyes shut. "You don't understand what I'm doing, Raveena."

"Then tell me!" My anger was coming off me in waves. I didn't realize I was clenching my fists until I felt my nails digging into my skin.

But even though I spoke out of turn *and* raised my voice *and* hurled accusations at her, Mama didn't say a thing. Of course.

She gave me a stern, thunderous look alongside another plate of meat loaf (barf! Who makes meat loaf twice in one week?), and told me to go to my room and think about what I said while she was out for another quick shift at the grocer. As *if*.

After scarfing down what I could of tonight's dinner, I flipped through the guidebook. I was in literal need of guidance. Paola had called herself our Guardian guidance counselor, but I didn't exactly have her on speed dial. I didn't even have a cell phone, thanks to my mother.

Why did everything come back to Mama? If she really *listened* to what I said earlier, maybe she'd see some sense in what I was saying. But *no*. She'd shut Grandmama away just like she abandoned her violin.

I wasn't going to give in so easily.

I kneeled on the side of my bed and placed the phone gently on the blankets. Then I splayed the guidebook open to a random page.

"*Guidebook for Guardians*, help me," I pleaded.

I half expected the pages to start flipping again on their own, like they had last night. That was a semi-freaky affair. But now things got even freakier.

On the bottom of a half-empty page, words started appearing in fine, black handwriting I didn't recognize:

Use the photograph.

The words faded just as easily as they came. I rubbed my eyes, wondering if they had even appeared in the first place.

I dug through my backpack and retrieved the photocopy of the picture I'd found in the archives. But this wasn't an heirloom. . . . Would it be strong enough to summon Grandmama? Not to mention there were other people in the picture. I wasn't entirely convinced this would work.

Use it.

The words appeared again, this time the ink breaking and splattering on the page, like it had taken whoever wrote this message more energy than I realized.

Could this be *Grandmama* writing to me? Any spirit in the in-between place could interact with the physical world, from what I'd learned over the past few days. Just like Mrs. Fitz and those potato chips. And the letters in the fog. Which meant only one of *those* spirits was able to write in the guidebook. But why not simply call the phone if they wanted to reach a Guardian?

I glanced back at the ink that splattered the page, watching as it disappeared. Were some spirits weaker than others? Did they need *help* reaching out? Elijah's heirloom rang in the back of my mind. When Mateo first came near the phone, he must have had something precious of his grandma's with him. His seashell necklace! I remembered his grandma making that for him.

And as for the triplets, what *heirlooms* did they have from Ruffles? Oh, yes—their tattoos. There was an identical one on each of their forearms. So maybe heirlooms didn't have to be totally physical hand-me-downs. It seemed that any heirloom, or a visible memento of the past, could strengthen a spirit enough to help it make a call.

Maybe this photograph truly *was* enough.

I placed the photo next to the phone and examined the chipped paint closely. Those burn marks stood out to me again. I closed my eyes and thought of Grandmama.

Come on, Grandmama. Just one call. Please. I need to hear your voice.

I peeked one eye open. Nothing. Not even a single *spark*.

I knew it wouldn't be that easy. I knew this whole idea was too much. If only I hadn't read what Elijah wrote about his dad. If only I wasn't so gullible—

Tears rose to my eyes, and before I knew it, they were falling off my face, crashing onto my blanket like raindrops tearfully pouring from the sky. I wanted to cry. I wanted to be angry. I wanted to feel everything I'd been feeling for six months and then *banish* it with a clap of my hands. It wasn't fair! Nothing about living without Grandmama was fair!

I got up and threw my tear-splattered pillow, making my desk lamp rattle. I grabbed the assignment handout on my desk and ripped it to shreds, my tears blinding me, my ire fueling me. What did it matter? What did *any* of this matter for, without Grandmama by my side?

I was shaken out of my stupor of rage by the ringing of a phone. It took me a second to realize...

The phantom phone.

A familiar glow filled the room, and my hands trembled as I lifted the handset. *Click.* "Hello?"

Something crackled on the other end of the line, like paper being scrunched together.

"Hello?" I sniffled. "Who's calling me?"

More static. The world of spirits was certainly electrified, just as Lillian presumed. But that wasn't what I cared about right now. I needed to know who was reaching out to me. Based on what we'd learned, it could only be someone related to the loved one who was close to the phone. And I was the only person in its vicinity. Technically, any of my deceased ancestors could be calling. But there was only one person whose voice I desperately needed to hear.

I swallowed the lump in my throat. "If you don't answer me, I'll hang right up."

No answer.

"I'm not kidding." I motioned to hang up, then froze in place.

"*Stay*," a voice shuddered out. It was so small, it could have belonged to a mouse. I shook my head.

"G-grandmama?" I held my breath, letting hope balloon in my chest. I wiped my snotty nose. "Grandmama, is that really you?"

The voice came back stronger this time. *"Yes, beti..."*

I nearly cried again—but this time in joy, as pure as sunlight breaking through after an endless rainstorm. The clouds had finally parted. Grandmama had called. I'd done it!

"Can you show yourself to me, Grandmama?" I choked out. I glanced around the room, expecting her spirit to materialize like Hockey Grandma in the rink or Ruffles in the shed. But that familiar white glow of a spirit was nowhere to be found.

"I am not... strong enough...."

"I'm learning about spirits from the guidebook. I'm a Guardian! I can figure out how to make you stronger—"

"Focus on my voice, Raveena," Grandmama said from the other side. Her voice warbled, like she was just getting used to using it again. Sort of like me after I got laryngitis two summers ago. I didn't blame her; she hadn't spoken to anyone in six months! At least, not in the physical plane, as Paola called it.

"Grandmama, I can't tell you how happy I am to hear from you!" I cried. Literally. The waterworks were dialed up to a ten, and I turned into a blubbering Wisteria Jones. I pinched myself once, twice. This was actually happening.

"Me too. I have so much to tell you.... But first, promise me something."

"Anything, Grandmama."

"Keep this a secret for now. Your mother might be frightened... your friends, too."

"I will." I didn't even have to think twice. Whatever Grandmama wanted, I would gladly give.

"*Good . . . Keep me in your heart, granddaughter. I will speak to you again.*"

"But we just started talking!" Panic set in. Oh no—I couldn't lose Grandmama.

Not again.

"Promise me you'll call," I begged.

"*I promise.*"

The phone's glow ceased. A beeping dial tone echoed from the phone. I didn't have it in me to hang up.

But I knew one thing: I had done what Elijah Hollow warned me against. I may have only ever guided two spirits, but I *was* an experienced enough Guardian.

I had successfully connected with my own grandmother through the phantom phone.

At school, I was practically buzzing with emotions. Good ones—relief, joy, elation.

Some were not as good. Anticipation, anxiety, dread. What if Grandmama really couldn't call me again? I had to focus harder this time—get her to call me with as much might as I could muster.

For now, though, this small interaction had to be enough. It *had* to.

"Raveena? You're chewing your fingernails. A lot. You okay?" Lillian asked while I was staring into the deep recesses of my locker. Or rather, the pile of binders I had yet to reorganize. I glanced down at my nails. Yikes—I would need to file those later.

"Just peachy," I said, shutting my locker as Aiko and Blair joined us. Grandmama's promise remained steadily in the back of my mind. No telling anyone. She was right. I might frighten away Mama, and I was already on her bad side. And my friends were still getting the hang of using the phone. As president, I needed to learn more about interacting with spirits first, before I presented all this information to the rest of the Fierce Four. In time, they would learn the truth.

Plus, I had a feeling Aiko was right about the whole destiny thing. Maybe Grandmama had been beside me all along, pushing me to go to City Hall, to find that photo of her in the old newspaper. It was just what I needed to summon her.

Now, two minutes after the lunch bell rang, it was time for the meeting the Fierce Four had booked with the Big Man himself. No, not *that* Big Man. Principal Hanover was the head honcho of Hollows' Peak Middle School, and despite having to give that doomsday speech at the beginning of the year, he was actually a pretty mellow dude. According to student gossip, he enjoyed swimming with pool floaties on his arms, listening to Kickin' Country Radio, and making daily phone calls to his mother.

Just as the four of us reached the principal's office, we stopped in our tracks. Another set of students was easing their way out of the room. The Keepin' It One Hunnid team sneered as they swaggered past us—all except one bringing up the rear. I nearly growled at the sight of him.

Mateo.

"Hey, Fierce Four," Mateo said as his cronies drifted ahead. "What's up?"

"The sky," Blair said. Dad joke, incoming!

Mateo frowned, clearly perturbed by Blair's attempt at comedy. "So, how's business, Raveena? Booming?"

"Yours must be," I said through gritted teeth. Over the past few days, I'd overheard his team members boasting about how any day now they'd have everything they needed for the Haunts, from sick new jerseys to fresh sneaks and shiny basketballs. Yes, *shiny*. Probably from all the sweat they would be dripping on them. Gross.

"Sure is. We're almost at our goal of one thousand—"

Aiko clasped a hand to her chest. *"One? Thousand? Dollars?"*

"Aiko, have a sip of water," Blair told her, fanning our friend.

"It's no biggie," Mateo said coolly. He gave me a subtle wink.

Erghhhh. That was *so* like him, riling me up. "Well, Get Everything Done! is getting a rebrand. In fact, we've already had a loyal set of customers come in, and they're going to recommend our service to all their friends."

"Rebrand? Sounds official. Well, good luck in there, I guess," Mateo said, his shoulder gently knocking against mine as he passed us on his way out of the office. OMG. Did he just brush me *off*?

I tried not to let it rattle me. After all, there were more important things to keep my eye on. Like the prize of getting the arts program back. Something Grandmama always clung to was the power of music, and she taught me to do the same. I couldn't live without it. It was hard enough living without *her*.

But hearing her voice last night gave me all the confidence I needed to make this meeting go my way. Principal Hanover was going to be so impressed. And Mateo? If I showed him up in the business competition, he and his cronies wouldn't *dare* talk back to me or my friends. In fact, they'd respect us. Mateo might even finally apologize.

Mission Make Spirit Service Win the School Business Competition was a go.

TWELVE

Mateo Who?

"Welcome, girls," Principal Hanover greeted us as we each took a seat in our respective armchairs. The kind where you practically sink into them and take a good, long nap. It was no wonder the principal spent most of his time here.

Principal Hanover seated himself opposite us before his grand oak desk, which was covered in bags of corn chips. (No surprise there.) He slid up the sleeves of his olive-green jacket before popping open a bag. Tapping the side of his headphones, he halted the blaring country tune and politely asked, "How's the business going, girls?"

"We've had a breakthrough!" Aiko cheered. "As you know, we were near the bottom of the business competition totals over the past few weeks. But we've got a new idea that can change *everything*."

I cleared my throat. I didn't want Aiko to get *too* excited—after all, we had to keep the actual phone a secret even from Principal Hanover. *No one* could know how our business practice worked outside of paying customers. But we still had to tell the principal what we were up to.

So I began. "We've come up with a grand new idea. We've found a way to bridge the weird and wacky ways of Hollows' Peak with a business idea that's out of this world."

"Literally," Blair added. She held up her phone and flipped through the slide deck she'd prepared eagerly.

"Do tell!" The principal's eyes widened as he offered us some corn chips. "Anyone?"

I shook my head. Time to come out with it. "We created a business that . . ." I took a deep breath. "Helpspeopletalktospirits."

"What now?" Principal Hanover said through a mouthful of corn chips. He read over Blair's slide deck just to be sure, which had the words SPIRIT COMMUNICATION = CHA-CHING! in red font.

"We have figured out a credible way to communicate with people from the beyond," Lillian said for me.

A corn chip fell out of Principal Hanover's mouth. "You mean . . . ghosts?"

Blair looked at us from the side of her eyes. She looked like she wanted to say *Mission abort!* Should we not have told the principal the truth of our business? But we had to. We couldn't lie about it to the *principal*. He was having meetings with all ten business teams to check in on our progress. Sure, we hadn't actually updated our business name on the school website—I was hoping to keep it a secret until we were able to snag more customers and raise our ranking. I wanted to *at least* be in second place before revealing the true nature of our business.

I couldn't wait to see the look on Mateo's face when I told him we beat his team by aiding spirits. Plus, the prize trophy didn't look too shabby either.

Mateo *who*? I only knew Mateo was going down!

"You . . . don't believe us?" Aiko frowned.

Principal Hanover's face darkened as he stuffed the fallen corn chip back in his mouth. "Girls . . . you don't know who you're talking to."

"What do you mean?" Blair chuckled nervously. She swapped glances with the rest of us, but none of us had any clue.

A chill slithered down my spine as the crunch of the corn chip became more and more ominous. Finally, his lips broke into a grin.

"Oh, I got you four good!" He wagged a finger at us. "You don't know who you're talking to . . . because I'm this school's resident spirit savant!"

"Savant?" I echoed.

"It means someone with detailed knowledge in a certain field," Aiko answered. She turned back to the principal, eyes sparkling. "You're telling me *you* love all things ghostly?"

"Only since I was a child! My mother would tell me stories about spirits. About the history of this town!" He swiveled a gilded framed photograph from his desk of an older-looking woman toward him. My guess, Mama Hanover. "Girls, this idea is *brilliant*! I just need to know one thing . . ." He leaned in conspiratorially, his bolo tie brushing his desk. "Are any of you . . . mediums?"

Lillian shook her head. "Well, actually, we found—"

"A way to communicate with ghosts," I said. "Yep. We're *in tune* with the other side, you could say."

"Hmm," Principal Hanover hummed under his breath. He eyed his now-empty corn chip bag with sorrow, then flicked his eyes up to mine with heavy interest. "You've communicated with spirits all on your own?"

"Mm-hmm!" Blair squeaked. If there was one thing she was terrible at, it was lying. "We're just *so* good at talking to ghosts!" she added through gritted teeth.

"Well, we might've gotten some *help*," I added to make things sound more believable. "Tía Paola from Paola's Predictions has been a great mentor."

Principal Hanover bobbed his head in approval.

"And we've gotten a customer already," Aiko said. "Anyone who needs to speak to a loved one's spirit—a spirit who hasn't moved on—can call . . . us! And we'll work our *magic*." She made jazz hands.

"We've lined up a few more clients for next week, too." Blair perked up.

I swiveled myself toward Blair, who was seated to my left. "This is the first I'm hearing of this."

Aiko whispered to me, "I didn't have time to tell you! You were totally spacing out during science!"

Was I spacing out this morning? All I could focus on was my phone conversation with Grandmama. Even now Lillian was snapping her fingers in front of me to grab my attention. Uh-oh, did someone say something?

"Earth to Raveena!"

Now *I* was the one who had to return from my mission to space.

"Or should we say, *Spirit world* to Raveena!" Principal Hanover guffawed. No, seriously. He laughed loud enough that he slapped a hand on his desk, causing the photograph to shake and teeter over picture-side up. The woman in the photo smiled at me, her lips turned sideways as if to hide a secret.

"Sorry," I said as the principal fixed the frame. "Principal Hanover, is it okay if you keep this under wraps for now?" Grandmama's words from last night rose to mind. "We don't want the competition knowing our secret." I winked.

"Of course," Principal Hanover said, leaning forward with his fingers tented. "Incredible work on your business model, I must say. I can't wait to see what comes of it! Hopefully a lot of"—he rubbed his forefingers and thumb together—"moolah?"

"Nobody says *moolah*, Principal Hanover," Blair said. "Respectfully!"

I didn't know anyone who used the term "cha-ching," either, but to each their own.

"Speaking of money," Principal Hanover said. "Remind me of your fundraising goals again?"

Blair began to speak, but I piped up, "One thousand!"

The girls gawked at me. Oh, pickles. Did I just word-vomit a new goal?

"Ambitious. I like it!" Principal Hanover rose and gestured toward the door. "Be sure to keep me in the loop."

We made our way out of his office, the girls staring daggers at me.

"Raveena, what was that—" Aiko began just as my backpack started ringing.

Correction: the phone *inside* my backpack started ringing.

"Raveena, is that . . . ?" Blair pulled me aside out of Principal Hanover's line of vision and unzipped my bag. An otherworldly glow filled the air, and Aiko shut the bag just as quickly as a secretary walked by. She headed to the front desk, confused by the office telephone not ringing.

"Raveena, why did you bring the phone to school?" Aiko whisper-yelled. "I thought you said you were going to keep it at home!"

"I—I *was*," I stammered. But after last night's chat with Grandmama, I couldn't *not* bring it to school. Maybe I was secretly hoping to contact Grandmama during lunch in one of the private bathrooms. "Muscle memory, I guess."

"We've had the phone for a little over a week," Blair remarked.

I blew out a puff of air. "C'mon, we need to answer the phone. Who knows when it'll stop ringing?"

The Fierce Four swept into an alcove in the office, and I unzipped my bag. "Hello?" I asked after picking up the receiver.

There was nothing but the sound of static.

"Who's calling?" Blair asked into the receiver. No one was around except us, Principal Hanover, and the secretary.

Still, no signature spirit voice came. Not even a dog's bark.

Alarm rose in my head—what if this was Grandmama contacting me again? What if the other girls heard her voice? Then they would know I was keeping a secret from them.

I slammed the receiver down before the girls could hear her.

"Wrong number?" I squeaked out, zipping my bag, the glow gone. Blair, Lillian, and Aiko eyed me like they could see through my lie. Unease crept onto their faces, but I waved them off.

"What?" I shrugged with a casualness I didn't feel.

"We can't risk bringing the phone to school again," Aiko warned me in a whisper. "And what was with you raising our fundraising goal?"

"It's no big deal," I said. "You're the one who said we had more clients, right?"

"Yeah, I guess," Aiko mumbled. Blair and Lillian stayed silent during the exchange.

My friends and I left the school office and headed to the cafeteria. My friends might have been worried about our new goal, but I knew what was most important.

There were some things sweeter than honey, including revenge against Mateo Pérez.

. . .

A frigid January week passed by, and not a spirit was stirring, not even a mouse. (Can you tell I still had Christmas music stuck in my head from over the winter break?) Well, I couldn't see the spirits stirring. But we had another customer, and that was all that mattered.

After chomping on El Grillo's famous churros Friday after school, Aiko and I headed over to our client's house. On the way, I read over the latest spirit slip added to the guidebook. Just yesterday, Blair and Lillian had helped Mr. Flounder, the local fishmonger, with his spirit conundrum. Apparently, he needed to speak to his long-gone brother about best fishing practices. Turned out Mr. Flounder was hanging on to his brother's favorite fishing pole, and his brother dissipated—another word for "disappeared into thin air"—shortly after he received it.

I rang the doorbell of Hardy Estate, one of the biggest mansions in Hollows' Peak. It was even located on a cliff, for crying out loud! They didn't call it Hollows' Peak for nothing.

The nearby lake crashed violently against the cliff, and dark, menacing storm clouds were brewing overhead. I *probably* should've taken Mama's advice and brought an umbrella this morning.

A young girl answered the door. "Can I help you?"

"We have a house call with Mr. Hardy," Aiko replied, holding out the phone. I let her keep it in her bag on the way over here, but I was still a bit frazzled that Grandmama hadn't called me back yet after that weird incident in the principal's office.

"Literally." The girl chuckled. She toyed with a fidget spinner. "Is that thing an antique? My grandpa likes collecting those, but they get all rusty and dusty."

"Sort of," I said as the girl welcomed us into the lobby. The estate could've doubled for a hotel, with its pristine glass chandelier and winding twin sets of stairs that met on the upper floor.

"Thank you, Ruby," said Mr. Hardy in a gruff but gentle voice as he wheeled into the room. "And thank you, girls, for agreeing to meet me here. Please, have a seat. I've already put on a kettle."

I officially met Mr. Hardy once at one of Mama's old violin shows a few years ago. She used to perform at the community center before Grandmama got sick. Mr. Hardy was a staunch believer that the strings were the best instruments to ever exist.

Mr. Hardy had a wheelchair to help him get around ever since I could remember, but since he didn't get out of the house much and lived alone—aside from his school-age granddaughter, Ruby—we decided to forgo a meeting at Spirit Service HQ. Plus, getting to go to an old mansion on a cliff? Totally an Aiko bucket list moment.

"How can we help you with our service, Mr. Hardy?"

"Please, girls, call me Dan. And before we get to the good stuff, what tea flavors do you each prefer?"

"Matcha, please. It's Mama's favorite. *Was.*" Aiko

adjusted herself on Mr. Hardy's leather ottoman. Ruby was right—her grandfather definitely enjoyed antiquing like Mama; you could tell from the cuckoo clock on his wall and the flower-printed wallpaper in just about every room.

"I like lemon hibiscus," I said. Mama and Grandmama preferred chai, but I wasn't accustomed to all those spices in my tea just yet.

"Well, I have neither of those, but how about we meet in the middle? Lemon . . . green tea?"

"Sounds good!" Aiko and I laughed.

Ruby came in with a tray and poured the tea. She placed a hand on her grandfather's shoulder. "You want some, Grandpa?"

"Oh no, dearest." Dan patted Ruby's hand. "I have some important business to attend to, so go ahead and play upstairs."

"You don't have to tell me twice!" Ruby scampered off. Aiko and I took small sips, enjoying the rush of warmth on such a frigid day.

"Now, girls," Dan said, turning his attention to us. "Is what your colleague said true? You can reach through the veil?"

By "colleague" he must have meant Blair. It made us sound so *profesh*.

"Well, the word 'reach' might be a reach." Aiko laughed as she set down her teacup. "But yes, we can help you communicate with someone you've lost." She placed the phone on the ornate table between us and Mr. Hardy. "You said you'd like to talk to someone named Leah?"

"Yes, precisely. Do you know if she will call this . . . rotary phone of yours?" He chuckled. "It looks like something my daughter would keep in her antique collection. You know, before she . . ."

I could fill in what he was trying to say. Aiko and I scooted closer to the phone just as a cool breeze skirted past me. I looked around, but I didn't see any windows open. Huh. Sure, it normally felt cold when spirits were around, but this didn't remind me of Hockey Grandma or Ruffles. This felt . . . different. Stronger, somehow.

The hairs on my arms stood up. Thunder rumbled overhead.

I thought back to Lillian's sixth-grade presentation on lightning and how it's created. Something about negative charges in the clouds, called electrons, wanting to touch the positive charges in the ground, called protons. The electrical charge in the air creates the quickest path it can to the protons, and bam—the result is lightning!

And didn't Lillian say that spirits were just energies, or electrical charges, passing through? Maybe with this weather, we had a better chance of receiving a true spirit call. Maybe *that's* what I was feeling—a spirit strengthened by the weather.

"We can't make guarantees, but . . ." I almost jumped for joy as the phone's familiar glow revealed itself to us once more. Looked like we had a spirit coming through!

"Time to take the call," Aiko said as the phone rang, nearly buzzing its way off the table. I held on to the base as Aiko picked up the handset. The whole time, Mr. Hardy watched in amazement.

"You've reached Spirit Service—Guardian speaking!" Aiko must've thought really hard about how she wanted to answer the phone on the way over. "How can we help you . . . move on?"

The glowing spirit revealed herself to us in an instant, floating right between the lobby and the living room. Taking the shape of a slim lady in a beret and flouncy dress, she spun around in her heels like she was asked to perform an encore.

"Leah!" Dan's eyes sparkled as he wheeled closer to the spirit.

"It's been so long since I've done that!" Leah said, doing a little two-step on the air. *"Oh, Papa! Is that you?"*

"I've missed you so much." Dan's lower lip wobbled as he tried to clasp hands with Leah but failed. "Ever since the car crash," he said, glancing down at his chair, "I always thought about you. And how I promised to take you to Paris. But one day, you grew up, and I never got to see the stars with you on the Seine."

"I never needed to see the stars on the Seine, Papa," Leah said. If ghosts could shed real tears, I'm pretty sure Leah's cheeks would be a watery mess. *"I saw them with you every night on the porch of this home. And that was enough."*

"I think we've got ourselves a level two!" Aiko whispered in my ear. I nodded, though honestly, I was barely registering what Aiko was saying.

I understood firsthand the loneliness and regret Mr. Hardy felt. But just as I was able to briefly communicate with Grandmama, Mr. Hardy could now speak to his deceased daughter one final time.

I just hoped my recent communication with Grandmama wasn't my last.

"How about we give them some privacy?" I told Aiko. "It seems like Dan needs more help from his daughter than the spirit needs from him." We tiptoed our way out of the room, but I was pretty sure Mr. Hardy didn't even notice.

"We'll give them a minute until the spirit crosses over," I reassured Aiko as we waited. Aiko twiddled her fingers, her cheeks looking splotchy.

"Are you okay?"

Aiko started. "Hmm? I'm fine. Just a bit under the weather." She patted her stomach. "Must have eaten too many churros."

Weird. Just an hour ago, Aiko had told me there was no such thing as eating too many churros.

"Any updates on your spirit board?" I asked Aiko to cheer her up.

Just as I'd hoped, Aiko perked up a bit. She showed me the board, where she'd added photographs of the town, including the bell tower and City Hall because of the terrible incident that had happened there. "That place is probably a major spirit zone after the fire."

I thought of all those lives lost in a terrible accident. "The phone wouldn't ring unless a spirit's loved one was nearby."

"Yeah," Aiko said, folding the board up. "But if that's true, who called the phone back outside Principal Hanover's office? You shut the phone off before we could find out."

My cheeks reddened with guilt. Should I have told Aiko about Grandmama? I'd already told her about the fog. To be honest, the secret was getting heavy to bear.

Before I could answer, a new voice interrupted. "Did I hear you both right? A *spirit* is in my house?"

Aiko and I both leapt with fright as we turned to find Ruby on the stairs, her white face peering out between the wrought-iron railing. "Sorry! Didn't mean to scare you." She skipped to the base of the stairs and went on her tippy-toes. "I've always wanted to see a spirit! But even in a mansion as old as this one, I've never seen one." She glanced into the room where Dan and Leah were having their private conversation. "Until right *now*!"

"You can see Leah?" Aiko blinked twice for good measure. Which meant that the spirit didn't just want to contact her father. She also wanted to contact Ruby. Leah must have been her—

"Mommy!" Ruby rushed down from the base of the stairs, and the spirit of Ruby's passed-on mother cupped her hands around her mouth.

Leah knelt on both knees and opened her arms for an embrace. Now Ruby could feel whatever the spirit wanted her to feel—the warmth of her arms as she hugged her, the soothing lull of her embrace.

Would Grandmama be able to do that with me one day too?

The spirit cried exuberantly, *"You've gotten so big, Ruby Red!"*

"I haven't heard that nickname in a long time," Ruby said, eyes wide with shock. She must not have seen her mother since she was a toddler. Ruby didn't cry, probably because this moment was surreal. And honestly, everyone handled their emotions differently. Take Mama, who didn't talk much about Grandmama but who I knew was hurting inside. Even still, I wished Mama would open up to me about her. Why did she have to change?

"Keep me in your heart, Ruby. I won't ever truly be gone."

Grandmama said the same thing.

"But—"

The spirit was already starting to fade. Mr. Hardy and Leah must have already had their emotional resolution, as all level twos required (and by the looks of it, their living loved ones, too). But Ruby barely had a chance to talk to her. Just like I barely had a chance to talk to my grandma.

I leapt back into the room. "Ruby, if you have something of your mother's, like an heirloom, it can make the spirit appear stronger. Maybe even give you more time with her!"

"Really?" Ruby's eyes widened.

"Yeah! Use a picture of her, or something important to her," I suggested, recalling what Elijah did with the chronograph.

Mr. Hardy pointed for Ruby to grab something from a nearby cabinet. Ruby withdrew a small painting of the manor on the cliffs. It was signed *Leah Hardy*. Leah stood at the front, sitting on the porch with her father and baby daughter.

"Portrait of a Family on the Cliffs . . ." Leah trailed off, no longer fading. She took a seat on a couch next to Mr. Hardy, with Ruby right by her side, squeezing her mother tight. It worked!

I turned away while Ruby, Leah, and Dan conversed longer, reminiscing in shared memories. I loved that word—"reminisce." It means looking back on things, usually fondly. It was so much sweeter than just remembering. It was holding that memory close to your heart.

Eventually it was clear their time was up. *"Goodbye, my loves."* Leah waved in farewell.

When Leah's spirit disappeared, Aiko hung up the phone. Its glow ceased. Mr. Hardy rifled through his wallet to pay us, but honestly, if I did this for free, it would be just as fulfilling.

"Thank you, girls," Mr. Hardy said, wheeling his way to the front door. "I didn't know how to move on without speaking to my daughter one more time. Maybe one day I'll paint a picture in Leah's honor."

"That sounds lovely," Aiko said.

I placed the phone in my backpack. "Bye, Mr. Hardy!"

Ruby skipped onto the porch. "I can't believe you both did that! Are you mediums?"

"Guardians," Aiko corrected proudly. "And it was amazing to see you connect with your mom again." Her eyes glistened.

"I always knew Mommy was near. Thanks for bringing her back, even for a little while." Ruby closed the door, and Aiko spun to me, worrying her lower lip.

"What's wrong?" I asked her. "Was it that weird cold wind inside the house?"

"I didn't feel anything," Aiko said, but her eyebrows frowned anyway. "You seemed to know a lot about heirlooms. Have you . . . tried contacting your grandma?"

Here was my moment to tell Aiko the truth. Instead, I blurted, "No!" like a knee-jerk response. Why was it so hard for me to admit it? "I mean, I want to, soon. *Really* badly. But it's . . . complicated."

"Things take time. I understand." Aiko gently squeezed my shoulder.

"I knew you would," I said. I wrapped Aiko in a hug. "You always do."

"Right. About that." Aiko swung on her heels. "Don't you think Blair and Lillian deserve to know about what you learned from Elijah Hollow's notes?"

Defensively, I asked, "Why?"

"Because they're part of Spirit Service too." Aiko scanned my features. "Raveena, is something going on? Is it your mom?"

"Yeah," I said half-heartedly. "My mom's just soooo out of it. She won't even give me a phone, and I've asked her, like, twenty times! Sometimes I wish she would just—"

I stopped, realizing what I was saying when I saw Aiko's expression close off. OMG. "Aiko, I didn't mean that!"

Aiko shook her head belatedly. "It's okay. Let's just move on. Wanna hang out at my place? We can watch reruns of *Mayhem, Misfortune, and Miniature Ponies*."

"As appealing as that sounds . . . I'm busy tonight," I said. "Catch you later?"

"Okay." She eyed my backpack. "But maybe I could keep the phone and guidebook over the weekend?"

"Not yet," I said curtly. Maybe *too* curtly. I amended, "I mean, I've got a little more *presidential research* to do. But I promise, I'll give it to you next week."

Aiko's expression dimmed before she stuck out her pinkie. "*Promise* promise?"

Hesitantly, I curled my pinkie around hers. "Yep. You'll get your turn with the phone."

But not before I made contact with Grandmama. *Tonight.*

THIRTEEN

Spirits, Possession, and Lots of Lessons

Back home in my room, I placed the phone in the middle of a blanket on the floor and put the photograph of Grandmama next to it. Thunder clapped outside, the winter mood making my blood chill as I glanced around. I remembered that strange wind I'd felt at Hardy Estate. Was it Leah, a level two spirit? Or something . . . else?

Just then a knock came at my door. Mama! I wrapped the blanket around the phone and pushed it under my bed right as she walked in.

"Hey, Raveena," she said, coming inside. She looked around my room—which was messy as usual—and eyed my unmade bed. "How many times have I asked you to make your bed?" She sighed, finding the blanket poking out from underneath it. She reached down and said, "And please, put away your laundry—"

I moved in front of her before she could yank the blanket—and the phone—out from under my bed. "Got it! I'll totally do it. Right after I . . . finish watching this season of *Short Island Medium*! Aiko's got me hooked!"

Mama raised a brow. "Since when do you watch ghost shows?"

"Since Aiko got me hooked!" I put on a big, toothy smile. Ugh, couldn't I come up with something other than *Aiko's got me hooked?*

Mama nodded as her gaze swept the room.

"Looking for something?" I wondered if she was finally searching for the phone she bought from Yoon's Antiques.

Mama bit her lower lip. "Nothing. I must've put it away already." She moved to leave the room, but I caught sight of her tired face before she could fully turn around.

"Mama," I called out, "maybe we could watch a show . . . together? Like we used to?"

Like we used to with Grandmama? I added silently.

Mama clutched the doorframe. "Maybe another time." Before she could turn away, I noticed something odd. Normally, her face was stoic and cold whenever I brought up the Good Old Days. But now her face was at war—one side trying to keep her emotions under wraps, the other desperately failing to conceal whatever was hiding within her.

What was Mama hiding?

Instead of leaving, Mama planted her feet firmly on the floor. "I . . . I have something to tell you, Raveena."

"You do?" My heart leapt in my chest. Was Mama finally going to agree to a movie or a mom-daughter bonding sesh? Was she going to recall all the good times we spent with Grandmama? Or worse . . . did she notice the phone was missing? I tried to keep my face void of my broiling inner commotions, even though that's the *exact opposite* of what Blair's therapist said to do. *Let your feelings out,* she advised Blair. *It's better than keeping it all bottled in.*

"Yes. I wanted to say . . ." The war brewing inside Mama must have called a ceasefire, because she righted herself and said, rather sternly, "Don't forget to study for your history quiz next week. I'll call you when dinner's ready."

My body deflated. I totally forgot about the quiz. With battling spirits and attending lessons with the town psychic, studying wasn't at the top of my to-do list. But I wasn't focusing on that statement so much as her previous one. *Maybe another time* was equivalent to *I'll think about it,* which really meant *I won't think about it.*

Mama and I used to cuddle on the couch together all the time, surrounded by paintings Grandmama brought from India. Now the walls downstairs were bare, with most of Grandmama's stuff in the basement. Mama had neatly tucked it all away, like Grandmama's things were nothing more than old junk. Like they weren't memories of our past.

Mama closed the door behind her. I couldn't dwell on the past; I had to focus on summoning Grandmama again.

I pulled the blanket out from under the bed and rearranged everything into the correct position. Then I raised my arms high and channeled my inner Aiko, calling out, "O Mighty Grandmother, please call the phantom phone!"

A white glow filled my fairy-lit room, nearly blinding my eyes for a second. As soon as the phone rang, I picked up, not wanting Mama to hear anything if she was still on this floor. "Grandmama? Are you there?"

Static. Then a voice, which sounded like it was fighting to come through. *"Yes, Raveena..."*

I grinned. "Yes, it worked again! I can't believe it! You must be getting stronger, aren't you?"

"You've always been smart, beti. I'm so glad."

Tears spilled down my cheeks. "Can you show yourself this time? You must be able to now!"

"I wish I could..." Her voice cracked. Was she not as strong as I thought? Was there anything in the guidebook about spirits who needed help showing themselves?

"But I know something that can help," Grandmama answered for me. *"An old heirloom that belonged to my friend Georgia."*

Georgia? I looked down at the photograph of three people in front of City Hall. Grandmama, a man named Hanbin, and a pale woman named Georgia.

"She gifted it to me, and it was so precious that it should be strong enough to help me step into this world."

"What do you mean, step into this world?" I gripped the phone so tightly, my knuckles hurt.

"I won't just be able to show myself as a spirit, Raveena," Grandmama croaked out. *"I will be able to..."*

"To do what?" My mind caught up with her words. "Wait. You mean you could . . ."

"Yes, beti. I have been stuck here for so long that I think I know a way to come back. For good."

"Really?" I nearly shouted before remembering to keep my voice down. "Tell me how, Grandmama," I whispered into the phone.

"Only the heirloom camera will do," Grandmama told me. "It is hidden in a time capsule somewhere in town."

"Time capsule?" Hadn't Mr. Bisson mentioned that it would be opened at the upcoming Hollows' Day Festival? "But where is it buried?"

"You must look for it," she told me. "The gift my friend gave me is hidden inside the capsule."

"I'll get it somehow, Grandmama," I said into the receiver. "I love you so much."

The line went cold. I dropped the receiver back into its place.

I couldn't believe it. I wasn't just going to see Grandmama's spirit. I was going to do something unimaginable.

Grandmama. Grandmama. Grandmama.

Her name echoed through my head the entire following morning as I headed to Main Street. It was time for another spirit lesson in Spooksville—pardon me, Tía Paola's shop.

"To kick things off," Paola began, "we will continue to enhance our teamwork skills! Guardians, take a look at the crafts I provided for you."

Lying before us were spools of yarn and knitting needles that could double as drumsticks. Turned out we were knitting Paola a sweater to "improve our teamwork and communication skills." Apparently, Guardians needed excellent communication in order to successfully aid ghosts and their respective loved ones.

Lillian and I were on arm duty, Blair on the turtleneck, and Aiko on the torso. I think Paola was just using our "lesson" as an excuse to give her a new look, which sort of backfired since we accidentally made three arms and no torso or neck hole.

"Tía, when are we going to start actually, er, *learning* about spirits?" Lillian inquired as she set her knitting needles down. "I hear learning is important for growing minds."

"So is knitting, but you don't hear that from the government," Paola muttered under her breath. "And I *have* been learning about spirits! I just wanted a new sweater for the winter!"

Paola harrumphed. "However, seeing as you girls are clearly not going to become master knitters anytime soon . . . it seems I should tell you that, thanks to my friends in Rosemary Heights, I've demystified a bit about level threes."

"Level threes?" Aiko rejoiced as Blair muttered, "Why couldn't we just keep knitting sweaters?"

Ignoring Blair, Paola said, "Can anyone tell me what they believe a level three spirit might entail?"

"A spirit who doesn't want to move on" came Aiko's

educated guess. "They choose to stay in the in-between place. They have unresolved issues like level ones and twos, but they can't just be helped with a material object or emotional reasoning."

"Good job, Aiko! Indeed, level threes are tricky beings. They don't want to move on—not because they're *evil* or anything of the sort, but because some sort of emotional trauma in their lives has festered within them, leaving these negative emotions to rot them from the inside out. These negative emotions thus change the spirits' bodies, manipulating anything from their appearances to their voices. They become... monstrous."

"How do negative emotions make level three spirits so... different?" Lillian inquired. She had her trusty scientific notebook out, plus a glitter pen and washi tape to make dividers on the page.

"I'm sure you girls have heard of stress pimples, haven't you?"

We all nodded.

"It's similar to that. When we have stress or other turmoil in our lives, it can manifest into something physical. Take zits for example. I had a whole host of them on my face last month when my mother-in-law kept calling me. I swear, she stresses me out more than doing my taxes." Paola shuddered. "The point is, level threes are very powerful, and the negative emotions residing within them are the root cause of why they choose not to move on. Their unresolved trauma turns these spirits into foul-looking versions of themselves. The only way to stop them—pardon me, to *help* them—is to suck away the negative emotions trapped inside by using a powerful object."

"What object?" Lillian was furiously scribbling notes.

"Rumor was that Carmela Hollow made one such device," Paola said.

I grabbed the guidebook from my backpack and flipped through it until I landed on a drawing. "Is this it?" I spun the book toward Tía Paola.

Aiko gaped. "Whoa. It looks like what the Ghostbusters used to suck up ghosts! The proton pack!"

"Carmela was alive and drawing this well before that franchise came out," Paola told Aiko. "Let me take a closer look at that, Raveena."

There was a caption written under the rendering of the device in what must have been Carmela's handwriting. "This device looks similar to the proton pack," Paola began, "but it doesn't seem to operate the same way. See this writing? Carmela wrote that instead of trapping spirits, the machine helps suck out the negativity and trauma that reside and fester in level threes."

"How?" Lillian examined the drawing. "Oh, magnets! Of course . . . the electrical charges of spirits must have something to do with it. But in order to only trap the emotions and not the entire spirit, the device has to locate the negative emotions and siphon them out. Maybe a positive charge connects to the negative emotions?"

I tried to hang on to every word Lillian said, but it was kind of hard having a science-loving bestie sometimes. "Umm. Can you rephrase that, please?"

"Remember what we learned about magnets in school? Negative and positive attract. So if the device has a positive charge, maybe the negative emotions act as a negative charge."

"Interesting," I said, even though I still didn't fully get it, or the device.

"Well?" Blair asked. "Where can we find it?"

"Unfortunately, the device is no longer in existence, according to my friends in Rosemary Heights," lamented Paola.

"But theoretically, it could be made again? With this drawing as a reference?" Lillian inquired.

"Yes, theoretically," Paola agreed. "Unfortunately, that is where my knowledge on level threes limits me."

Out of nowhere, Tía Paola pulled down a projector screen. Why she had one in her reading room, I didn't know. She scampered her way behind us and turned on the projector, which now displayed an image on the screen.

"Why are we seeing your grocery list?" I asked. I didn't know what was so frightening about doing groceries, besides the skyrocketing price of produce. The image Tía Paola had selected was a long shopping list of boring adult stuff and a bunch of coupon cutouts. *Save fifty cents on milk before it gets spoiled this Friday! Remember, there's no use crying over spoiled milk!*

"I believe the saying is spilled milk," Aiko noted as Paola quickly shuffled through the images on her camera roll.

"Ah, there it is." On the screen appeared an image of a skeleton with something overlain on top of it, like a screen of white smoke. "Do you girls know what this is right here?"

"Next week's science lesson?" droned Blair.

"No, girls, it's one of *Medium Lovers* magazine's depictions of... *spirit possession!*"

She said the word the way one might shout *Bingo!* at a seniors' game night.

"I thought you said you didn't know anything else about level threes?" said Lillian.

"This has nothing to do with level three spirits, my dear," Paola said. "This has everything to do with *all* spirits. You see, I wanted to show you girls exactly what all tricky spirits can do. This X-ray right here shows not only a human skeleton, but a ghost on top of it. Or *inside it.*" Tía Paola wiggled her eyebrows.

"A ghost in a human body? Spirits can do that?" I'd seen my fair share of ghost movies from Aiko's marathons, but to be honest, I didn't know a lot about possession. I was also pretty afraid of possessed dolls.

"Yes! Based on my research, every level of spirit from ones to threes has the ability to escape the in-between and travel into a host body. This body allows the spirit to stay in our physical plane for a longer visit than a spirit could do on its own. And spirits are *not* supposed to remain long in our realm—or in our bodies!"

"So you're telling me spirits can go possessing people all willy-nilly?" Blair peered around the reading room like she was next on the list for spirit possession.

"Not willy-nilly, girls! It takes a lot of a spirit's strength to possess someone. But remember—possession is not the same as *control*. It's more like having a voice in your head that can affect the words you say out loud, or make your brain work differently. Like a conscience. Or a good vitamin. I'm partial to omega-3s."

"How can you tell if a person's possessed?" I wondered.

"Usually, they will begin to act strange; their body movements might be stiffer. Emotionally, they might begin acting more aggressively—not necessarily because the spirit is angry, but because two separate entities in one body can be very confusing for the mind, hence amplifying one's emotions."

Aiko beamed. "Imagine being possessed by a *spirit*! The things I could learn about the other side!"

Blair said, "I'd like to stay firmly on *this* side of the physical plane, thank you very much."

Meanwhile, Lillian was fervently jotting down all of Paola's nuggets of wisdom. But I had something else nagging at the back of my mind. In my notebook, I drew an old-school vintage camera, using a pencil to shade in the details. Grandmama needed it soon. *I* needed it.

I needed *her*.

"Interesting drawing you've got there. Would you

like to share it with the class?" Paola's owl-sharp eyes landed on mine.

I closed my book with a thud, cheeks turning splotchy. I'd been so absorbed in my drawing, I'd almost ripped right through the paper. "No thanks."

"Distractions do not make for good Guardians, Ms. Gill," the psychic reminded me with a stern raised eyebrow. Her words reminded me of a Robert Frost poem we read in class once about good fences. Or good neighbors. Or both—I wasn't much of a poet.

"She's been like that all week," Lillian said. When I glared at her, she merely shrugged. "What? It's true."

"I guess I have been distracted." Ever since my initial call with Grandmama, I'd been falling behind on my Hollows' Peak assignment. "Sorry, guys."

"Don't beat yourself up about it," Aiko said with a smile and shoulder bump. Once again, I could always count on my bestie to be there for me. I owed her bigtime.

"Back to spirits," Aiko said, grabbing Paola's attention. "What happens if a spirit *does* get out and possesses somebody, right here in Hollows' Peak?"

Paola's voice was grave. "That would be very troubling, girls. Very troubling indeed."

FOURTEEN

Note to Self—Always Eat Corn *Off* the Cob

February rolled through with blustering wind and a chilled embrace. Helping spirits wasn't the only chilly thing going on around Hollows' Peak. Mother Nature was doing her thing—or maybe that was climate change.

Paola's vivid tarot card reading came back to me. How had it already been two weeks since we'd told Tía Paola about the phantom phone? What Paola didn't know was that the card was referencing my *grandma* being able to speak to me again!

The stars were literally aligning. And today I was prepared for an adventure.

Okay, it wasn't an adventure so much as a research trip. I knocked on my old babysitter Janice Hollow's front door, admiring the cottagecore vibes of her screened porch, from the muted orange of the doorway to the wicker chairs out front. Plant tendrils were growing wildly all over the white railings.

I smiled widely as she swung open the door.

"Hey, Raveena," Janice said, letting me step over the threshold. "What's up?"

Janice was in her early twenties and a recent

university grad. Her hair was pulled back from her warm brown face in a messy bun, and she wore an NSYNC tee. Whoever that was.

"I'm actually doing some research for a school project," I told Janice, slipping off my backpack. I told Mama I was going to hang out with the rest of the Fierce Four, and I told them I was out of commission for the day due to a fever. Which were white lies. Saturdays were usually reserved for bubble tea and movies with the girls, but I had something more important on my mind.

"Cool. How can I help?" Janice asked, leading me to the kitchen. I hadn't been here in almost four years, but I always remembered how Janice would make me the cutest cucumber sandwiches shaped like Hello Kitty.

"I'm working on an assignment about Hollows' Peak history. Could you tell me anything you know about a time capsule hidden somewhere in town?" I figured if anyone had information about Hollows' Peak's hidden treasures, it would be a Hollow themselves. Plus, I didn't want to ask Mr. Bisson any questions—I was falling behind on my City Hall assignment as it was and didn't need another reminder.

"Sorry, Raveena." Janice frowned. "I don't know where my grandfather hid the time capsule."

Grandfather? Right, Janice used to tell me stories about her ancestors, the Hollows. He must've been mayor of Hollows' Peak in the seventies. Too bad I couldn't ask him myself. . . .

But couldn't I?

"Janice, do you have any heirlooms of your grandfather's?"

"Sure." She fiddled with the frame of her glasses. "These belonged to him back in the day. They were his favorite. I got the lenses replaced, of course."

I unzipped my backpack on the kitchen island and revealed the phantom phone. It was so heavy, my fingers turned stiff as I plopped it down on the marble countertop. Some might call the phone cugly—a cross between cute and ugly. If anything, those burn marks added character.

I pointed at the phantom phone, specifically the inscription, which read PROPERTY OF THE HOLLOWS.

"Whoa!" Janice ran her fingers delicately over the handset. "This thing must be a hundred years old!"

"It is."

"How'd you get it?" Janice wondered.

"My mom found it in Yoon's Antiques. I'm not even sure how it got there. But look." I spun the dial around. "Neat, isn't it?"

"Totally vintage," Janice said, and I could tell she was into that sort of thing from the flower scrunchie in her hair to her tortoiseshell glasses and her whole "plant mom" vibe.

"Well, you can't tell anyone this, but the phone has . . . a power."

Janice leaned in. "Spill."

Knowing from her babysitting days that Janice could keep a secret, I confessed the truth about the phantom phone—from vanquishing Hockey Grandma to visiting the glamorous old Hardy Estate. "We've created a business called Spirit Service to help people communicate with loved ones who haven't moved on," I finished.

"No way. How does it work?"

I was about to answer when I felt a strange wind pass me by. My body chilled, like I'd felt a spirit. Maybe I was just overthinking things.

"Well, typically an heirloom of the deceased strengthens the connection. Your glasses?" I held out a palm. Janice dutifully handed them over, squinting.

The phone's ring filled the air.

"Whoa—you weren't joking," Janice said. She rubbed her eyes. "Am I seeing this right?"

"Yep. The phone is glowing," I assured her. I had to project confidence as a Guardian, and although I wasn't expecting to contact a spirit today, it was my duty to answer the call.

I picked up after the second ring. "Spirit Service Guardian here. How can I help you?"

The spirit revealed himself from the bottom up. Straitlaced loafers, well-pressed trousers, a matching blazer and bow tie, a pencil 'stache, and a fedora topping a totally seventies hairdo. He would've fit right in with the Jones triplets.

"Pop Pop?" Janice fitted her glasses back on her face. "Is that you?"

"In the flesh! Well . . . more like in spirit. Literally."

Janice's grandfather walked on air as he approached the fridge. It actually swung open. *"Got any OJ? I could use a sip. I'm parched! Haven't had a drink in almost twenty years! Or better yet, I'll take some Haunting Hollow Crunchies!"*

"What's that?" Janice asked, still taking in her grandfather's spirit form. She poked a finger into his belly, and her hand almost went right through.

"That tickles! And it's my favorite cereal, of course! Don't tell me you're fresh out."

Janice swiveled around the kitchen island and gasped at her grandfather with a revelatory grin. "It really *is* you!"

"Yes, granddaughter. You see, Janice, I have not been able to move on to the afterlife on my own. I may have had a wonderful life as mayor of this town, but I need your help."

"What do you need?" Janice panicked. "Haunting Hollow Crunchies? They probably don't even make those anymore!"

"No, dear! It's something else . . . something I can't quite put my finger on . . ."

Oh no. Did that mean he was a level two? I did *not* have time for a twenty-years-in-the-making therapy session.

The spirit soared right through the island, into the wall, and appeared on the other side. *"Hey, this is kinda fun,"* said Pop Pop.

Janice and I ran into the living room, where her

grandpa was currently examining a set of old baseball cards being kept in a drawer.

"You mean you can't do this otherwise?" I asked. "Sorry, I haven't even introduced myself—I'm a Guardian of the phone, Raveena Gill."

"*What a familiar surname...*" He trailed off. "*Pleasure to make your acquaintance. I'm Mayor Hollow—Colin for short. And no, not always. It takes a lot of energy to move or even touch things in the physical world from the in-between one. But since you answered the phone, I feel like I have a new pep in my step!*"

Whoa. I was learning so much!

"I can't believe the phone call *worked*," Janice said in awe. "Did it really belong to my ancestors?"

Mayor Hollow chuckled. "*My grandmother Rose created that phone. In fact, her children were so proud of her invention that anyone who married into the family kept the Hollow name. Cool, right? We were kind of famous, including my mother, Carmela, may she rest in peace! But enough of the history lesson.*" Mayor Hollow adjusted his bow tie. "*In order to answer your question, I'll have to go far, far back to my golden days in 1975....*"

Janice and I seated ourselves as Mayor Hollow got comfy on the nearby piano. The keys started moving up and down—if someone other than Janice or me came a'knockin', they would see a pretty weird piano ... playing *itself*.

"*They called me the hippest and snazziest mayor*

in all of Hollows' Peak history. I was shakin' my groove thang every night on the dance floor—"

"Pop Pop!" Janice plugged her ears. Even I couldn't deal with the utter cringe.

"Did you say your name was Raveena Gill?" Mayor Hollow ignored Janice and turned to me. *"Now I know why the name 'Gill' sounded so familiar. That was Avneet's last name!"*

I gasped. "You knew my grandmother?"

"Of course!" said the old mayor. He stroked his pencil 'stache and gazed at the ceiling. *"Yes, I remember it all as clear as day. She and her friends saved my life!"*

"My grandmother and her . . . friends saved your life?"

"You haven't heard the tale?" The mayor peered down at me. *"The origin of reverse birthdays!"*

Janice nodded, ears unplugged. "Raveena knows the story! I taught it to her."

I shuffled back through my memory. "You mean the day the mayor"—I pointed at Mayor Hollow—"choked on his tooth after eating corn on the cob? That was you?" The day was deemed so un-birthday-like—who wants to choke in front of a crowd of partygoers?—that all residents started having reverse birthday parties from then on.

The mayor nodded. *"It was three immigrants, new to Hollows' Peak, who saved my life. They were volunteering at City Hall, where my birthday party was being held. I gave them the phone as a gift for rescuing me from my choking incident."*

"That's a . . . unique gift."

"It had been lying dormant for years. With my generation no longer practicing speaking to spirits as my ancestors used to, our family Gift was waning. Only mediums could use the phone, of course, but I figured the phone would be like a key to the city—a present only a Hollows' Peak resident would appreciate! Well, in this case, three residents."

I thought of that photograph of Grandmama and two others outside City Hall.

"Were their names Avneet, Hanbin, and Georgia?" I asked.

"Yes, exactly! The newly married Avneet Kaur Gill, her friend Hanbin Yoon, and—"

"Hanbin Yoon? That explains it!" It all made sense. The three of them volunteered together in 1975, which wasn't long after Grandmama immigrated here from India and the Philippines. I turned to Janice. "That must be why Yoon's Antiques had the phone. Mr. Yoon's dad is Hanbin!"

Janice added, "Who knew history was so cool? I mean, I *majored* in history, but still? Egypt's pyramids don't compare to this!"

I turned back to the spirit. "Mayor Hollow . . . I'm working on a school assignment and need some help. Would you happen to know anything about where the time capsule is hidden? The one that was buried fifty years ago?" I wasn't planning on writing about the time capsule for my assignment, but considering Grandmama told me to find it, I figured now was my only chance to learn more information.

Mayor Hollow exclaimed, "Fifty years already! I locked away that capsule myself at the town's fiftieth anniversary festival!" He scratched the top of his fedora. "Where did I put that time capsule . . . Aha! It was kept under lock and key in my office, where it remains in City Hall to this day."

"Sweet." I rubbed my hands together, and Janice raised an eyebrow. "For my assignment, I mean. It'll really . . . liven it up, all these details."

"Well, I'm glad to be of help! But I think I know why I haven't moved on. My baseball card collection is sitting right here, untouched! My poor babies!"

Mayor Hollow leapt off the piano while Janice retrieved the cards. She handed them to her grandfather. "I hope you can rest easy now, Pop Pop."

"Me too." The mayor's form started to fade, turning pale. Oh, pickles. I wasn't done asking my questions yet!

"Mayor Hollow, you mentioned the capsule has a lock?"

"A numerical padlock," he confirmed, his voice waning. He sat back on the piano keys, waiting to be taken to the afterlife, waiting for the peace he'd been craving all these years.

"What's your date of birth?" I asked. That was usually people's passcodes, and if I had that, maybe I could open the time capsule myself.

Still . . . it begged the question. Why couldn't

Grandmama wait until the time capsule was opened in just a few weeks? The festival was right around the corner. But then again, why wait? I might be able to bring Grandmama back. That would go down in history! My name would be enshrined in every Hollows' Peak history book. *Raveena Gill, phantom phone Guardian who discovered how to permanently return spirits to the land of the living!*

Mayor Hollow's spirit began fading into the ether; I couldn't even see his face. All that was left was his dangling legs, already disappearing.

"It's January 25, 1935," said Janice, grabbing my backpack for me. "Why'd you want to know?"

"For my assignment," I lied. I gave Janice a big hug and placed the phone in my bag, zipping it tight.

Don't worry, Grandmama. I'll find the camera and bring you back . . . for good.

The bus stop greeted me just a few blocks away from Janice's house. With Mayor Hollow's spirit vanquished, I flipped open the guidebook to write down my experiences—and Mayor Hollow's date of birth, before I could forget.

> Guidebook Log, 02/01/25
> Guardian Name: Raveena Gill
>
> Spirit Category: Level one
>   Spirit Issue: This client was given a

> surprise call, so no issue to report.
>
> How I Aided the Spirit: Former Mayor Colin Hollow required his baseball collection to help him be at peace in the afterlife. . . .

Partway through my writing, I noticed a fresh set of splotched ink on the following page. How did that get there? I tried to rub it away, but instead, my eyes trailed down to a message written at the bottom of the guidebook.

DON'T TRUST HER.

Huh? I had never seen this message before. And the last time I saw handwriting in the book, it read: *Use the photograph. Use it.*

Except this handwriting wasn't the same. Even the ink color was different. How could that be possible?

Who was I not supposed to trust?

I quietly closed the book and tucked it into my backpack. I think I'd had enough of this guidebook, and aiding spirits, for today.

"Raveena?"

I peeked out of the bus shelter. Standing with their mouths agape were Aiko, Lillian, and Blair.

Uh-oh.

"Hey, guys," I said as nonchalantly as possible. "What's up?"

"We thought you were at home." Aiko glanced me up and down. "Sick."

"Oh." I faked a terrible cough. "Mama gave me some of her famous chicken noodle soup and *bam*! I'm all better."

"Mm-hmm." Blair tapped her foot like she wasn't buying it. "Are you sure you had a fever?"

"What's with the third degree?" I shouldered my bag uncomfortably. Could they tell I was carrying the phone? Were they onto me?

Aiko's eyes grew heavy with suspicion.

"Okay. The truth is . . . my mom wanted me to run errands for her. Hence my heavy backpack." I winced as I clutched the straps of my bag. TBH, this phone really was weighing me down. Not to mention my neck had become so stiff lately from hunching over the guidebook for nights on end. But my friends couldn't know that.

I continued. "I know it's been a while since we all hung out—for fun, not for business—and I didn't want to disappoint you guys."

Partially true. I *didn't* want to disappoint my closest friends. Which was why I was keeping my trip to see Janice close to the vest. I had a lot on my plate—things my friends just couldn't understand—and I didn't want to break Grandmama's trust in me. Not when I was getting so close to fulfilling her request.

"You could never disappoint us, Raveena!" Lillian gave me an encouraging punch on the arm. Why did that make me feel even guiltier than before?

I turned to Aiko with a watery smile. Her suspicion had melted into something else. I'd seen that look before, like something was bothering her.

I checked my watch. "Looks like the bus is late. I—I better run."

Cheeks red with embarrassment, I stumbled all the way back home.

Since I was already at three strikes, Mama had told me to come home early today. I didn't want her to be suspicious of where I was, so I arrived at five on the dot. Responsible kid? I was your girl.

Apparently, my mother didn't think so.

"What were you up to today?" Mama asked, folding laundry on the couch as I locked the front door.

My cheeks were now red from embarrassment *and* running home. "Uhh—not much. Just chillin' with the Fierce Four like usual."

I was surprised how easily the lie slipped past my mouth. But skipping hanging out with my besties was totally worth it in exchange for the information I got from Mayor Hollow. Aside from him *shakin' his groove thang*, everything else he mentioned was pretty critical—at least toward helping Grandmama.

So why was that seed of guilt inside me growing?

"Aiko called the house earlier. She said she was sorry you couldn't make it to the movie marathon today. She also said she and the girls hoped you would *feel better soon.*"

I audibly gulped.

If Mama were a dragon, her nostrils would be smoking. "Where were you, Raveena?"

"Relax, Mama," I said with as much joviality as I could muster. There was another vocab word for you. "I needed to speak to Janice Hollow at her house. You can totally call and confirm with her. We were just catching up, like old times!"

Mama separated the lights from the darks. She shook her head. "I sincerely hope that's true. But lying to your mother? To your friends?"

"I'm sorry," I said, that guilt spreading deeper, like a tree growing its roots. "It won't happen again."

"And another thing. I got an email from your school today."

Schools sent emails on *Saturdays*?

"Well, it was yesterday, but I forgot to check my inbox or my voicemails. Mr. Bisson says you performed poorly on his last history quiz."

"I'm great at history!" I eked out.

"I know. Which is why I think I should sit down with him and see what's going on. He said you've been out of sorts these past few weeks. You haven't even handed in the first draft of your assignment on the history of City Hall."

"I swear, I'm doing so much research!" I might have missed the first draft deadline, but that was a small price to pay for the research I was *actually* conducting to help Grandmama.

"You don't need to talk to Mr. Bisson. I'll apologize to him on Monday." I paused. "I'm sorry, Mama. Honest."

"I know you are. And just to be sure this doesn't happen again, I'm revoking your television privileges."

Okay, I deserved that. *Days of the Glorious*, one of Lillian's favorite soaps, could wait.

"No talking on the phone with your friends, either, or hanging out with them after school. You're grounded for a week."

"But—" I paused before I could dig myself into an even deeper hole. Mama had never used the G-word with me before. That's how I knew she was serious. "What about the school business competition? I still need to help out."

"Once this week," Mama conceded. "But that's your limit."

Mama returned her attention to the laundry bin. I forced myself to fold, only to ensure Mama's punishment wouldn't escalate.

When I was younger, we used to make laundry days a whole event of fun and shenanigans. I used to say, "Laundry patrol officer, on duty! I'll write you up if the socks are mismatched or the white sheets turn pink!"

Mama would let out a closed-lip chuckle. She would place a gentle kiss on my forehead and hug me so fiercely, she wrinkled my freshly ironed clothes. Back then laundry wasn't really about getting a few fresh sheets. It was mostly about being together.

I'd forgotten what those kisses, what that touch, felt like.

I needed to remind my mother that she could heal. That she could be her old self again. If we raised enough money through Spirit Service and brought the arts program back, both Mama and Grandmama would be so proud of me.

All these distractions, my schoolwork going unfinished, my friends questioning me—it would be worth it in the end. It would make all the difference to help the one I loved most.

FIFTEEN

Meltdown in Aisle Two

A week slogged by in a February haze. Since I got G-worded, I reluctantly gave up the phone to Secretary Blair so my friends could handle anything else that came up. Thankfully, Aiko's suspicion receded over the endless days of my punishment. Not that we could even hang out, outside of our one client. Nor could I sneak off to City Hall to search for that time capsule. The good thing was I could really focus on school. (Yeah, I know. Mama was right. I hated saying that.)

After apologizing to Mr. Bisson, I stayed after class twice to go over my history quiz mistakes. Apparently, the year 1066 was a hot time for conquests.

Yesterday I completed my makeup test. And guess what? I got a B+. Not Lillian's usual straight-A standard, but hey, I was catching up.

When I was finally ungrounded, Mama allowed me to invite the rest of the Fierce Four for a sleepover. It was a truce of sorts. Mama and I signed an invisible peace treaty, and I promised her we'd all behave. No spirit communications would be had tonight.

"Thanks for the popcorn, Ms. Gill!" called Lillian

from the foot of the couch. Her perfect bucket of popcorn had to include extra butter and a sprinkle of nutritional yeast, or nooch for short.

The Fierce Four were currently gathered in my living room for the ultimate sleepover party, which we'd been planning all through yesterday's lunch period. Lillian brought the board games (the Game of Afterlife was totally fitting); Aiko had the movie recs down pat and a fancy screen projector to boot; and Blair brought the snacks, from slices of her peanut butter no-bake cheesecake to tangy chocolate-dipped Twizzlers.

"Anytime, girls," Mama said. Faint eye bags rimmed her eyes. She'd been working overtime, and I guess my lying incident last week didn't help with her stress. I still felt guilty about what I did. I hoped this sleepover was a way to make up for it and then some. And luckily, Mama agreed.

After a round of the Afterlife—the game, not the real deal—in which Lillian "won" by becoming an undead zombie (how unrealistic), we put on a ghost flick. We all burrowed into our sleeping bags, ready to put our brains at ease with mindless spooky content.

We were just ten minutes in when Blair hit the pause button.

"Hey, there wasn't even a jump scare!" Aiko bemoaned.

"Sorry! That scene with the ghost who just slipped out of a shoe box was so tacky. I mean, clearly the director never heard of a phantom phone—nor do they understand anything about spirits at all!"

"You're right. It's hard to be impressed by special effects when we've seen the real deal," Aiko said, shutting off the projector. "Should we consult the *Guidebook for Guardians*? I'm sure there's *tons* of information in there. Blair?"

After a groan, Blair retrieved the phone and guidebook from her duffel bag.

"Are you guys sure about this?" My voice cracked, a different pitch than usual. I cleared it before saying, "I thought tonight was a chill hangout, you know? No spirits, no phone."

What my friends *didn't* know was I worried over Grandmama calling out of the blue and the girls discovering my secret. I didn't even know Blair had brought the phone!

Lillian said, nonchalant, "It couldn't hurt to see what more we find. It's not like we're dealing with a client."

That was true. To be honest, I wished I could share my secret with someone other than the voices in my head. My besties would be so interested to hear about my contacting a spirit from the great beyond, just like Elijah Hollow did. And maybe they would be able to help me find the time capsule too. After all, four minds were better than one, especially when they were as tight as the Fierce Four.

Grandmama told me to keep things a secret. But how long could this secret last?

"OMG, this book is chock-full of stuff I didn't even see before. It's like the pages are never-ending!" Aiko zipped through the pages with wide, eager eyes, and my friends followed suit, amazed by all the nuggets of wisdom provided by past Guardians. Weeks ago, I was amazed too.

I cleared my throat. "There's something I have to say about the phone."

"It's okay. We already talked about it on the way over and worked out a new schedule," Aiko said, shutting the book.

"Hold up—a schedule?" My friends clearly didn't know I was just about to drop a total truth bomb about Grandmama. "For what?"

Blair yanked on her Twizzler. "For rotating the phone between us. Get it? Rotate the *rotary* phone?" Blair slapped her knee. It was kind of a dad joke, but that happened to be her specialty—sometimes she used it as a defense mechanism for times she got too scared to be herself around people. She said her therapist called it social anxiety.

"Oh. I just thought, since I'm the president—"

"Here we go again," Aiko muttered.

I stiffened. "Come again?"

Aiko huffed. "I asked you for the phone two weeks ago, after we helped Mr. Hardy's daughter move on. You pinkie-promised I would get it, but then you only gave it up to Blair when you were grounded."

"I know," I realized. "I'm sorry. Everything's gotten

away from me, with my makeup test and catching up on schoolwork—"

"It's okay, Raveena," Lillian said, patting my leg reassuringly.

"Honestly?" Aiko swallowed like there was a lump in her throat. "It's not. Ever since we got this phone, you've changed. First you brought the phone to school, even when you promised you'd keep it at home. Then you *lied* to us about being sick. I know you had the phone in your backpack that day. So tell me—what were you really up to?"

I'd never heard Aiko be so direct with me before. "Okay, yeah, I was bringing the phone to school... and to Janice Hollow's house that day at the bus stop. I spoke to the spirit of her grandfather, the old town mayor!"

"You contacted a spirit... without telling us?" Lillian asked quietly.

"I was doing research," I countered. "It was for a good reason!" I looked over at Blair. "In fact, now that I'm ungrounded, I think I need the phone back for just a little longer...."

"Really?" Aiko retorted. "I get that you're the president of Spirit Service, but hogging the phone? It's not cool, Raveena. In fact, it's just plain selfish."

"Are you calling me a phone hogger?" I asked before realizing Aiko had just called me selfish.

Self-centered. Self-absorbed.

My heart raced. We *never* called each other words like that before.

"Yeah, I am."

I turned to Lillian, simmering with anger. "And you agree with her?"

"Well . . . a little. C'mon, Raveena, wouldn't it be fun if each of us had a chance to hold on to the phone? We could swap houses each weekend, like the phone's going on a little sleepover. Just like we are now! It's no biggie."

But it *was* a biggie. The girls just didn't know why.

"I'm not sure that's a good idea," I mumbled.

Aiko scoffed, eyes narrowing. "What's with you, Raveena? You really expect us to believe you want the phone back for *research*? We deserve the truth!"

I balled my hands. That simmer was now frothing into a full-on boil. "You guys wouldn't even understand! I need the phone—because . . . because . . ."

My friends each stared at me wordlessly.

"Because I contacted Grandmama!" I blurted.

Silence. My stomach fell into a deep, dark pit and burrowed there, all my previous conviction now lost as the enormity of what I said crashed down on us.

"Um . . . *what?!*" Aiko's voice punctured the silence. Blair held her sleeping bag to her nose with fright. Lillian whistled in disbelief.

"I know. It's a lot to take in. That's why I was waiting to tell you all." I paused. "So? I bet now you can understand why I've been a bit distant. It wasn't anything you guys did, I swear. I've just been so focused on Grandmama. On talking to her again!"

Blair crossed herself. Lillian anxiously nibbled on her peanut butter cheesecake.

"So that day at the Hardy Estate, when I asked you if you contacted her . . . you were lying?" Aiko shook her head, like she knew all along.

I gawked. "I can't believe you're accusing me of that!"

"Well?" Aiko's lower lip trembled, hard. I couldn't tell if she wanted to cry or shout. "*Were* you?"

"I . . . I . . ."

My hesitation was enough of an answer. Aiko stood furiously. My other friends exchanged an uneasy look.

"Great. So you *were* lying to me, just so you could keep your hands on the phone. Just so you could talk to *your* grandma and not let me talk to my—" Aiko stopped herself before she could spill the truth. But deep down something told me exactly what she meant to say.

"Your *mom*," I realized. All those moments we'd brought up her mother hurtled back to me: reminiscing while we made mochi; recalling at the Hardy Estate how much her mother loved matcha; and finally, brushing off my flippant remark about Mama not giving me a cell phone.

"You . . . wanted to talk to your mom?" Blair asked.

"Why didn't you tell us?" Lillian added.

Aiko looked down. "It doesn't matter. Raveena should've known I wanted the phone. She *promised*. It's not like she's the only one who's lost someone important!"

I began shaking. Every emotion—every bit of sadness, rage, grief—bubbling up inside me poured out.

"It's different for you, Aiko. You don't get it. You don't know what it's like having a mom who doesn't care. Who doesn't treasure my grandma's memory. You and your dad keep your mom's memory alive every day. You make mochi, and watch old movies, and look back on the good times. But me? I don't have that luxury! I don't have that connection! So forgive me for wanting to speak to my grandma—for wanting her *back*."

Aiko's eyes glazed over with tears. "I want my mother back too, Raveena. Just because your mom handles grief differently doesn't mean I'm any less worthy of hearing from my loved one. Don't you get it? We're the same. And I hate that. I hate that what we have in common is ripping us apart!"

"Guys!" Lillian got up from sleeping bag, holding her hands out. "Aiko, Raveena, let's calm down. Aiko—your anger is valid. Raveena, yours is too. But the issue is, *you've* been acting different."

"Going on solo research trips, making excuses to avoid hanging out with us . . ." Blair jumped in. "I'm sorry to say it, Raveena, but Lillian's right. I think . . . I think something's wrong."

"Wrong? Nothing's wrong! I've got everything under control!" My voice cracked as the lie escaped my mouth.

The girls each turned to me then. But they weren't angry. No . . . they were scared.

Of *me*.

No one had ever looked at me that way before. Like I was a monster.

"Remember what Tía Paola said during our last lesson? About spirits possessing others, changing their emotions?" Aiko reminded us.

"It amplifies a person's emotions," Blair recalled. "Their aggression."

Usually, they will begin to act strange, Paola had told us. *Their body movements might be stiffer. They might begin acting more aggressively.*

"Wait a minute." I cooled myself down enough to laugh without mirth. "You think *I'm* possessed? Guys, come on. I've been a bit out of sorts, sure, but there's no way you can accuse me of *that*."

"Never say never." Aiko draped her arms in front of her in a menacing stance. "Raveena, I think we all agree you need a break from the phone. Now."

If I could hear my heart shattering, it wouldn't be the same as broken glass. It would be stitches of fabric ripped one by one—slow, haunting, torturing.

I grabbed the phone, not even caring if it looked like I was hogging it at this point.

"I'm the president, and we all agreed that I should be the one to keep the phone. You guys don't understand. I'm onto something huge. Just let me explain—"

"I don't want to hear your explanation," Aiko spat. "Guardians are supposed to work together. But you haven't been acting much like a Guardian lately, have you?"

"Maybe we should break for some hot cocoa?" Blair tried tugging Aiko in one direction as Lillian brought me to another. But I wasn't finished. Aiko was a fighter, and so was I.

"Well, *you* haven't been acting much like a friend!"

In an instant I realized I'd stepped too far.

Those seeds of guilt had sprouted into a full-on forest. If I wasn't careful, I would be part of the forest itself—or worse.

Consumed by it.

Aiko's eyes watered. "I backed you up at our spirit lesson with Tía Paola. I've always been there for you, always been patient. How about you? What did you do in return?"

Nothing, my brain replied coldly. Nothing at all. I'd been so wrapped up in helping my grandma that I'd abandoned my own friends' needs. But I was too far in now to stop, like a train veering off the tracks. I couldn't give up on my family, my blood. Not when Grandmama was depending on me.

"Give me the phone," Aiko demanded. She wasn't asking, but I wasn't going to give in. I could feel my cheeks turning blotchy and red.

"No. I'm keeping it." When Aiko learned why—what I was doing to bring Grandmama back for good—she would understand.

"I knew I shouldn't have trusted your pinkie promise!" Tears escaped Aiko's eyes.

Aiko tried to take the phone from me, and I tugged it back. The cord threatened to snap.

"Stop!" Lillian cried.

Aiko didn't let up. But she wasn't angry—she was sorrowful. I'd seen that exact look of sadness, of desperation, on my own face in the mirror. She wanted to speak to her mother as badly as I needed to speak to Grandmama. One part of me said I *was* being selfish. But the other couldn't bear the heartbreak if I never heard from my grandmother again.

I didn't realize I'd been tugging on the phone so hard that it slipped out of my grasp. The phone struck the hardwood floor.

Crack!

Silence. Then—the phone began to glow, the handset already having slipped off the base. But this glow wasn't the familiar white light that normally filled a room when the phone rang.

It was *red*.

"I d-don't think that's a good sign," Blair stuttered.

We all watched as white wisps swirled out of the phone, escaping through the closed window.

"Now look at what you did," Aiko accused me. I wasn't going to let her have the last word. And whatever just happened, there was *no* way the phone broke.

I checked it for good measure, placing the handset back on the base. The glowing stopped. "See? Only a small crack." There was a fissure near the base of the phone, but it was practically as good as new.

"Raveena, maybe Aiko's right," Blair said with newfound confidence. She leveled her gaze with mine. "The phone is messing with your head, making you think things that aren't real. We're all besties, okay? But even besties need to tell each other when they're in the wrong."

"Blair," I said, but that was all I could manage before tears welled up and my throat closed. Aiko placed the phone and guidebook in her backpack and rolled up her sleeping pouch. The other girls followed suit.

"Whether you're possessed by a spirit or not, I don't care." Aiko shouldered her backpack. "All I know is the girl I've been friends with for years would never treat me this way. The girl who learned Japanese with me at recess, who hugged me when I cried . . . she's gone."

A jagged line ripped through my heart.

"Girls, what is the meaning of this?" Mama emerged from the basement. What was she doing down there? We'd already cleaned up most of Grandmama's stuff, plus those dusty photo albums. "I heard a racket. Is everyone okay?"

We all mumbled different things, but we definitely weren't okay.

"I think I'll be calling my dad to pick me up, Ms. Gill," Aiko said, not even looking my way. All the terrible things I'd said to her were roaring like blood in my ears.

A small part of me—the angry, bitter, sad, scared girl within—wondered if I really was possessed. It would explain the way I'd been acting to my friends and the aggression I felt. But nothing needed to possess me to remind me that my grandma came first. That she would always, always come first.

"Is something the matter?" Mama asked. "We haven't even had hot cocoa yet."

"Not right now, Mama," I told my mom, slipping past her. My footsteps were as quiet as a ghost's as I stumbled upstairs. There was no hiding the tears burning in my eyes as I shut the door on my friends, on the phone . . . and on myself.

SIXTEEN
Cinnamon Hearts and Candy Crushes

Valentine's Day arrived in a flurry of hot pinks and crimson reds. Heart-shaped cinnamon candies lined students' desks, along with cute cards from besties to besties. (Or in some seventh-grade rumors, classmates-turned-more-than-friends.) If this were any other year, I would've been laughing and gossiping with the rest of the Fierce Four about who got who a punny card or an anonymous rose delivery. But this year was different. A pretzel of worry knotted in my stomach, and not because I wasn't getting any cards this year.

A few days had passed since the Incident. Since then, I'd been avoiding talking to Aiko and just barely keeping in touch with Blair and Lillian. A weird wedge sat between us, as if I'd drawn a line in the sand. One day at lunch, I even almost sat at our usual table. Lillian had worn a welcoming smile, but when Aiko dismissed me, Lillian glanced away like she wasn't sure what to do.

No, Aiko didn't merely dismiss me. She *ignored* me. Level two pettiness, but I was probably a level three, because I ignored her right back.

I didn't blame Lillian or Blair for having lunch with

Aiko instead of me. I'd pushed them away. *I'd* said all those mean, terrible things straight to Aiko's face. I was the one in the wrong.

But the worst thing? I couldn't find it in me to apologize. Not when the situation was still so fresh. Not when my once-fierce family thought I was lashing out and ignoring them because I was possessed by a spirit. How ridiculous was that? Me, Raveena Gill, *possessed*?

Aiko's words snaked through me. *The girl I've been friends with for years would never treat me this way.*

Was I showing the signs? Aggression? Check. Stiffness in my body. Double check.

So what if I'm possessed? challenged a deep, dark part of me. *So what if I'm changing?*

After an excruciating game of dodgeball during gym class—I had been pummeled like a piñata—lunch finally arrived. I was on duty to help Blair run a booth in the cafeteria for the Valentine's Day bake sale. Lots of competitors in the business competition were taking part to make some extra dough, literally. By the time I got changed out of my nasty gym socks and into a cute but affordable pink jumpsuit, I found the cafeteria and looked around for our booth.

A pair of familiar brown eyes and a sweeping brown ponytail greeted me. "Raveena!" Blair called from behind a table covered in a heart-patterned tablecloth. A light box sign read BLAIR'S DELECTABLE BAKES! and a three-tier dessert stand showcased all of Blair's confections, from heart-shaped macarons to fudgy triple chocolate brownies. (There was cocoa powder, chocolate chunks, *and* chocolate syrup in those bad boys.)

"Thank goodness you made it—I'm swamped!"

The cafeteria was buzzing from all the kids checking out the pretty-in-pink booths. Some students were selling candy grams, store-bought frosted cookies, and even batches of fresh-cut flowers to go with the baked goods. All of it was overseen by Principal Hanover himself, who peered carefully over the proceedings with watchful eyes—and a bag of corn chips.

Next to the principal, Mayor Clayton made a welcome appearance, doling out advice to the young entrepreneurs and saying "Keep up the good work!" Today's bake sale was probably an excuse for him to get out of his office and snack on some delicious treats while he was at it.

"Where were you after school yesterday?" Blair asked as she finalized a sale. I came behind the table and put on the apron Blair made for each of the Fierce Four with our names on them. "Lillian and I were looking for you."

"You were?" Mama wanted me to come home right after school every day as part of my punishment for acting out at the sleepover. It's not like I was purposely avoiding Blair or Lillian—I just didn't want to address . . . the *meltdown*.

Hope lit inside me until I realized the unspoken words in her sentence. *Aiko wasn't looking for me.*

"Guess what? We've got two more bookings this

week!" Blair said, pulling me from my reverie. "I guess Valentine's Day really is a great time for reconnecting spirits with their loved ones. Lillian and I have already agreed to connect Mrs. Fitz and her potato-chip-obsessed husband after school. The next booking is tomorrow. Do you want to handle it?"

"Alone?"

Blair looked left and right, her cheerful expression falling. "Well, seeing as you and—"

"I can do it," I cut in, waving to my classmates—or prospective customers—and showing them the array of confections Blair had baked last night. "No big deal."

"Great." Blair looked more than relieved. "I would help, but I've got therapy, and Lillian has saxophone lessons."

Since Lillian's parents wanted her to keep up with playing music due to the loss of the arts program, they'd recently enrolled her in extracurriculars funded by the local government. I missed playing my flute too. Every press of the keys, every lilt of the notes, reminded me of Grandmama.

"Speaking of bookings . . ." Blair spun me so we were facing away from the customers. "These will be our first customers since . . . everything." She jerked her chin at Aiko's apron sitting lonely in a cardboard box. "You don't think the crack in the phone will affect anything, right?"

"Of course not," I said with false confidence. I had to keep up pretenses as much as possible—and pretend like I wasn't thinking about our fight or the red glow from the phone. "It was a small fissure. Bet it still works like a charm."

"But what about those white wisps—"

"These heart-shaped macarons look great," a voice claimed. "I'll take two."

"M-Mateo?" Blair's eyes widened as we spun back around. She looked between me and my semi-nemesis, then straightened herself and said, "Oh, yeah. Totally. That'll be five dollars."

Mateo handed over a bill while I avoided his gaze. Why was he buying from *our* booth? It would only help us climb higher in the school competition ranks, and at this point, based on the school website, we were currently in third place.

From my vantage point, I could see Mateo's cronies were selling something in little Chinese takeout containers—popcorn drizzled with ruby chocolate. Did that even count as a baked good? Ugh. They were clearly pushing both a Valentine's and Lunar New Year theme. Why didn't we think of that? Every year, Aiko gave us wagashi, special Japanese confections typically served with green tea. It would've been cool if we did something like that . . . except this year we weren't talking. No Aiko, no sweets, and definitely no friendship in sight.

The pretzel-knotting sensation returned.

"How's the bake sale coming along?" asked Mateo while Blair went to go grab some food bags from another table now that we'd run out.

"Swimmingly," I gritted out. I couldn't take it any longer. I didn't need Mateo here causing problems with everything else I had going on. "What are you *really* doing here? Spying for your teammates?"

"I'm not here to spy. I wanted to say hello. We used to hang out all the time."

"*Used to*," I reminded him. He hadn't apologized to me yet about ditching me last year, and I doubted he was going to now. "Friends change."

"Is that what's happening to you right now? I noticed you haven't been hanging out with Aiko."

"It's nothing," I told him, even though it was really something. I had never fought like that with Aiko before. We'd been friends for years! Just thinking about what happened brought prickling tears to my eyes, but I blinked them back before Mateo could see.

"Well, whatever's going on, I'm here to talk if you want to."

Mateo was being uncharacteristically polite. The pretzel in my stomach slowly unspooled. I didn't have time to say anything, not even a "thank you," before he got up and rejoined his buddies.

Mateo was being nice and Aiko wasn't. What happened to the world? Did it flip upside down while I was sleeping?

Principal Hanover waded over to our booth. "Absolutely exquisite work, Blair and Raveena. These will be sure to ramp up the sales!"

"And help us get closer to winning for the arts

program," Blair reminded him. "Do you think next year our school could offer a home economics class? I really think it's important for kids to learn cooking skills."

"Great idea, Blair," Principal Hanover said, glancing into his half-empty bag of corn chips. "Unfortunately, it's not my decision to make—but I will be sure to tell the school board! Now keep selling! Sell, sell, sell!" he urged the students as he walked past the other booths and out of the cafeteria, fist-bumping Mateo's team on his way out.

I stared at Mateo, and as if he could sense me looking, he turned my way. My cheeks blazed as I gazed back down at the treats strewn along our table. Did he always have that annoyingly pretty-to-look-at face? Maybe Valentine's Day was messing with my head.

I had something more important to focus on. Tomorrow I was going to scooch a spirit into the afterlife—and get a hefty tip.

The spirit rose to life wearing a very dapper three-piece suit.

He stretched his arms wide as if waking up from a long nap and said, *"Finally, the smell of the open earth! It gets quite tight in the place in between our world and the next, you know. I think I got some premature wrinkles waiting around for my turn into the afterlife. Well, lookie here, my suit still fits!"*

I was sitting in Lillian's (other) neighbor's living room, taking our Valentine's week house call. This technically wasn't my first time talking to a spirit without help from any of the Fierce Four, but it *was* the first time facing one who was on the docket for Spirit Service. I'd have to be quick, though; Mama still didn't trust me to stay out late after school after what happened with the Fierce Four.

"Do you want to talk to me about what happened?" she'd wondered the Monday following the sleepover. First I'd lied to her about my whereabouts and schoolwork, and now this blowup with my BFFs? Obviously, something was wrong. Still, I said nothing. I didn't exactly want to tell her *I'm falling behind on schoolwork because I'm obsessed with contacting my dead grandmother—and hey, my friends think I'm possessed because I'm acting aggressive! Now, what's for dinner?*

Maybe I was becoming more like Mama. Burying my feelings instead of dealing with them.

I faced Miss Evermore, whose deep complexion blanched at the sight of the spirit. "M-Magnus? Is that you?" she asked with a creaky-croaky voice. Miss Evermore's voice shook in general, since she was pushing ninety-seven; but when facing a spirit? Her jaw was practically flapping open.

"It seems that Magnus has something very important to tell you," I told Miss Evermore. When she'd told Blair she felt a "presence" hovering nearby her and then noticed the posters in the community center, she felt it was only right to book a session with us. And who was better to take the call than the president?

Raveena Gill, at your Spirit Service!

"*My darling love,*" Magnus said with a bass voice, swooping toward Miss Evermore. "*I've missed you so much, Missy.*"

"I . . . I haven't seen you since—"

"*1944? I wish I hadn't tragically passed in the Fabulous Forties. That's what I called the decade after the Dirty Thirties*"—he winked at me—"*but the war was calling, and my sacrifice with it. I'm so sorry I was never able to give you this.*" He produced a ring from behind his back.

My eyes bulged. "You wanted to get married?" How fitting was it that I was helping two long-lost lovers right after Valentine's Day? Level two spirit—check.

"*I had hoped to give it to Missy upon my return from Britain. Will you accept it now?*"

Wow. Magnus had been waiting over eighty years to give Missy an engagement ring. Talk about playing the long game!

I tried imagining holding that kind of love for someone for so long. I thought of my friendship with Aiko—four solid years without so much as a squabble, most definitely not like the fight we'd had at our sleepover. Four years didn't hold a candle to eighty, but it still felt like a long time.

An even longer time since we'd stopped speaking.

The spirit handed over the ring, which sparkled like my and Aiko's friendship bracelets we'd made in third grade. I tugged at the bracelet absentmindedly as the ring landed in Miss Evermore's palm, as solid and real as anything I'd ever seen.

"Of course, Magnus," Miss Evermore said. "I waited for you, too. I'm so glad I got to speak with you one last time."

Magnus smiled forlornly. *"Until we meet again, my love."*

I turned to the spirit. "Thank you for waiting all these years. But I have to ask—why didn't you reach out through the phone back when Elijah and Carmela's family had it? You could've given the ring a lot sooner."

"The phone's power was beginning to fade with disuse, I'm afraid," the spirit told me. *"Besides . . . I didn't want Missy thinking about a fallen soldier—I wanted her to find love in this lifetime."*

"I did," Miss Evermore said, "but I never married. No one was the right fit, not like my Magnus. He was my soulmate." Lillian's neighbor dried her wet eyes with a handkerchief. Even my eyes began welling up as I thought of Aiko.

And with that the lovers said goodbye. I blinked the tears away and hung up the phone, which I'd collected from Blair today before she left for therapy. During the trade, she told me our bake sale was a huge success, putting us in second place right behind Keepin' It One Hunnid.

If I never saw another *100* emoji again, it'd be too soon.

I collected the cash from Miss Evermore, who told me to come over anytime with Lillian to have a snack. Miss Evermore made a mean hummus and ranch dip combo.

I was *totally* right about getting that hefty tip. And it seemed like nothing was wrong with the phone if Blair was able to use it yesterday successfully, followed by me today. Take that, Team Mateo!

With or without Aiko, I would make sure Spirit Service took first place.

I stepped onto Miss Evermore's front porch to find Lillian waiting for me, saxophone case in hand.

"My lesson ended early. Wanna hit up El Grillo for Taco Saturday?"

In Hollows' Peak, we had Taco Saturdays, not Taco Tuesdays. That alliteration was too basic. (But we did like to use *some* alliterations, like our business name, Spirit Service. That one slapped.)

"Sure." I could go for their newest creation, chicken tinga tacos. I saw it on their Instagram page on Mama's phone last week and *literally* drooled. Guiding spirits to the afterlife made me hangry, and if I didn't get a taco soon, I might go full level three on this sidewalk!

If a spirit isn't possessing me already, whispered a voice in my head.

I shook away the thought. "We're doing great on the spirit business front," I told Lillian as we walked to El Grillo. It was only minutes away, and we reached the arched front door in no time. The scent of fresh spicy salsa wafted toward us. "How was yesterday's appointment? Did you and Blair handle a level one or two? Or maybe a *three*?"

"Actually, it was Aiko who helped the spirit of Mrs. Fitz's husband—you know, potato chip guy? She kinda showed up at the shed last minute. Her stomach had been hurting earlier, but she felt better after some Pepto."

"Oh." I tried not to sound bothered. "Well? Was it a one or a two?"

"Maybe you could ask Aiko yourself?" Lillian asked me as we passed the hostess stand.

I stopped in my tracks as we spotted Blair waving us over from a booth at the back. And across from her, her back facing us, was Aiko.

I spun on my heel and made for the exit.

"Wait!" Lillian cried out.

I turned back to her, anger scrawled across my face. "Was this some kind of setup? Lure me with tacos and then make me talk with my frenemy!"

"Aiko isn't your *frenemy*," Lillian reminded me. "We're besties. We always will be. Blair and I wanted to remind you of that."

I simmered down as I took in Lillian's words. Okay, so maybe I was overreacting with the frenemy thing. But Aiko and I still weren't on speaking terms, and that was practically enemy territory.

"Fine," I mumbled, letting Lillian lead me to the table. I plopped down next to Aiko, who gave me a subtle nod of her chin in hello.

"So," Blair began, sitting straight. "I got back from therapy an hour ago. And let's just say, therapists rock!

Aside from working through some of my anxiety, I told her all about our little . . . situation. And she agreed that we needed to do something about it."

Lillian confessed, "I won't lie to you, Raveena. Blair and I have been getting kind of tired of acting like an owl carrying messages between you guys."

Blair's and Lillian's earnest expressions made my heart dip in my chest. Was this really how they felt? I couldn't believe I'd made my own best friends feel like go-betweens. They were so much more than that.

They were the glue keeping us together.

"Even if you two aren't ready to talk, Lillian and I needed to get this off our chests," Blair said. "We have to keep things professional for Spirit Service. Agreed?"

Aiko and I exchanged quick glances. They were right. I wasn't ready to talk to Aiko yet, but if we wanted to reach our goal, we had to be able to at least work together. Nothing personal, just business. "Agreed. I'm sorry we made you feel that way."

"Me too," Aiko added.

"And we don't have to talk about what happened at the sleepover if you're not ready," Blair said. "My therapist says that sometimes these things take time."

I definitely needed that. But I worried that the more time we took, the closer we'd be getting to the Fierce Four being no longer. Maybe Blair was right—I did need that break from the phone.

And the most surprising part? It actually felt *good* not having to keep it around me all the time. Although

I still hadn't forgotten about looking for the heirloom camera, I was slowly learning that my friends' trust wasn't something to take for granted.

So I placed it on the table in front of Aiko. "You can have it back."

She wordlessly stuffed the phone into her backpack and continued ignoring me, glancing at the menu.

Well, I guess that answered that.

"You're right, Blair. I'm not ready to talk about the sleepover yet." Or what I'd blabbed about me speaking to my grandma. I'd already broken her wish for me not to tell anyone about our meetings. But I was breaking a lot of things these days.

Promises. Friendships.

Lillian leaned in, her coils bouncing. "And that's not the only reason we invited you both here today. I've been working on something super epic."

Aiko perked up at those words. We leaned in while Lillian pulled something out of her bag that looked an awful lot like Carmela's device drawn in the *Guidebook for Guardians*.

"I know it's not much," Lillian began, "but Blair and I have been working super hard this week to make a device that can sap out negative energy and emotions like Tía Paola taught us."

"This is so cool!" Aiko said brightly. Meanwhile, I asked, "Does it work?" while poking at the long stick that looked almost like a metal detector.

"We're not sure yet. There's no way to test if it will

suck out negative energy and capture it into the device until we meet a level three spirit. But it *can* do something else."

"What?" Aiko and I asked in unison. We both looked at each other awkwardly, cleared our throats, and sat back.

"It can measure the strength of a spirit using a frequency meter," Lillian answered. "Since spirits have a strong electric charge, the device can measure it. The more difficult a spirit is to help—the higher the level—the stronger its frequency seems to be."

"Theoretically," Blair amended.

"That's amazing. Thanks so much for being proactive and working on this device, guys. Seriously—you two have been a great help with Spirit Service."

"Thanks, bestie. And it is pretty cool, huh?" Lillian said, tucking it away as a waiter approached our table. "The device should be ready within the next couple of weeks, before the Hollows' Day Festival. Who knows—a celebration of this strange town could bring about a lot of level threes."

Lillian was right. As I ordered the taco special, I wondered to myself, *When would we have to face a real level three spirit?*

SEVENTEEN

Key, Please?

Come Monday morning, City Hall was packed with kids roaming about like explorers in a new land, or a Mickey Mouse fanatic at Disney World. No kid could resist a good field trip or a chance to skip Mr. Bisson's lesson on the history of cursive writing.

"Come along, classes," Principal Hanover called to the groups the seventh-grade teachers were currently ushering through the lobby.

It was the principal's idea to bring the classes to City Hall in honor of the upcoming festival in Hollow Square in two weeks. You know, to learn more about the town, get inspired for our assignments, yadda yadda. All I knew was I had a mission to accomplish.

Grandmama had waited long enough for me now. Here I was in City Hall, and I wasn't about to waste this perfect, just-fell-into-my-lap opportunity to open that time capsule!

"This way for MY GROUP," Mrs. Nkosi said from the front of our pack. I wasn't certain why she was yelling—she used her indoor librarian voice *everywhere*. Not to mention she wasn't even wearing her glasses!

Blair and Aiko were in their history class's group,

and I'd decided to join Mrs. Nkosi's group of "future librarians"—or so that was what she called us. Lillian stood next to me, wearing a crossbody bag with pins on the strap that read FUTURE SCIENTIST and E=MC².

The other classes needed a tour guide, but since Mrs. Nkosi volunteered at City Hall, she was practically already one.

"OVER—here," she said, clearing her hoarse voice. She shook her head, as if confused as to why she was yelling before motioning for us to follow her into an exclusive "exhibit" on Hollows' Peak history. "Here you'll find an entirely reconstructed area of City Hall. Does anyone know why this part was reconstructed?"

Raising my hand, I said, "The fire from fifty years ago?"

"Precisely. Great job, Raveena." But after she said those words, Mrs. Nkosi's eyes darkened. "To this day, the origin of the FIRE is debated. Some say that the bell tower was struck by lightning, causing an electrical issue. But others believe there is more to the story than a simple lightning storm."

"What else would explain the fire but lightning?" Lillian whispered into my ear.

I didn't know, nor did I have time to find out the answer. Our group was now splitting off, scouring the exhibit displaying one hundred years of Hollows' Peak, from inventions to kooky fashion. Even Lillian was enraptured by the scientific advancements the Hollows had accomplished during their lifetimes.

I approached Mrs. Nkosi and asked sweetly, "May I

use your key to get into the staff bathroom? The public one has a line."

"Of COURSE, Raveena! And excellent job on your research project. I heard from Mr. Bisson that you've been doing extra credit?"

"Oh. Yeah, I am." Guilt threaded through my stomach, threatening to bloom into a banyan tree. I was only doing extra credit because I was so wrapped up with the phantom phone.

"Well, I think kids should have NO HOMEWORK at all!" Mrs. Nkosi boomed before she cleared her throat. "Sorry, Raveena, my voice is a little hoarse. That's what I get for going to a Taylor Swift concert two nights in a row!" She rubbed at her shoulders, stretching them out.

"Ummm, okay, Mrs. Nkosi," I said before the librarian could belt out a tune. I plucked the keys, which were attached to a coiled bracelet, from her hand. "Sorry. Nature calls!"

I slipped away from the exhibit hall and into a secluded area by the staircase. I had to get up there and into the mayor's office without anyone seeing.

Just as I was about to climb the staircase, I bumped into someone with long raven-dark locks and piercing silver eyes.

"T-Tía Paola?"

"Oh, hello, dear Guardian! Come to enjoy some fine art?"

I pointed to the herds of kids. "Actually, I'm on a field trip."

"Hmm." Paola squinted at the kids; it seemed she didn't need glasses for reading—as in her "readings"—but rather for long distance. "I've got a season's pass to the City Hall museum's paid exhibits, so I thought I'd better use it! Art is like a window to the soul, just as reading one's hand is a window into the future!"

"Never thought of it that way," I admitted, getting antsy as I looked up the staircase. Thankfully, Mayor Clayton was currently embroiled in a conversation with Principal Hanover on the importance of corn chips in one's diet. I didn't care *what* they were talking about—as long as I didn't get caught.

"Tía, I have to—"

"Is there something grieving you?" Paola asked me suddenly. "I sense a difference about your aura."

I should've known I couldn't get anything past the local psychic with spidey-senses to the nth degree. "It's nothing," I lied.

She tutted. "Nothing should get in the way of young friendship."

Did she somehow know I was in a rut with my friends? That I was caught between them and Grandmama? Aiko and I clearly had trust issues in need of mending.

My mind swam back to the words I'd seen in the guidebook outside Janice's house. *Don't trust her.* Who wrote that? Aiko had the book and phone now, so I couldn't check.

Aiko. Just thinking of her name made me tumble

back into the hole of guilt I wished to bury myself in. But what if I didn't have to bury my feelings?

I turned to Paola and said, "You're right. Nothing *should* get in the way, but something is, and I have to get it off my chest."

"Well then, speak, Guardian!" Paola boomed.

"A few people think I've . . . *changed* recently. And maybe I have. Some days it feels like the old Raveena can't answer the phone right now." Mrs. Nkosi would be proud of that reference. "Is that part of growing up? Feeling like you've left your old self behind?"

"Oh my, I didn't think I'd be having the puberty conversation today. . . ." Paola dabbed at the sweat beading on her forehead with a mystic handkerchief. "You see, Raveena, as you get older, your body—"

"No! Not like that," I shouted, embarrassment rising twofold. First of all: I'd learned all about that in school, thank you very much. And second: I didn't need *Paola*, of all people, schooling me on the dos and don'ts of teenager-dom.

I mustered up the courage to say, "Lately I've been acting out at my friends. Blaming them. Feeling sad and angry—not just at them, but at the whole world."

"Oh, we all have those days. Did you try writing down your feelings?" Paola asked before muttering, "My mother-in-law could use that same advice. . . ."

"Yeah. It helped, but I think something bigger might be going on." I steeled myself. "My friend Aiko thinks that I've been acting differently because of how obsessed

I've become with the phone. In fact, she thinks I'm . . ." I glanced around. *"Possessed."*

"Oh!" Paola placed her handkerchief in her purse and tutted. "What makes you think that?"

I shrugged. "Everything you taught us about spirits being able to slip into town and possess humans . . . What if it's already happened? What if *I'm* being affected?"

Could that truly be the reason I'd been acting so differently? Aside from losing Grandmama, something *else* must have been going on to make me react to Aiko in such a horrible way. To make *me* the bad guy. Because Raveena Gill was a good friend. Maybe not the most patient or the most keen, but I loved my friends just like I loved my family. What I'd said to Aiko—that wasn't the real me.

It couldn't be.

"Well, I can't say I know for sure whether you are indeed possessed—I specialize in futures, as you know, but I believe yours will be bright indeed." Paola gave me a reassuring pat on the shoulder. She was probably just happy she didn't have to have the *P-word* convo.

I gripped Mrs. Nkosi's keys and thanked Paola. But before I could turn away, Paola's eyes narrowed. "Remember what I taught you, Raveena. If a spirit *is* indeed on the loose, terrible things might happen. Not every spirit is kind. Some are tricksters—like Loki! Oh, but I do love a bad boy with a heart of gold. . . ."

I wasn't so sure about the heart-of-gold thing. To

get away, I muttered something about the bathroom and did "the pee dance." That sent her zooming in the other direction.

Time for my mission.

I slunk up the staircase as fast as I could. I tried putting nearly every key in Mayor Clayton's lock, but none of them worked. Finally, I was down to one key. This *had* to work.

And when it did, I did a different dance. Score! I was in! How was this so easy?

Before I could cross the threshold, a voice in the back of my head tickled my thoughts. But it wasn't my own—it was my friends'.

Aiko. *So you were lying to me.*

Lillian. *You've been acting different.*

Blair. *I think something's wrong.*

Here I was, breaking into the mayor's office without an ounce of remorse. *Could* I really be changing? Was there a voice in my head whispering to me—making me act all out of sorts?

Even if there was . . . no one could stop me. I had to do this.

I snuck into the mayor's office, which was decorated with more kitten pictures than a *Cat Lover's Monthly* subscriber, and set to work. There, in the middle of the office, was a large treasure chest. The time capsule.

Double score! I hurried toward it and found a combination lock. I spun the dials to match up with Janice's grandfather's birthday and pulled.

No luck.

Drat. I knew it couldn't be that easy.

I tried spinning the lock again, reorganizing the date of birth as many times as possible, but no dice. I tried putting in the date the town was formed in 1925, and when that didn't work, I tried putting in the year the time capsule was made—1975. After all, Mayor Hollow *was* shaking his groove thang on the dance floor back then.

I removed the nightmare-inducing image from my mind and focused. I had maybe a minute longer before Mrs. Nkosi would start to wonder where I went.

"C'mon, Raveena," I told myself. "You need to do this for Grandmama. You have to . . ." A sprinkling of familiar memories dusted my mind—the smell of daal simmering on the stove when Grandmama made it for me and Mama, finished with her signature spice blend and a smattering of coriander leaves. The sound of Grandmama cooing me to sleep while her handheld radio was on, the lull of voices drifting on the air. The look on Grandmama's face when she smiled, her eyes crinkling and lines sprouting out of them like the weathered veins on a leaf.

I had so many good memories with Grandmama. More than some others get to have with their grandparents.

"I thought I heard someone . . . ," a voice called from down the corridor. I froze, a hand on the combination lock as another voice followed: "No, I think it came from the other direction. . . ."

The second voice sounded familiar. But I couldn't place it, and I didn't have time to mull it over. I frantically sought out a place to hide as the footsteps grew louder. I spotted a cabinet and forced myself into it, shutting the doors just as two figures entered Mayor Clayton's office.

"Now, what was it that you wanted to talk to me about, Hugo? Something about getting the arts program back on track?" asked the first voice. The mayor!

"Yes, of course . . . ," the second voice—Hugo—replied. Why was that voice so familiar? I went onto my tippy-toes, trying to peer into a small hole in the cabinet so I could get a look at who was talking, but it was too high up.

Their voices became hushed as they conversed. I pressed my ear as close to the cabinet door as I dared.

"During the Hollows' Day Festival, all will be revealed," the second voice said cryptically. "But first, where is that time capsule you were telling me about?"

"Oh, thank you for reminding me. I was just about to move it to a secondary location to prepare for the festival—"

"No!" The word leapt out of my mouth unbidden.

The voices faltered. Footsteps approached the cabinet, and a blinding light struck me as the doors were flung open.

My face burned. "P-Principal Hanover?"

He looked down at me. For a moment, I could've sworn his eyes flashed red.

I squinted—no, it must've been a trick of the light.

Now they were flashing with confusion and, to my chagrin, disappointment.

"Raveena Gill." Principal Hanover's face creased with recognition. "What do you think you're doing here?"

"I—I—" No excuses came to mind. I sheepishly exited the cabinet. "I'm sorry, Principal Hanover and Mayor Clayton."

"Breaking and entering is the last thing I expected from a bright student of Hollows' Peak Middle," the mayor said scornfully, his expression darkening. "I must ask, what prompted such an outburst?"

"I don't know what I was thinking. I'm sorry. I'm . . ." I stopped myself. I had lied to my friends, to my own mother. I couldn't keep going like this—I had to get the truth off my chest. "Honestly, I wanted to get a look inside the time capsule early."

"The time capsule? Well, that's a perfectly suitable reason," Principal Hanover said with a sudden joviality, like I had just offered him the world's biggest bag of corn chips. "For your history assignment, I presume?"

Not really, but I nodded nonetheless, too embarrassed to reveal the truth.

"Still," the principal conceded after noticing his colleague's expression. "I myself am an enthusiast of studying the past, but I think this little stunt warrants a call to your mother."

It did. And oh, was I dreading it.

· · ·

"What were you thinking, Raveena?" Mama asked me as she drove me home early from school that day. Talk about going from probation back to jail time. "Snooping around in the mayor's office?"

My silence was proof enough of my guilty conscience.

Mama turned onto our street. "Honey, I know the past several months have been tough."

Understatement of the year. "It would be easier if we spoke about it," I said. "About *Grandmama*."

For a hopeful moment, it almost appeared like my mother agreed. But at the last second she clamped her mouth into a tight line, and I swore I saw her eyes glisten.

"Mama, why don't you ever talk about her?"

"Because," Mama said, discreetly wiping her eyes. "It's too difficult."

I swallowed the lump in my throat. If Mama wasn't going to talk, then I would. "I snuck into Mayor Clayton's office because I'm trying to do something that will bring us all back together. I want to see you happy again."

Mama's brows creased. "Nothing is going to bring Grandmama back, honey." She brushed the hair out of my eyes for the first time in forever. "And is that what you think? That I'm not happy?"

I shrugged, turning away. "You don't seem like it. You don't even touch your violin anymore."

Mama pulled over on the side of the street. She put her head on the steering wheel before glancing at me and tucking a strand of loose hair behind my ear.

I didn't know what she was doing until she gave me a full-on bear hug.

"There's something I've been meaning to tell you, Raveena. But I haven't found the courage to yet."

"Why not? You're the bravest person I know." It was true. Even though Mama had been different since Grandmama left, I'd still never forget how she comforted Mateo's mom after Gabriela's passing. Or when she performed onstage with her violin in front of all of Hollows' Peak. She would always be the bravest to me.

Mama's eyes welled with tears. "I wasn't brave when Grandmama died. I was scared. I didn't know what to do, so I hid away from you—from everyone." Her voice cracked. "But then, a few months ago, I found a place that helps people like me. People who need to grieve."

"Like how Blair goes to therapy?"

Mama nodded. "Exactly. It's called the Hollows' Peak Grief Counseling Center."

I thought of all those times Mama was busy, unable to spend time with me lately like we used to. "You mean that's where you've been going all this time? You've been . . . attending grief sessions?"

She nodded. "I'm so sorry I wasn't there for you, Raveena. Maybe if I were—"

"No," I cut in. "You needed help. You shouldn't apologize for that."

Mama's eyes touched mine—and for a moment I saw something in them I hadn't seen in a long time. Hope.

"Sometimes it feels like the moments my mother and

I shared, all the happy times and the sad ones, were a long-forgotten dream." She sighed. "I know you think that I haven't been prioritizing Grandmama since she passed. That I should be doing more to honor her memory. The truth is that I have, in my own way. But I've been hiding it from you and acting like nothing ever happened. I thought I needed to protect you from my grief, but it turns out, I ended up pushing you away in the process."

Mama was choking on her words now. Tears sprang to my eyes. I was what Lillian called an empath, which meant I felt a lot of feelings, especially what other people were feeling, even if I wasn't going through whatever they were. Everything Mama said broke my heart, because grief wasn't something we should go through alone. It should be shared—to lighten the load and remind us that we're not alone.

I was crying full-on tears now too.

Not just for Grandmama, but for my mother. Because as unfair as it was that I didn't have a cell phone, that didn't truly matter. What mattered was that Mama and I could bond again. Could remember, little by little.

Mama hugged me, then blew her nose. "I haven't hidden away every piece of Grandmama from my life. I brought many of her things to my sessions." From the glove box, she retrieved a framed photograph that used to rest on our fireplace mantel.

There was a streak in the glass, like someone had touched it. Mama.

I could picture her rubbing a thumb over the glass to

see Grandmama more clearly. Wrinkles formed around her beaming smile, her white hair smoothed up in a perfect bun. Her eyes sparkled with mischief. We always snuck around Mama and played games on her iPad way past my bedtime. Back then Mama would scold me, but she did it gently, always brushing my hair back and wetting my forehead with an overexaggerated kiss. *Gross!* I would say, rushing to my bathroom to wipe it off and prepare for bed.

"I'm sorry that I kept my grief a secret from you, and I'm sorry I didn't create a safe space for you to talk to me about your feelings." Mama squeezed my hands before taking a deep breath. "But I'm not quite ready to talk about it all yet. I might be going to counseling, but it's going to take time. Can you give me that? A little more time?"

It took bravery to admit you needed help, to admit you weren't ready, to admit that you were scared. And bravery deserved to be rewarded. I nodded. "Of course, Mama. And I'm sorry about what I did. Really."

Besides, if Mama could admit all that to me, then it was only fair that I admit the truth to her . . . soon. I needed a bit of time, too, to confess my own hardships.

I made myself a promise, bound by the beat of my slowly mending heart, that Mama was going to hear them all.

EIGHTEEN
Would You Like Fries with That Taco?

All week at school, kids whispered intensely and stared as I passed by. I could tell what they were thinking: *Did Goody Two-shoes Raveena Gill get caught in the mayor's office?* Little did they know I wasn't a Goody Two-shoes—not after everything I'd done to my friends.

I needed to clean up my act. *After* detention, of course, which I'd been attending every day after school. It was a fitting punishment; I was forced to write *I will not sneak into the mayor's cabinets or take my librarian's keys* thirty times over.

"Is Aiko coming?" I asked Blair after detention. We were due for a meeting at Spirit Service HQ before our next lesson with Tía Paola. El Grillo's warm pendant lights glowed nearby.

"I think she's . . . busy, but she'll be coming for the lesson," Blair said, avoiding eye contact with me. I knew it was just an excuse, but it hurt. What I'd said to her must've hurt even more.

"But on to business." Blair flipped her phone toward us, showing the school website. The business competition rankings were fluctuating like crazy ever since a team of eighth graders with killer weed-whacking skills climbed into second place last week. (You tell *me* why residents of Hollows' Peak wanted their weeds whacked in the middle of winter.) Yet somehow Mateo's team was still going strong.

"Without any bookings lately, we slipped into fourth," Lillian said. "Even if we do get more bookings, I don't think any of us would have time for them. I've been busy trying to re-create Carmela's device...."

I zoned out as I thought of what Paola told me during my dreaded City Hall field trip. She knew my future would be bright. But she couldn't say for sure whether I was possessed like Aiko thought.

I couldn't keep in my thoughts any longer.

"Can we hold off on talking business for a sec? I have something personal to share. About what Aiko accused me of at the sleepover."

"Being a phone hogger? Because you kind of were. Sorry, not sorry," Lillian said with a shrug. Direct, but I appreciated it.

"Yeah, that was true, but it's about something else she said. About me being possessed. What if I'm not being myself because . . . well . . . someone *else* is controlling me?" I steeled myself as I finally let out, "I think I know what needs to be done. I need to have . . . an exorcism."

Blair and Lillian exchanged a loaded glance before bursting into laughter.

"Oh, an exorcism is definitely the answer." Lillian chuckled, while I frowned.

"Hang on while I get the holy water!" Blair doubled over from laughter, clutching her stomach.

I heaved a sigh. "Ha ha. Very funny, guys. But I'm being serious! Something about me has changed."

"Honestly, at the sleepover, it did feel like you changed," Blair admitted. "But remember what Paola said? Spirits can possess people, not control them. The way they affect them is more subtle. Like entering their conscience and changing their decision habits, the way they speak, stuff like that."

"Well, my decisions haven't been all that good," I said. From lying to my friends and to my own mother, getting grounded, and then sneaking into the mayor's office—I wasn't sure who I was at all anymore. "You said it yourself, Blair. Something was wrong with me."

"Because something *was* wrong—but not because of a spirit."

"What do you mean?"

Blair carefully asked me, "Have you ever considered that maybe your decisions *have* been your own? And blaming them on a supernatural being is sort of . . . a shield? A defense mechanism, like my dad jokes?"

Wow. Her therapy lessons were really coming through.

"I never thought of it that way." My shoulders dropped—I hadn't realized I'd been holding so much tension in them. Is that why I was always stiff? From everything that had been going on? From carrying around the phone in my backpack? Or the weight of what my grandma was asking me to do? For the past few weeks, I'd actually believed Aiko might be right about my being possessed. But deep down we both knew that wasn't true.

It was time to own up to my mistakes. "It was all me. I can't keep blaming my poor actions on an imaginary spirit. *I* made those decisions. I'm sorry. I can't say I've done enough to earn your friendship back, but—"

"Hey, you never lost it to begin with," Lillian said reassuringly. "Remember what I always say? *We contain multitudes.* Courtesy of Walt Whitman. Do you know what that means?"

"We're not all good and perfect. We're walking contradictions—people with different interests, hobbies, and life choices. We all have our highs and lows," I said, remembering what our Language Arts teacher taught us last month.

"Exactly!" Lillian was burning up with enthusiasm now. "In science, we don't always deal in facts, but hypotheses. My hypothesis? You are a deeply passionate friend, Raveena, so much so that sometimes your passion blinds you. But it makes you who you are."

My eyes watered. I was so, so grateful.

Now if only I could win Aiko back too.

Three knocks came from the door. I wiped my eyes and pulled it open, hoping to see Aiko but instead finding a pair of hazel eyes that looked too sweet to be coming from someone so *not*.

I thought I felt something flutter in my stomach—butterflies? No. This was a hornet's nest that had been knocked over and was currently thrashing in my belly.

Coolcoolcool.

"Hey, Fierce... Three," Mateo said, glancing around and noticing Aiko's absence. "Mia's got another secret recipe for you guys to try out. It's taco fries."

"What are taco fries?" Blair asked, hurrying over. "Never mind. They look delicious—I don't care what they are." She grabbed a fry from the plate, which was doused with tajin seasoning, and munched. "Oh, now I get it! They're tortilla strips, not potatoes!"

"Bingo! Mia knew you'd get it, Blair." Mateo wore a wide grin. I thought again of what Mama said about needing time after Grandmama's death. Yes, she needed space, but she also needed someone to be there for her, just as I needed someone to be there for me. Mateo had recently gone through the same thing with Gabriela's passing. I was certainly no comfort to him this past year.

"I'm gonna head back—waiter duty calls," Mateo said, leaving the extra fries for us to clean off. Blair was practically licking her fingers. I glared at her.

"What? They're so good! Just a hint of spice from the jalapeño, paired with the savory heirloom tomato salsa and..."

Chef Blair trailed off, probably dreaming of mouthwatering food combinations. At this point, she could be a judge on *Minced Junior*. Meanwhile, I hurried toward

Mateo, who was about to open the back door to El Grillo.

"Hey," I said, pausing him in his tracks. "You were right about the Fierce Three. Something happened, and it was my fault."

Mateo blinked. "I thought you guys would be friends forever."

"We will be." After hearing of Blair's and Lillian's support, newfound confidence was growing inside me. I didn't have to pretend to be calm, casual, and noncommittal anymore. I could just be myself.

My friends helped me face my problems head-on, and it was time to cross another one off my list.

"I thought the same thing about us, you know. That we'd be friends forever . . . until you ditched me." There they were, the words I'd been waiting to divulge for months. My heart began to beat as fast as a hummingbird's.

"Oh," he realized slowly, glancing at his sneakers. "You mean the talent show last year. That's when my grandma started getting sick. And I know yours passed not long after."

"She did," I said. "I lost my grandmother and my best friend in a matter of weeks."

His eyes shot up to mine. "Is that how you felt? That you'd . . . lost me?"

My cheeks reddened. "I dunno. You started hanging out with those eighth graders. . . ."

"Jaiden and his buddies were there for me. I skipped

the talent show to hang out with them. I guess I wanted some guy friends, you know?"

"That doesn't mean you had to abandon me."

"You're right," he admitted. "Honestly? I thought hanging out with them would keep my mind off my grandma's illness. I didn't feel like I could tell anyone how I felt, so distracting myself with new friends was just . . . easier. Wrong, I know. But easy. And then they invited me to be a part of their business team—how could I say no?"

"By saying no," I said, only half joking.

Mateo laughed. I hadn't heard that laugh in a long time. For some reason it made my stomach flip in a way I'd never felt before.

Were Mateo and I seriously talking again—like the friends we once were?

Boys. Are. Confusing.

But in all honesty, it felt good talking to Mateo again instead of stewing at his back.

"Jaiden and his friends aren't *real* friends like you, Blair, Lillian, and Aiko. I'm sorry for ditching you, Raveena."

Mateo expelled a breath, like that took a lot out of him. Like Mama, Mateo struggled with confronting grief. I couldn't keep blaming him for not confiding in me after his grandma's death.

"Thanks, Mateo. That means a lot," I told him. It felt good clearing the air. Maybe this meant I finally had my friend back.

Now it was time to get back another.

. . .

Blair, Lillian, Aiko, and I took our seats in Tía Paola's reading room. It was decorated with fake palm trees, twinkling lights, and glittery seashells. Brochures spilled across the table, reading: SAN DIEGO PSYCHIC CON, THE ULTIMATE DESTINATION FOR CLAIRVOYANTS!

"Who needs Comic Con when you can go to Psychic Con?" Paola exclaimed as she entered the room. "I've gathered you girls for one final meeting before I jet off. Unfortunately, I won't be here this weekend for the festival, because I'm a featured panelist at Psychic Con!" She waited for us to do something. Cheer. Clap. But we only swapped confused looks.

"Girls, I'll be speaking on a panel about the *dos* and *don'ts* of cleaning crystal balls! This is *huge!*"

"Yay," we droned, Blair's and Lillian's voices sounding slightly more excited than mine and Aiko's.

The tension in the air could've been cut with a mystical pen. (Trust Aiko, they were sharper than they looked.) We hadn't had a lesson with Paola since the fight, but it was about time I organized a meeting with the girls, with Paola's help to boot.

"Well, enough about me! Raveena was the brave Guardian who called you all here to my esteemed psychic shop. I think I'll let her take the floor."

"Thanks, Tía." I rose from my wingback chair, wobbling for an uneasy second. "There's a reason I asked Paola if we could gather here today. This was the place where we learned how to become Guardians, and I'm hoping it's the place where we'll become a team again. Remember what Paola taught us during our first lesson?"

"Teamwork is key!" Blair and Lillian harped in unison.

I glanced sideways at Aiko, noticing that she was wearing the friendship bracelets we'd made for each other. She hadn't taken hers off, just like I hadn't taken off mine.

Maybe I wasn't losing my best friend. Maybe, just maybe—I could save this. Save *us*.

"A few weeks ago, I said terrible things to you, Aiko. For a second there, I blamed it on being possessed by a rogue spirit. Now I know it wasn't anyone's fault but my own." I heaved a deep breath. "I *was* hogging the phone, and I needed a break from it. I didn't realize how much I was depending on it . . . depending on getting a call from Grandmama."

The girls glanced down. They had all met my nani on multiple occasions and knew that her kisses could heal and her touch was warmth.

I held back a bay of tears as I said, "Plus, I lied to you—all of you—multiple times, and that's not fair. So I'm really, really sorry, Aiko. I hope you can forgive me."

Silence. I already knew I was forgiven by my two besties, Blair and Lillian. But what about Aiko? Had I irreversibly changed the course of our friendship?

"I have something to say." Aiko's voice startled me. She stood and turned in my direction. "I was really hurt by what you said at the sleepover. I was hurt that you didn't consider how much I wanted to talk to my mom. I was hurt that you were jealous of the relationship I had with my dad and how we treasured my mom's memory. And most of all, I hated that you didn't have the same kind of relationship with your mom. That you felt like you didn't have anyone to lean on, or talk to, or trust with your secrets. But you do. You have all of us."

Aiko turned to Blair and Lillian, then Paola, and finally, back to me.

"I accused you of being a bad Guardian, but the truth is, just like spirits, Guardians need help once in a while, too. So I don't want to keep being angry. I want to do what any good spirit might do—move on. Move forward."

I bit my lip to stop from crying. It didn't work.

"Hey, we're supposed to laugh together and grow old like the Jones triplets!" Aiko chuckled, but it turned into a small sob as she turned to face all of us. "I didn't tell you guys *why* I wanted to talk to my mom so badly. It's because . . . I got my first period. I wasn't sure who to tell; only my dad knows. And he doesn't get it, and I wanted someone who *did* get it, and I wanted my mom to be there for me so I wouldn't feel alone—"

Now Aiko was blubbering, and my tears couldn't be held back. The dam broke, and Aiko and I hugged each other. Fiercely. Because when the Fierce Four hugged it out and apologized, it couldn't be done any other way.

"I'm so sorry, Aiko. I had no idea," I said. But honestly, I should've been there for Aiko, should've asked her what was wrong. That explained why her stomach was hurting at the Hardy Estate. From what I heard, period cramps were the worst. And not having anyone to talk to about it probably felt even more lonesome.

Aiko sniffled. "I tried getting my mom to call the phone, but it didn't work."

"It's possible you didn't receive a call from your mother because she's already moved on," Paola noted gently. Aiko looked at peace with that.

"I'm glad you told us," Blair said. "Sometimes it's easy to keep secrets from each other. But it's so much better to get things off your chest. To talk about the hard stuff. *That's* how we stay besties."

"Another piece of therapy wisdom?" I asked.

"No, that was all Blair Ricci."

I hugged my friends again. Things weren't going to be the same as they once were. But maybe, with all our feelings out in the open, they would be even better.

"Great job, girls. I can sense your auras have been cleared. And good thing, because I couldn't in good faith hop on a plane to Psychic Con and sip on my peach Bellinis with you girls arguing. But now that I know the issue is resolved, I can travel in peace." Paola relaxed in her seat, clearly dreaming of those Bellinis awaiting her.

"No more lies, and no more secrets," I said resolutely as we returned to our seats. It was time I told my friends the whole truth. "We weren't really able to talk about it because of our fight, but Grandmama didn't just want to talk to me. She asked me to do something for her: sneak into the mayor's office and steal a camera from the time capsule."

"Hold the phone." Blair held up her hands. "Pun aside, your *grandma's spirit* told you to steal something from the mayor? Am I hearing that right?"

"Yeah," I said, only just now realizing how strange that sounded. From the looks on the girls' faces, they were picking up on the oddness of the situation too.

"Something seems off...." Paola studied the mirrors littered along the table with an otherworldly intensity. Was she getting a message from the beyond? Surveying what the future held?

"What do you see?" Blair asked.

"Wrinkles." Paola pouted. "I'm turning into my mother-in-law!"

I turned away from Paola and toward my friends. "Honestly, Tía Paola is right. I think something is off.... I just can't put my finger on what."

I told the girls the rest of the story—how the camera was a powerful heirloom gifted by her friend Georgia, how it might contain the power to bring her back to life for good.

Paola hummed with disbelief. "I've never heard of spirits being called back to the physical plane for good. One cannot be resurrected—such power of necromancy is beyond my knowledge," she finished gravely.

Aiko frowned. "You know I love all things resurrection, creepy clowns, and possessed dolls. But even I'm not totally convinced of how your grandma's story lines up."

I felt silly for believing resurrection could be possible now too. But why would Grandmama tell me otherwise? What was she hoping to gain from getting that camera?

"Okay, wild idea," Blair said, "but do you think maybe your grandma is trying to tell you something is wrong? Maybe she was talking in some kind of code?"

I thought of the message in the guidebook. *Don't trust her.* Was Grandmama writing to me in the book? But it didn't match the handwriting of her first note— *use the photograph.* And why wouldn't she just tell me who I couldn't trust on the phone?

I was starting to sense that something was *very* wrong with Grandmama's requests.

"Well, I can't give you all the answers, girls," Paola said, "mainly because my brain is on vacation mode, and mentally I'm sipping drinks by the pool. Now, it's a shame I'll be missing the Hollows' Day Festival this weekend—my fortune-telling booth is always a hit—so allow me to give you girls a reading on the house."

We hadn't gotten a real reading since my Mother Nature card and Lillian's dry hand situation (if that even counted), so we turned to our Guardian guidance counselor with fragile excitement.

Tía Paola closed her eyes and let her fingers wiggle and wander over the flickering candle flames. I could've sworn some of them leapt higher, drawn to her hands like magnets.

"Well?" I shook my leg. "What do you see?"

"It's not about what I *see* but what I *sense*," Paola corrected. "When I offer a reading for my loyal clients, I focus on their auras. It's not something you see but something you *feel*, pulsing around like electricity." She hummed thoughtfully. "Yes, it's coming to me now. . . . Lillian, your saxophone will need a tune-up. Blair, your socks will be mismatched tomorrow. And, Aiko, avoid Jerry for at least three days."

"I don't even know a Jerry!"

"Hmm. I might have mixed that one up. Ah, here we go—avoid *dairy*."

"B-but I love ice cream!"

"Well, my reading is telling me that dairy will cause an ill-fated future . . . or an extra trip to the bathroom."

"Are we sure this reading is accurate?" Blair asked us out of the side of her mouth.

Paola ignored her, pressing her fingers to her temples like she was giving them a massage. "I'm getting something else. . . ."

When Paola's eyes popped open, the fire reflected in them like two darkly lit matches. "Darkness."

"Darkness?" I shivered. "Where?"

"At the Hollows' Day Festival."

My friends and I exchanged trepid looks.

Paola frowned. "Keep your eyes peeled, girls. Someone's true nature will be revealed, and chaos will ensue."

Lillian wondered, "True nature?" while Blair wailed, "*Chaos?*"

As Paola finished her reading, her silver eyes bored into mine. Somehow, they were even more menacing when she was in the middle of a reading. *Spooky.*

"What does that mean?" I asked, but Paola had no answer. And that was the spookiest thing of all.

NINETEEN

Avoid the Kissing Booth at All Costs

The morning of the Hollows' Day Festival, my friends and I met up outside Hollows' Peak Middle. Lillian had an important update for us all before the festival went down tonight in Hollow Square, located right by the school. For weeks my classmates had been preparing to present our assignments to festival attendees, and thankfully Aiko helped me put the finishing touches on my board last night. Volunteers, including Mama and other residents of Hollows' Peak, passed by holding ladders as they prepared to hang banners for this evening's festivities.

Lillian squealed as we all huddled outside the school entrance. "I've finished it!" She pulled something out of her backpack—the device she and Blair were making to mimic Carmela's negativity- and trauma-sucking machine. Honestly, it could've put the Ghostbusters' proton pack to shame—it was spooktacular!

"OMG!" Aiko fawned over it with doe-like eyes.

"Blair and I fiddled with Carmela's schematics, and guess what? The machine can do more than we initially thought! It can also measure the strength of different spirits, thanks to some magnets and an old radio my parents tossed away that can read frequencies."

I smiled. My bestie was *on it*.

"I've even come up with a name for it. I call it . . . the Phantom Energy Evaporator!"

"You just wanted to use the term 'energy evaporator' since you suggested it as our business title," Aiko joked.

Blair stifled a laugh. "Phantom Energy Evaporator . . . PEE for short!"

It was an unfortunate acronym, but also pretty funny. "So? Let's test it out!" I said.

As one, we watched Lillian power on the battery-operated machine.

"Whoa," Aiko said in awe. Bright green lights dotted the surface, and the machine let out a long beep as we approached the school's front doors. We opened them and trotted inside, scanning for areas where the frequency grew higher.

"This way," Lillian said, heading for the principal's office. Now the frequency meter was jumping to the max. No way—was there a spirit in the school *office*?

"It's picking up more activity to the right, too." Aiko took the device and retreated from the office. She stopped right in front of the teachers' lounge.

The machine let out another beep, this time longer. Was it sensing even *more* spirits nearby?

I pressed my ear against the lounge door. Sure enough, I heard a few of the teachers "spilling the tea," but I wasn't sure if it was gossip or *actual* tea. What were they even doing here on a Sunday?

And why was Lillian's device picking up spirits in there?

To clear our minds, the Fierce Four took a quick trip to grab boba and come up with a game plan. Paola had said something big was going to happen tonight. Coupling that with her highly vague warning that "chaos will ensue," we needed to be prepared for anything.

We currently sat in Benny's Boba, sipping on our brown sugar tapioca-filled creations, which the barista was unnecessarily rude about—so what if I wanted half sugar? Sue me!

"Lillian, do you have the itinerary?" I asked.

Lillian squared her shoulders. "At approximately six o'clock, the festival will begin. Booths will be operating, hot dogs will be flying—"

"Flying?" Blair cried.

Lillian ignored her. "According to the town website, Mayor Clayton will make some opening remarks at seven and then unlock the time capsule. You know, the thing Raveena's grandma wanted her to open."

"Right," Aiko said, "and in order to stop any possible *chaos*, we'll keep an eye out for more spirit activity. Lillian, keep your machine on. The rest of us can watch different areas of Hollow Square."

"I'll watch the school," I suggested. The students would have booths where townspeople could roam by and hear about our projects, so it wouldn't be hard to keep an eye on suspicious activity while I was at it.

"Then I'll watch the festival entrance," Blair added. "As long as I can avoid Mrs. Fitz's kissing booth."

The girls' mouths puckered at the thought. Pro tip: Don't visit Mrs. Fitz's kissing booth. It's not a kiss from Mrs. Fitz you'll be getting, but a whiskery "kiss" from her cat, Jelly Bean. She will give you a scratch and a cruel *meow* and Mrs. Fitz will say, "That'll be three dollars, please."

Our sour expressions lifted as the boba shop door swung open. The Jones triplets walked in with seventies-style coiffed hair and matching glittery headbands. Their identical T-shirts read, I LOVE ROCK 'N RUFFLES!

"Hi, girls!" called the triplets in unison. They swaggered over to our table as Wisteria said, "We're just swinging by for the festival! Thank you *so* much again for helping our little boy Ruffles move on. You know"—she glanced around, but the chatter of the boba shop was thankfully covering up our conversation—"to the big *doghouse in the sky*." She made an overexaggerated wink.

"Nice code word, Ms. Jones," Aiko said. "Hey, Tía Paola told us that there might be something . . . unsavory happening tonight. Do you have any advice for us?"

"Well, if it's spirits who come calling, literally, don't ignore them," Iris advised. "They need answering and get so bored in the in-between world!"

"Yeah, like me at that mahjong tournament last weekend," Dahlia said, wiping her bifocals. She squinted at us as she continued. "As long as you don't have spirits traveling about between humans' bodies or controlling other spirits—"

"Hold up. *Controlling?*" I asked. From Tía Paola, we had learned a handful of facts about spirits.

#1: All levels of spirits are capable of possessing humans.

#2: Level threes do not want to move on because of the negative emotions they harbor, which can rot them from the inside out and change them physically. Their unresolved trauma turns them into monstrous versions of themselves and can even alter how their voices sound.

#3: Spirits can . . . *control* other spirits? How? Scratch that. Paola never mentioned anything about control.

I said as much to the triplets, who merely chuckled between each other.

"Well, what can you expect? Paola isn't a spirit expert like us! She thinks that because she has the biggest psychic shop in a hundred miles she's all that!" Wisteria huffed.

"Well, she kind of is," Dahlia argued under her breath. "And yes, girls—a very strong spirit can actually control *other* spirits, leading them like the general of an army. Like calls to like; spirit calls to spirit. You didn't know? It's basic Medium 101 training."

"Very strong? Like a level three spirit?" I asked. I thought of the way the device had been beeping wildly earlier. Was there a level three spirit lurking somewhere in Hollows' Peak?

"I've never used levels to describe spirits before," Wisteria said, "but the Hollows must have written about them in that guidebook of yours. Oh yes, I know about that. Paola has quite the flap on that trap, if you know what I mean." She made a talking motion with her hand.

With that, Dahlia left to order her drink. When she returned, she had the strangest look on her face, and her eyes looked dead inside. She wasn't even wearing her bifocals!

"I asked for no tapioca and the barista just *stared at me*. Stared! In Rosemary Heights, we DON'T DO STARING. OR TAPIOCA."

"Ooookay." I shifted in my seat with discomfort. Why was Dahlia acting so strange?

"And DON'T get me STARTED on popping BOBA—" Dahlia started coughing on her words. Her voice had suddenly gotten hoarse.

Mrs. Nkosi's voice had been oddly hoarse not long ago too. Either Dahlia was also a major Swiftie, or something strange was going on.

"She prattles on too much, this one," Iris said as she and Wisteria ushered their sister to the door. "Come, sister, let's get some fresh air."

"In a town that's made up of all things weird, even *I* found that weird," Lillian said after they left. "What do you think the Joneses meant when they said spirits can control other spirits? Tía Paola taught us about *possession*, not control."

"Paola might be a psychic, but she definitely doesn't know everything," Blair said. "Case in point, her decorating skills—no one would call her reading room mid-century modern."

A chill swept through me as I glanced out the window. Soon residents would begin closing their shops and opening their booths, all in preparation for the hundredth anniversary of Hollows' Peak.

The town was certainly getting in the spirit—I just hoped it wasn't literally.

At 6:37 p.m., full on three refills of boba and a wide array of a nearby booth's ghost-shaped sugar cookies, I stood next to my display board. It had a whole bunch of newspaper printouts about the 1975 fire and even obituaries of the deceased.

"Olivia Dare enjoyed planting tulips in her garden," I told a young couple as they strolled past me. "Betsy Crane loved injecting music into her everyday life. Then there was Jedidiah Craven, who studied amphibians' mating habits until his untimely death. I made a mural to help townspeople remember all these lost souls, and more."

My speech was drawing a crowd—the fire was a hot topic, quite literally. Just yesterday Aiko lent me her paintbrushes so I could create my mural on the poster board, and it turned out better than I imagined.

Mr. Bisson parted the crowd, wearing an approving

smile. "Great work, Raveena. I can really see your sense of dedication to learning about Hollows' Peak history!"

I beamed. After all my failings, all my mistakes, I knew he was right. But I wasn't just learning about the *town*'s history; I'd unearthed facts about *Grandmama*'s history. And that was most rewarding of all.

After finishing up, I headed to the town festival's main stage to meet up with the rest of the Fierce Four. On the way, I meandered past the booths, admiring everyone from the local bakers to El Grillo's pop-up. Their birria chimichangas and achiote chicken tostadas brought the heat!

Next to them was a dunk tank for charity—all you had to do was throw a dodgeball at the target to dump the volunteer into the sudsy tub of water. Principal Hanover dangled his toes over the water, waiting for his soapy fate.

It felt so good to see my whole community come together. Mrs. Wang sold Bodacious Blueberry lipstick, a local vendor hawked popcorn of every color in the rainbow, and the Yoons displayed some of their antique art for people to peruse and enjoy. Blair joined me after she finished working the Journalists of Tomorrow Club's booth, where they were showing off old editions of the school paper and even the tech they used to use, from VHS players to projector screens.

The main stage was set up in the center of Hollow Square, with the bell tower and City Hall rising behind it. A full moon rose in the sky, brightening the dark, cloudless night. A lone mic stood in the middle of the makeshift stage, awaiting Mayor Clayton's arrival, and a bumping beat blared from the speakers.

In the thick of the crowd, I spotted some of the townspeople we'd helped with Spirit Service: Mrs. Fitz, still clinging to a bag of potato chips; Miss Evermore, wearing her engagement ring; the Joneses, pulling off some disco moves to the music (Dahlia participated with a scowl); and even Mr. Hardy and his granddaughter, Ruby, who spotted me and gave me a big wave. I became teary-eyed just thinking of how many people we'd helped in such a short period of time.

"The time capsule reopening should start any minute now." Blair checked the time on her phone. Two minutes to go. "How was spirit-hunting, Lill?"

Lillian appeared at my other side with Aiko, each of them decked out in all white as if they were trying to be part of the Ghostbusters squad. I must've missed the memo. "My device is definitely picking up spirits in the area. But why aren't any of them calling the phone?"

"Maybe their loved ones aren't around?" I asked, peering into Aiko's bag, where she was keeping the phone. She was right—no glow. My eyes found the fissure, and an image flashed unbidden in my head. *The phone, glowing red. Wisps escaping out my living room window.*

But what if those weren't just smoky wisps that had escaped? What if they were . . . ?

I whispered my thoughts to my friends, who each went paler than a ghost itself.

"But spirits aren't trapped in the phone. They're trapped in the in-between," Lillian reasoned.

"Unless these spirits are different," Aiko said. "Season 2, episode 14 of *Short Island Medium* explores spirits who are trapped in a mirror. When the mirror cracked, the spirits were released."

"But whose spirits did we release?" Blair asked.

A tense silence followed. Great. We did *exactly* what Paola told us not to do—we let spirits loose without helping them move on. Her words hovered in my mind, coating my body like coarse, wet grains of sand.

That would be very troubling, girls. Very troubling indeed.

Before any of us could delve deeper, a stream of fireworks lit up Hollow Square as Mayor Clayton took the stage. Applause thundered through the crowd. Mayor Clayton made a motion, and a few City Hall workers dragged the treasure chest—the time capsule—onto the stage.

"Welcome one, welcome all!" Mayor Clayton beamed while fixing his 'fro. "I'm pleased to be onstage for yet another year of Hollows' Day Festivities. As you all might know, many, many years ago, our town mayors were Hollows themselves. While I'm no Hollow, I think I can certainly speak for the town when I say that the Hollows built our lovely community from the ground up. And look at us now—one hundred years later to the day, still thriving!"

More applause and cheering. Mayor Clayton bent

down to enter the combination lock I so desperately needed not long ago. The time capsule clicked open.

"And here it is! Our fifty-year-old time capsule is officially open. Let's see what we have here...."

In true Hollows' Peak fashion, Mayor Clayton drew out an old sock, a broken necklace, a pair of bell-bottoms straight out of the Joneses' closet, and a now-expired jar of mustard. Apparently that brand of mustard was all the rage, along with Haunting Hollow Crunchies.

"And lastly, we have ... a camera? Well, it's certainly vintage, isn't it?" Mayor Clayton held up the camera for us all to see. It fit neatly in his hand but was bulky, nothing like the cameras of today.

Why did Grandmama need it so badly?

"Weird ... spirit activity is increasing," Lillian said, checking her PEE device. The thing was, the activity looked to be coming from all around us, so there was no way to pinpoint the source.

"And now I'd like to bring a revered member of our community up to the stage to say a few words." Mayor Clayton returned the camera to the time capsule and clapped as the figure wound his way out of the crowd.

Principal Hanover—still dry despite many attempts to dunk him into a water tank—meandered onto the stage, giving a well-mannered wave to the audience.

"Greetings, residents, students, and teachers I hired," Principal Hanover said into the mic, laughing, as Mayor Clayton withdrew from the stage. The crowd laughed along with him. "What a beautiful evening this is, a chance for us all to come together and celebrate our spooky little town. I hope tonight is all going according to plan."

Odd choice of words, but there was a smattering of claps.

"I know it will be for me."

Townspeople around us stirred, like they felt a rock in their boot or an ant crawling up their arm. Energy crackled in the sea of bodies. Thunder rumbled overhead, and rain spat down in thick, warm droplets. Where had this weather come from? It had been completely cloudless minutes ago. The angry gray clouds had seemingly gathered right over Hollow Square.

"Is it time yet?" one townsperson shouted with agitation, nearly crushing a handful of uprooted tulips in their hands.

"We've been waiting for fifty years," growled Mrs. Wang. She wasn't even wearing her Bodacious Blueberry lipstick anymore, instead opting for a slime-green shade that matched her new I <3 FROGGIES crewneck.

"I say we take back our home," another festivalgoer shouted. "The one we were torn from!"

"Let's start a fire and show *them* what it feels like!" another roared.

Raucous cheers filled the air. Principal Hanover drew his gaze over the crowd with a sly smile, but my mind was going a mile a minute. *Fifty years. Tulips. Amphibians.*

Fire.

Olivia Dare planted tulips in her garden—Jedidiah

Craven studied frogs and other amphibious creatures.

The principal cracked his neck from side to side. "Patience," he exhaled. "First I must get what I have been seeking...."

Principal Hanover reached into the time capsule and retrieved the vintage heirloom camera. He opened the tape compartment, looking pleased for a moment before a scowl tugged at his mouth.

He stared at the empty slot. "Where is it?" he hissed. When no one responded, he boomed, *"Where is the tape?!"*

Looks of confusion fell on my friends' faces.

"You," the principal spat, wagging a stern finger at me. "You and your friends did this, didn't you? Didn't you!"

"No—" I started, but the crowd was already turning to face me. Cold fingers crawled over my skin as I took in their eyes—hollow, black, and sunken. Like they were... *possessed.*

And they were looking at me like I was their next meal.

I thought of Principal Hanover's flashing red eyes at City Hall. His cryptic statement—*During the Hollows' Day Festival, all will be revealed.* His obsession with ghosts, as a self-proclaimed "spirit savant."

I racked my brain for all the strange encounters that had happened today, like Lillian's device beeping nearby the teachers' lounge . . . and just outside the principal's office.

The principal raised his arms, eyes flashing red. I shuddered as the truth dawned on me—was Principal Hanover not just a savant . . . but a spirit himself?

"Spirits, I command you to cause havoc and destruction!" he ordered, his voice doubling, like there was another being trapped inside him. As one, the townspeople spilled forward, and Paola's vision of the future came true.

Pure. Chaos.

Mrs. Fitz turned on me, holding up her cat, who nearly scratched my eyes out. My friends grabbed on to each other and slipped between the bodies as arms and legs thrashed, as words were spewed and eyes flashed a deep, all-consuming black—

Nearby, glass shattered, and I watched as Janice Hollow's spirit-possessed body tossed baseballs, probably from her grandpa's collection, at the school windows. I covered my head with my arms as I spotted Mrs. Nkosi. Finally, an adult who could help us!

"Mrs. Nkosi—"

Her neck snapped to the right, her eyes deep and dark and focused intently on mine. No glasses, either. "Yoo-hoo, Fierce Four . . . why don't you girls come over here to chitchat with your favorite librarian?"

We froze, glancing at each other.

"I SAID LET'S CHITCHAT!" She cleared her throat, inching closer to us like a tiger zeroing in on its prey.

Somehow, my librarian had turned a T-Swizzle song into a menacing remark. Had Mrs. Nkosi been possessed by *Betsy Crane*, the music-obsessed woman who died in the fire, since way back at the City Hall trip? Her hoarse voice must've been from her aggressive, heightened emotions. And it seemed spirits didn't need glasses. Now it made sense why Dahlia had removed her bifocals. In the boba shop, Dahlia had been acting fine until she came back with her order of bubble tea. What if the *barista* was possessed, and then the spirit decided to change things up and enter Dahlia's body, where they now resided?

Thankfully, Mr. Bisson appeared next to the librarian. I'd never been so grateful to see my teacher in my life.

"Mr. Bisson, help!"

"Oh, *I* need help," Mr. Bisson said, eyes like black holes. "Don't you girls agree that TEACHERS DESERVE BETTER WAGES?!"

Oh no. *He'd* been possessed too!

Freeze. Mr. Bisson was right about the wages thing—teachers were criminally underpaid—but it appeared that the spirit inside him was only making him all the more vocal about it. It was no wonder the device had been beeping like crazy outside the teachers' lounge!

Okay, unfreeze.

"Guys!" Lillian tugged on my arm as my librarian reached out for us, nails ready to dig into skin.

We dove for safety. Screams erupted in the air, and panic took over. An unmanned cotton candy booth was our only salvation, and we slid behind it, our breaths locked in our beating throats.

Aiko quivered. "Didn't the Joneses teach us that any

spirit, if strong enough, could control *other* spirits?"

"You're saying Principal Hanover is . . . a *spirit?*" Blair gasped.

I nodded, face grave.

We let that sink in as chaos reigned around us. How it all made sense, I wasn't sure. But he wanted something on the camera's tape—maybe even something Grandmama had wanted—and I was determined to find out what.

"And I think I know whose spirits we let out of the cracked phone," I told the girls, jittering all over. "The townspeople who died in the fire in 1975."

"*That* was why they mentioned waiting for fifty years . . . for their revenge!" Aiko exploded with the realization.

"Revenge for what? The fire was an accident," I explained. "At least, that's how the story goes."

But Mrs. Nkosi brought up that the origin of the fire was a debated topic. What really happened that night fifty years ago?

As Lillian and Blair exchanged tense looks, I dared to peer over the booth.

Ten paces away, a horde of residents with soulless eyes grabbed spray paint from the community center's booth and went to town, vandalizing booths and tearing into signs. One even found an unlit match and searched for a lighter. I thought of the fatal fire. If we didn't act fast, town history would be doomed to repeat itself.

Moments later wisps of white light escaped the

bodies of the vandalizing residents, and their eyes returned to their normal shades. They turned to one another like, *What just happened? And why am I holding spray paint?*

I tracked the wisps as they found new hosts. Bodies shuddered as the spirits entered residents through their mouths and took over their souls. They marched forward, ready to terrorize the town.

One spirit even traveled from a human to the inside of the festival's photo booth. Next thing we knew, the booth was jittering like an overheated kettle. Printouts zoomed out of that thing at the speed of light and sliced into passersby. Death by a thousand cuts had never been so literal.

Pro tip #2: Skip out on the possessed photo booth.

"We have to do something!" I said before zeroing in on someone. Principal Hanover lurked through the crowd, pausing in his tracks when he spotted me. His eyes flashed red again, and I knew for certain what he was.

Not just any spirit. A level three.

TWENTY

The Truth about 1975

To be honest, it was a brave assumption—but we had no other logic to go off. Principal Hanover's office was the source of the loud beeps. He must have been a strong level three spirit to control an army of possessed residents. But how could he himself be a spirit if he looked like a regular corn-chip-loving dude?

"A plan would be nice right about now!" Aiko blurted out of the corner of her mouth.

"We need to lead him away from Hollow Square, get him somewhere private," I told my friends.

"I know just the place." Lillian pointed to the school. "Leave it to me."

My friends dashed out from behind the cotton candy stand. I made to follow them, but someone caught on to my jacket sleeve, and I recoiled, thinking of Mrs. Nkosi sinking her claws into my skin—

"Raveena? Raveena!"

I almost cried in relief. Mama gave me an even bigger bear hug than the one after the City Hall trip. This time it wasn't out of sadness but desperation.

"What's going on? One minute I was listening to

Mayor Clayton and your principal onstage, and the next—"

"Spirits," I said firmly.

Mama blinked twice. "Come again?"

I did my best to explain the situation while leaving out the phantom phone.

"Are you serious about this? Townspeople are being . . . *possessed* by spirits who haven't moved on to the afterlife?" For someone who just learned about spirits, my mom had the gist of it down pretty fast.

A baseball zoomed our way, and we ducked. A nearby popcorn machine was overflowing, and townspeople tripped and flailed within the sea of corn goodness.

"Get to safety, girls. I'll find one of your teachers—"

Mama didn't have time to finish her sentence. A stray baseball knocked down the cotton candy machine, and I leapt with fright as Mama stopped the machine from toppling over.

"But, Mama—"

"Just go! Be safe!" my mom cried, arms buckling under the weight. A hand dragged me back—Aiko's—and I had no choice but to follow.

Lillian led the charge, waving down the principal to grab his attention. "Hey, Principal Hanover! We've got your tape!"

"And corn chips! Extra crunchy!" enticed Blair.

I caught on to their ruse. "Meet us in the office, or you'll never get the tape."

Principal Hanover's eyes flickered different shades of red. He growled. Clearly taking the bait, he broke into a sprint.

"Okay, now we run!" I yelled. We were panting for breath by the time we peeled into the school. We landed in Principal Hanover's office, turning to find him just steps behind us. He smoothed a few greasy strands of hair out of his face in an attempt to feign composure, but his eyes, no longer red, were still wild with desperation.

"There's no need to look so afraid, girls," Principal Hanover began, his voice ragged. He took a menacing step toward us. "Now give me what I want."

"What are you talking about?" Lillian's voice turned high-pitched as she glanced over at me. We hadn't come up with the next part of our plan yet.

"Don't be coy. The tape." He opened the camera to show us an empty compartment, probably where a tape was supposed to go to record whatever the camera captured.

"First tell us how you controlled all those spirits outside," I demanded. "That must mean you're a level three spirit!"

The other girls balked at my conclusion.

"That's ridiculous! I'm not a *spirit*," the principal spat, making a *gimme, gimme* motion with his hands. "Now hand me the tape. I know you girls must have the evidence!"

"What evidence?" Aiko asked me. I shook my head.

"We don't actually have the tape," Blair revealed, appearing to grow a few inches taller as she faced down our principal. "It was all a ploy. So tell us what's really going on!"

I would've gone teary-eyed with pride at Blair's assertiveness if we weren't currently being grilled by our principal.

The principal's eyes slid over to mine. "I should've known better than to trust a . . . what's it called again? A *Guardian*."

"How do you know about Guardians?" My voice quivered.

"I've heard all sorts of stories about them. I know a lot about that little phone of yours too. Don't think I didn't see it in your bag that day in my office. I know that's how you've been communicating with spirits!"

"Well, yeah, duh," Aiko said like it was nothing. "How do *you* know about the phone?"

The principal snickered humorlessly. "It all stems back to the story of Colin Hollow, who choked on a loose front tooth and declared reverse birthdays forevermore in this odd little town. What a silly tradition. But I suppose I have Colin to thank for giving the phone as a present to the three immigrants who saved his life."

"Avneet, Hanbin, and Georgia," I recalled, pulling the photograph of my grandma and her two friends out of my coat pocket.

"Georgia?" Blair asked me, looking at the photograph. "As in your grandma's friend?"

"The one who gave your grandma the camera?" Lillian added.

"You're all quite keen on your history. Especially you, Raveena. Your grandmother was apparently much like that too."

"Grandmama?" How did the principal know my grandmother? "What do you know about—"

"Let me finish," Principal Hanover interjected. "When these three immigrants were granted their gift—the spirit phone—they became so mesmerized by it, despite it being dormant and unused, that they tried to find a way, as non-mediums, to use it. Georgia led the charge one night, when the forecast predicted a horrid lightning storm. She decided to host an experiment in their secret club house at the bottom of the bell tower. She put the phone there, hoping a strike of lightning might be powerful enough to activate it once more."

Was he talking about the day of the freak lightning accident at the bell tower? The day Olivia, Jedidiah, Betsy, and dozens of others were killed?

Principal Hanover continued. "Avneet and Hanbin warned Georgia something might go wrong, but she didn't listen. The three of them watched from nearby as lightning struck the bell tower and the electricity coursed all the way down to the phone. Georgia captured the footage of the strike on her camera—she wanted her paranormal discoveries to be known all around the world someday—but it seemed nothing *actually* paranormal took place. Their phone had become singed and the power cord frayed."

"The power cord..." Aiko trailed off, glancing at the phone in her backpack.

Lillian's eyes grew wide. "The burn marks!"

"But that wasn't the worst of it," the principal barreled on. "The three newfound friends had caused something terrible to happen, inadvertently, of course. The phone attracts electricity—it made the lightning all the more intense. The nearby City Hall went up in flames. A group of people who were trapped inside perished."

I couldn't believe it—Grandmama and her friends *caused* the fire? It was an accident, but I still couldn't wrap my head around something so terrible, so tragic.

So close to home.

"Knowing the damage they created, the group decided to hide the phone and promised to never speak of it. But in secret, despite the guilt eating her up inside, Georgia discovered things about the phone that the group never anticipated. The lightning must have triggered the phone to reactivate from its dormant state. With the paranormal phone causing the fire..."

"The spirits of those who died became trapped in the phone itself," I pieced together.

Principal Hanover's lips curved into a slippery smile. "But this story doesn't end there. Georgia found notes from these so-called 'fire spirits' in the guidebook and told her friend Avneet all about them. The fire spirits wrote about their deaths and how they were trapped inside a strange phone, trying to be freed so they could move on to the afterlife."

My skin iced over. We were the reason these fire spirits were set loose in our town. We caused this problem. But it all stemmed back to Grandmama—no, to Georgia. This was *her* fault, not my grandmother's—even if she was partially an accomplice.

"How do you know all this?" I asked. "How can we trust that your story is true? You don't exactly seem like a trustworthy principal anymore."

The principal schooled his features into a state of calm. "Because I'm connected to all this. You do know how, don't you, Raveena?" He lifted the framed photograph on his desk into his hands and admired it longingly. The woman in the picture had the same face as the one in the photograph with Grandmama.

His words from our first business meeting right in this office flooded back to me. *My mother would tell me stories about spirits. About the history of this town...*

"You already knew about the phone," I said. "Because of your mother."

"It was a treasured possession of hers." The principal's voice deepened, growing hoarse. "And now she has returned to me once more, with the phone right within our grasp...."

Aiko gripped her backpack straps tighter.

Principal Hanover's eyes flashed crimson. "Would you like to meet my mother? She's been eager to speak to you all."

We all stood, speechless, as the principal's eyes rolled toward the back of his head, showing only the whites. A new voice poured out of the principal—a woman's, deep and commanding.

"*Well, well, well, if it isn't my friend Avneet's granddaughter,*" she told me with a wicked smile.

TWENTY-ONE

I'll Take the Midnight Train to—

"Georgia?" we cried in unison.

Principal Hanover—no, *Georgia*—smiled using her son's lips. Our principal's eyes unrolled from the back of his head, and I swore that image would haunt me for the rest of my days. In her voice, she said, *"Hello, girls. I gather you know the truth now? Oh, how long I've been waiting for this day to come...."*

"You're the level three spirit!" Blair cried. "You're possessing Principal Hanover!"

"How is this possible?" Aiko shuddered, looking at us for help. "She never called the phone!"

"But I did," Georgia revealed. *"And it's all thanks to Raveena."*

I blanched as the other girls looked at me.

"The Mother Nature card," I whispered to myself. Paola's premonition from her first reading: *This card only appears when a mother, or a maternal figure, is about to cause upheaval.*

The card was never talking about my mom or my grandma. It was talking about Georgia.

"That day next to the principal's office," I said, "the

phone rang, but no one spoke." I steeled myself and looked up into Georgia's eyes. "You called the phone."

Georgia offered me an oily smile. *"How could I not? My son had to be able to see my spirit somehow. But spirits cannot remain in this world for long, not without a host body. Luckily, my son was the perfect vessel."* Her eyes focused on mine. *"But little did you know that that wasn't the first time I contacted you through the phantom phone. When you lifted the receiver before our first call, you unwittingly released my spirit from the in-between world...."*

I thought of that first phone call with Grandmama. Scribbled words had appeared in the guidebook—the first set of handwriting. *Use the photograph.*

The photograph of Grandmama, Hanbin . . . and Georgia.

Tears reached my eyes as the realization hit me. "Grandmama never called me." The day I'd used the photograph to summon Grandmama, I hadn't summoned her. I'd summoned Georgia.

Don't trust her. Don't trust *Georgia.* The second set of handwriting—Grandmama's—must have been telling me that Georgia was sneakily impersonating her.

My voice shook as I recalled what Paola taught me. "Level three spirits can manipulate their voices. You tricked me!"

"It was all too easy," Georgia revealed, *"answering your call. You're a stronger Guardian than you realize to call someone who is not your loved one. But the photo-*

graph including me and your grandmother, plus your desperation, did the trick. I chose not to show you my spirit-self—it's quite ugly, and you thought I was Avneet. All I had to do was call you beti, like Avneet did with her own child. And you were oh so willing to believe the lie."

My heart turned molten. I couldn't believe I thought this vile spirit was my grandmother. How could I have been so foolish?

Georgia continued. *"Oh, how I was dying to be freed. But when I realized I could get you to listen to whatever your grandma wanted . . . what I wanted . . . I asked that you keep our little rendezvous a secret and carry the phone around with you at all times, hoping you might bring it to school. And like a dog in search of a bone, you followed my every order. You brought the phone into my son's office, where it was close enough that I could make the call and show myself to him—well, 'possess' him, for lack of a better term."*

I sneered with distaste, my molten heart cooling into glass. "You would possess your own son?"

"Like you for your grandmother, my son will do anything for me. When I told him about the evidence of the cause of the fire on my camera, hidden in the time capsule, the two of us concocted a plan. For phase one, I asked you to retrieve the camera, and my son ever so dutifully organized a school 'research' trip to help you get to City Hall. Of course, it wasn't until I followed you to Janice Hollow's house that I learned where the time capsule was hidden. You did feel my presence that day, didn't you?"

I thought of the strange wind I'd felt at the Hardy Estate—and then again at Janice's house. Because of her—Georgia Hanover. Watching me.

Spying on me.

"Why not just retrieve the camera yourself? Your son could've done your dirty work," Lillian said scathingly.

"Oh, he did. He even tried to get into Mayor Clayton's good graces by inviting him to silly bake sales and conversing with him over bags of corn chips, hoping to sway him to open the time capsule early. But the mayor wouldn't fall for my son's tactics. Thankfully, we had Raveena as our insurance policy. Too bad the mayor returned to his office before she could accomplish my simple task." Her look of reproach speared through me.

"I needed that camera for the next step of my plan: getting rid of the evidence that I caused the fire that night. I couldn't have that coming out at the Hollows' Day Festival this year, ruining my son's image! But when I discovered the tape was gone..."

"You broke down and ordered the townspeople to chase us. You ordered them to cause havoc!" Aiko retorted. She wasn't even the least bit scared of a level three. I think I knew why; spirits weren't of our world. But friends and family? Those were fragile things that needed love and care. Those were things we couldn't afford to lose.

"You know, back when I was alive, I watched that tape over and over, hoping I missed something crucial, a vital spirit discovery somewhere in the footage. But

there was nothing there but the proof of the murderous accident we had caused. Then, one day, before I could destroy the tape, it disappeared. Someone left me a note that they had stolen it and the camera and buried it in the time capsule. I needed to get that tape back from whoever buried it—likely Hanbin or even my best friend, Avneet, were the culprits. They hid it in the one place that would be locked and inaccessible for decades. They wanted the truth of our crimes to come to light in fifty years—they said the truth would set us all free. How preposterous. Why reveal our crimes when we can erase the past? Now, where is that tape!"

"We don't have it!" Blair repeated.

The spirit wasn't happy with that answer.

"You're lucky I'm not in a foul mood," Georgia gritted out. This was her on a good day?

"My son will help me find that tape, and we'll keep looking until our fingers bleed."

Again, not a pretty visual.

"Do you know how tenacious my son is?" Georgia snarled. *"For years he's been taking trips around the world to speak to mediums and see if other phantom phones might exist. He's fascinated by spirits just as I was. Of course, those trips came with a hefty price tag. Which is why the poor arts program had to take a blow . . . and why the school business competition was such a brilliant plan."*

"Wait—Principal Hanover is the reason the arts program was cut? He was funneling the funds?!" Aiko blurted. "I've always wanted to say that alliteration, but not under *these* circumstances!"

I gawked at the principal-slash-mother-spirit. "I can't believe it. He said there was no budget this year—but he took the money for himself! I bet he never really had a plan to bring the arts program back!"

"And he was planning on using our hard-earned money from the school competition, too?" Blair's ears were practically steaming. "That's a new low, Hanover!"

"My son wasn't low," Georgia snapped. *"He was audacious. Of course, our plans changed when I showed up. My son wasn't thinking big enough. I had to show him that this phone was still in existence, and in your girls' hands. And now we'd like to take it from you and put it back where it rightfully belongs. With us."*

I had a feeling Georgia wasn't asking. Like mother, like son.

"No," I said firmly.

Georgia growled. *"Do you know what this phone means to me? It was MY gift from the mayor. And I was the only one of my friends to take charge and REALLY uncover this phone's properties. And when I get the phone back, my son can show the world all our amazing discoveries. We'll be revered in the paranormal community as geniuses!"*

"Lillian, take out your device!" I managed out of the corner of my mouth. Lillian powered it on. But the spirit wasn't easily distracted by her own spiel.

"Do you think you can seriously capture me?" Georgia

scowled derisively at the device. *"I am a level three spirit! I am too powerful for you girls to ever help move on—and I'm going to keep it that way."*

The spirit of Georgia escaped out of her son's mouth, and Principal Hanover slumped to the ground, unconscious, as his mother revealed her true self for the first time.

Monstrous wasn't enough to describe it. Paola's pimple metaphor barely scratched the surface.

Georgia was herself . . . but not. Her features had been enhanced, or rather, uglified. Her brows were long and spiky, and so were her lashes. Her nails curled like a hawk's talons. Her lips were covered in warts, fangs protruding. But she didn't look like a witch or a vampire. More like a sad, depleted, decrepit ghost with straw-like hair and a mournful face. And her eyes . . .

They flashed a deep, hypnotic red. *"I won't be kept waiting. It's time for me to find that tape."*

"Lillian, now!"

Lillian aimed her device right at the spirit, clicking a button to suck out its negative energy. She narrowly missed as the spirit flew aside, cackling.

"Forgot something? Spirits can float through walls." Georgia escaped out of the principal's study.

"Follow her!"

In the hallway, the spirit spiraled through the air, dodging all of Lillian's attempts at siphoning the trauma within her. I followed Lillian, pointing out where to aim the device next, but the spirit was too fast.

We chased the spirit, spilling out into the school foyer. Without hesitation, Lillian leveled the device at the ghost—

Georgia turned on us and snatched the device from Lillian's hands. She broke it in two with her taloned hands, baring sharp fangs.

"My PEE machine!"

I stared in utter horror as Georgia tossed the device aside. Its green lights flickered and glitched, powering down with a dismayed wail.

Our chance at vanquishing a level three spirit was gone.

There was no time to mourn the loss of Lillian's device. Georgia's monstrous form was evolving by the second, and nothing could dampen the spirit's rage. She spread her hands out, just like the Mother Nature card in Paola's tarot deck, head upturned as if to summon a phantom wind.

But Mother Nature had nothing on a level three.

A burst of red light flooded out of Georgia's chest, momentarily blinding us. I shielded my gaze, peering out to find the light was now emanating from Georgia's eyes and mouth. The light funneled into glowing chains, darting like vines for our wrists. In seconds, each of us was shackled in Georgia's trap.

"Help!" I struggled to break free, but the chains were too strong, searing my skin with their magma-hot touch. Georgia was gaining strength by the minute, the glow spreading from her chest to the very tips of her gnarled fingers. If we didn't stop this soon, the light—her unresolved trauma—wouldn't just strengthen. It would take over her form, her being, for good.

Pot lights flickered overhead, and the ground quaked, causing a nearby trophy case to shudder. The largest trophy fell forward, shattering the glass so it rained onto the ground. Aiko shielded her head from the assault, hands still shackled. I tried to run and help my friend before noticing my feet were restrained too.

"We need to distract Georgia!" Lillian yelled.

"How?" Blair squirmed, chains squeezing her arms to her sides.

We needed to appeal to Georgia's mind. To her reason.

"We can't help you find the tape if you keep us trapped!" I shouted.

"And if you keep fighting us, we can't help you move on!" Aiko persuaded. I wondered if my friend got that from a trusty television show or if she'd caught on to my plan.

"You don't get it, do you?" Georgia barked. The chains clamped harder on my wrists, squeezing into my skin. "A level three spirit doesn't *want* to move on . . . not just because of our trauma but because we want others to feel our pain. To remind them of *their* trauma too!"

I stared down at the shackles. In the red light, scenes played out before my eyes. Grandmama getting sick. Grandmama taking her medicine. Grandmama wiping my tears with a wrinkled finger. Grandmama singing me to sleep. Grandmama's eyes closing, maybe for the last time.

The scene shifted. I saw my friends and I finding the phone for the first time. Our fight at the sleepover. The phone cracking. Our friendship breaking.

Tears blurred my vision, but it didn't matter. All my traumas played on a loop against my eyelids.

And I understood why level threes didn't want to bear the burden of their pain. Why they wanted to share it. Because when Grandmama died, it felt like I had no shoulder to cry on—that *I* had to carry the weight of her loss myself.

But when I spoke to Mama—when she finally opened up to me—I learned none of that was true.

My community, my friends, my family, that was what set me free.

The shackles turned icy cold. With one final yank, the chains shattered to the ground.

I rushed toward my friends. Blair squeezed her eyes hard, scrunched her nose, and broke the chains apart. Lillian followed suit.

Aiko hesitated.

"You can do it, Aiko."

"She can't," Georgia said in an acidic tone. But I could tell she was taken aback by how three of us had already escaped.

Aiko stared down at her chains, hissing as they burned her skin. "I—I can," she choked out. "I have to."

A beat passed as the chains' glow softened. "For my mom," she warbled out. Frost began to creep over the red-hot chains. "For my dad." More frost, faster this time. Finally, she sucked in a deep breath. "And for my friends."

Aiko grunted as her chains completely cooled. With a thrust, she broke free of the chains, and they collapsed like shards of glass.

"See?" I turned to face Georgia. "You don't need to do this. Spreading your pain to others won't stop your own."

Georgia fumed. "Maybe you won't share in my pain," she said, clearly not quelled by our display of friendship, "but I *will* stop you from getting in my way. The supernatural world will revere my son—and the first step is to destroy that tape."

At those words, the television screen above Georgia's head flickered on. Usually it displayed important school events, the weather, and other news, but now static filled the screen. And then—

Words, flickering on and off.

PLAY THE TAPE.

Was this Georgia's doing? No—as she followed our gazes, she appeared just as befuddled as the rest of us.

"But where is it?" I asked.

The static returned before four new words filled the screen.

IN THE CLUBHOUSE.

The words didn't last long before the static resumed.

Everything Lillian taught us about spirits and energy coursed back to me. Spirits could manipulate electricity. Whoever was sending us this message wanted me and my friends to find the tape and see the evidence. But why?

My friends exchanged lost looks. By the time we turned back to Georgia, she was gone.

TWENTY-TWO

Keep Calm and Ghost On, Part Deux

"She escaped!" Blair tore her gaze over the lobby, as if Georgia's glowing shackles might reappear.

My mind raced. A clubhouse, as in a secret meeting place. Hadn't Principal Hanover just mentioned his mother had a secret clubhouse under the bell tower, where everything that fateful day went wrong?

I spun to find Blair, her plaited hair now frizzy from the scuffle. "We have to get to the tape first, before she destroys it."

"This way!" I took off like a shot toward the bell tower, the girls on my heels. Within minutes we skidded to a halt as the tower loomed over us.

Georgia's monstrous form darted around the base of the tower—the clubhouse—and the four of us approached cautiously, wading in like we were entering the maw of a monster.

"*Where is it?*" Georgia's nostrils flared. Incensed, she gathered a beam of red light in her palms and drove it downward. Dirt erupted from the ground like a volcano, and we were each blasted back from the impact. The soil hissed and fizzed beneath us, and the smell of rotten mulch filled the air. I winced as I regained my footing.

"No, no, no!" Georgia panted in agony when all she found were empty holes void of hidden treasures. She dug through them with a feral gleam in her eyes. *"Was that television screen a trick? A ploy to get me back to the place that still haunts me like no ghost ever could?"*

"It was no trick," Aiko declared. "Trust me, I'm no good at technology!"

Georgia growled, plunging back into the dirt just as a strange movement caught my eye. I turned to find ghostly fingers of light beckoning to me, rising higher, higher . . .

To the bell itself.

"Follow," a voice croaked, as faint as a hum. My stomach flip-flopped from the familiarity of it. Could it be . . . ?

There was no time to think. My eyes fell over the cold steel bars and screws holding the tower together. I glanced at the rope attached to the bell, but it was too high up. I needed to climb the bars.

"Aiko, I need a boost."

My friend complied, and I vaulted up to grab the first bar. *This is just like rock climbing in gym class,* I told myself. *Except if I fall now . . .*

No. Georgia wanted us to fall into our fears. I had to climb out of them, quite literally.

One bar, another. I pulled my weight inch by inch until I was close enough to grab the rope. I swung for it with an open hand, narrowly missing and grabbing a fistful of air instead. My muscles screamed as I reset myself to try again. One . . . two . . .

Gotcha.

Rope in hand, I tugged *hard.*

The bell, rusty from disuse, screeched before it pealed. The sound crashed like a wave over our eardrums. I let go and clamped one hand down over my ear, watching as something fell from up high. Blair caught it expertly in her hands.

"I've got the tape!"

Relief washed over me. Back on solid ground, my friends and I performed our signature handshake. We'd done it.

We all turned to Georgia, bracing for her next inevitable attack. But all that power Georgia expended earlier was catching up to her. She appeared hollow, defeated. Heavy chains now circled each of her wrists, pulling her toward the ground. Manacles of her own making.

"Fierce fam, I think we're forgetting something."

Georgia's sunken eyes found mine.

"Tía Paola taught us that we're Guardians. A Guardian is a protector of spirits, a helper of ghosts. Which means it's *our* responsibility not to banish a level three . . . but to save it from itself."

"How?" questioned Lillian.

"By facing the trauma head-on and realizing it doesn't define you, like we all did back in the school. Can you do that, Georgia?"

"My past is too dark to relive." Georgia shook her head. *"It is too late for me."*

"I don't believe that. I think you're more than your past." I turned to my friends. "Isn't she?"

"Yes," Lillian agreed. "She's a fierce and protective mother."

"She'll go to any length to protect the one she loves," Blair added.

"She puts up a heck of a fight," Aiko stated.

Georgia stared down as her ghostly body began to change. Small pinprick holes of light poked out of her spirit form. *"W-what's happening? What are you girls doing?"*

"Don't panic," I told her. "We're here to help."

In a matter of moments, a sparkling light emitted from within her. Georgia thrashed, trying to fight the flares of light, of joy, until she became still. Her warty face smoothed to a supple veneer, and her eyes were now a bright shade of blue. Her fangs retracted until I could see a hint of the smile she wore in that photograph on Principal Hanover's desk. She examined her untaloned hands and touched her face as if for the first time.

"See? It's working. You're overcoming your trauma, bit by bit, by remembering the goodness within you. It's not enough to erase the past, but it's a start."

"But my shackles . . ." Georgia hadn't fully returned to her normal self. If I peered closely, the chains were still tethered to her wrists, her ankles.

I gently grabbed the tape from Blair. "I know just what to do."

The Journalists of Tomorrow booth was up and running in no time. With the projector screen lowered—and some other old-school tech running in the background—it was almost time to execute my plan.

Thankfully, the fire spirits were currently subdued, now that Georgia was no longer commanding them to cause havoc. Instead, she was hovering just paces away from the Fierce Four, gnawing at her lip. Festivalgoers gathered in a packed circle around the booth, and even Mama joined my side.

"Are you sure about this?" Lillian asked me.

I nodded firmly. Whatever spirit had told us to play the tape must have also conjured that ghostly light to help us find it. I had to believe the evidence that was on here would help Georgia somehow.

My finger shook as I hit play.

The film spurred to life. I expected to see the bell tower—the night of the terrible fire—but instead I found three friends in front of City Hall hugging each other with beaming smiles: Avneet, Hanbin, and Georgia. The day they saved the mayor's life. My eyes teared over at the sight of this younger Grandmama and the friends she'd created memories with over many months.

Nearby, although no one but the Fierce Four could see, Georgia's mouth fell open and she absently floated closer to the screen.

"Meet my best friends, Georgia and Hanbin," Grandmama's voice-over began. "When this tape is unearthed, I want everyone to see what amazing people they are. How much we helped each other integrate with society. It isn't easy to cross oceans, but we all did. And that makes us all braver than we know."

Mama began to weep as the tape showed Grandmama cooking for Hanbin and Georgia for the first time. Later, Georgia played with her baby son in a courtyard that I recognized as the one outside Hollows' Peak Middle.

"We made mistakes in our lives," Grandmama's voice continued. "And one day they will come to light. But for now I want to show the world who we truly are. These are the friends I want the world to remember. Love, from 1975."

The tape ended. Both Mama and I were crying now.

"Georgia never needed to find the evidence," I said to my friends, "because there wasn't any." Grandmama was never planning on revealing the truth of that day to the world—instead, she'd offered to show the good side of both her friends, the side she'd gotten to know and cherish during her young life.

Principal Hanover, now awake, hobbled through the crowd. He must have seen the tape because tears glistened in his eyes. His eyes traced from the projector screen to Georgia.

"Mother. It's really you."

"Yes," she said, pulling him aside. My friends and

I followed, drawing away from the crowd. *"I feel . . . different. Better. Those girls helped me find myself again. My true self."*

"But the tape . . . it wasn't from that night?"

"No." Georgia sobbed in relief. *"No, it wasn't. But watching that tape made me remember what I'd long forgotten: that it's our bond, not the phone, that ties us together. Friendship, love . . . I forgot what that felt like."*

"I—I forgot about that too," he hiccuped. "We've been so focused on the phone when we could have been treasuring this time with each other instead. I could've helped you find peace."

"I think I know how to make this right," she said, and then whispered in her son's ear.

The principal nodded. He stepped back toward the crowd with unshakable resolve.

"What you all just witnessed on that tape was my mother, Georgia, and her two friends, long before she passed." The crowd exchanged hushed whispers. "I shared so many wonderful memories with her. My mother buying corn chips from the corner store for our backyard movie nights. My mother carrying me up the stairs when I fell asleep on the couch, even though I was wide-awake—I just liked being in her arms." He laughed softly. "She was the strongest single mother I knew. I wish I was as strong as she was. But maybe the first step to finding that strength is to admit my wrongs."

He steeled himself with a long inhale.

"My mother was part of a terrible atrocity that cost many of you here their lives. While none of you can hear her, I can, in my heart. She apologizes tenfold. And I do too. Because my own greed cost Hollows' Peak Middle their arts budget. Yes, I slashed the funds in hopes of pocketing the money for myself . . . and devised the business competition to feed my own gains." He turned to look back at the Fierce Four. "I even tried to steal a prized object from a group of four brilliantly brave girls, and I hope they'll find it in them to one day forgive me."

Shocked murmurs echoed through the crowd, but no one moved. Even my fierce fam was rapt.

I stepped to the principal's side and spoke in a low voice. "It's not about forgiveness, Principal Hanover. It's about understanding. I know why you wanted to be close to your mother again. You didn't just want to learn about ghosts—you wanted to reconnect with her. But in my time as a Guardian, I've learned the ones we've lost never truly leave us. We can still speak to them, even without a phantom phone to guide the way."

Behind us, Georgia glimmered with light. With hope.

"So, Georgia? What do you say?" I asked.

"I studied the spirit realm for so many years," bemoaned Georgia. *"I consulted books. I spoke to mediums. I did whatever I could to learn more—to DO more. All I wanted was to forget the pain of my wrongdoings and reconnect with my son."* She faced the principal, approaching him and taking his hands into hers. *"I can't believe the trauma I harbored turned me into such*

a foul thing. I can't believe I possessed my own son. I'm so sorry, Hugo."

Her spirit shone brighter, brighter, like every memory, every moment of light and hope and happiness, was there to fill the well of the trauma that had been depleted from her. Her shackles broke apart and dissipated into mist.

"I don't blame you for what you did, Mother. I only hoped we could be reunited once more." I had never seen my principal cry, but as Blair always said, letting it out was better than keeping it in.

"I feel the tug to the afterlife—you four Guardians have freed me from my shackles. I must move on. . . ."

"Is this really farewell, Mother?" sniffled the principal.

"It is time for me to go. Goodbye, my son."

"Goodbye," croaked Principal Hanover tearfully.

And with that, Georgia's spirit floated off into space like a hundred glittering stars, and our once-possessed principal fell to his knees.

Night wrapped me in its cool embrace. I shivered, my breath coming out in puffs, before spotting a police cruiser arrive. A group of officers swept toward Principal Hanover and placed handcuffs over his wrists.

"Thank you, girls," the principal admitted before ducking into the cruiser. "Thank you for helping me speak to my mother one last time."

I watched the back of the cruiser disappear in a

cloud of fog. I was about to turn around when I noticed the fog thickening, separating into words two by two:

THANK YOU . . .

FOR HELPING . . .

MY FRIEND.

The fog swirled, and seconds later the words disappeared. I blinked back tears. Grandmama was the one sending me messages on the screen, telling me to play the tape. Grandmama was the one to lead me to the bell.

Grandmama was with me all along.

"I hope the trial is televised. I love a good courtroom show," Lillian said from my side. "I'm sure the judge will see how sorry he was. He confessed to the town. Now he just has to appeal to a jury."

Principal Hanover *had* committed a crime with the school funds, and it was only fair that he paid for it. But maybe the jury would also see how much had changed after the spirit of his ghostly mother disappeared—what he'd learned by helping her move on.

Mama, who was just paces behind me (as she always was, keeping an eye out), spoke up. "I would say spirits take the cake for oddest discovery of the day, but your principal cutting the arts program to fund his own trips?" My mother *tsked* before lowering herself so that we were at eye level. "I should have known you had the phone I got from Yoon's Antiques all along. I bought it for a reason, you know. My mother once told me stories about a special phone that could connect with spirits. . . ." She chuckled to herself. "I didn't believe her. But with her gone, I thought I'd look for it at Yoon's Antiques and see if it really worked."

My eyes bulged. "So you knew the phone could connect to spirits?"

"I think there's a difference between *knowing* and *believing*," Mama said. "C'mon, Raveena. Let's get you home."

"Wait!" I glanced at the townspeople. Some of them still hosted spirits. "My friends and I have one last job to do."

"I need a stuffed bear for Ella," Blair called out.

In the aftermath of the principal being taken to the *other* kind of doghouse, the Fierce Four got to work. We were currently dividing the possessed townspeople into two assembly lines—one for level ones, the other for level twos—to help the spirits move on to the afterlife. One of Ella's loved ones approached with the level one spirit's bear, and she gratefully floated out of her host's body. Aiko and I aided a group of spirits who were all family members by connecting them with the living descendants who they'd hardly gotten to know.

After a solid thirty minutes—and a lot of *Spirit Service Guardian, here to help you move on*—we were down to our last possessed townsperson. Dahlia Jones.

"Was I possessed?" Dahlia asked after the soul within her parted.

"Well, now you can check that off your bucket list," Iris remarked.

"Sisters, I think this is our last trip to Hollows' Peak for a while. Next mahjong tournament is happening in Rosemary Heights, and I don't care who says no!" Wisteria commanded.

And off the triplets went.

The fire spirits were saved. Despite their unfair and traumatic deaths, they were finally freed from the phone—and ready to rest for eternity in the afterlife. Of all the possessed townspeople, I was most happy to see Mrs. Nkosi return to her true self, placing her chained glasses back on her face and bumbling on about how much the Archive Room needed organizing.

The festival wrapped up, and finally it was time to go home.

"I'm so proud of you," Mama said as we walked to the car. "Helping those poor souls—it's nothing a kid should handle. But you made it look effortless. I think a lot of neighbors will be requiring your service." She winked.

"It's our responsibility. We were chosen," I said, thinking of that fateful *zap*. The moment my fierce fam turned to fierce Guardians.

Mama offered me a warm smile. "You're growing up so fast, hon. Which means I think it's time you got your own cell phone."

"Wait, really? Thank you, thank you!" I wrapped my mom in a steely embrace. When I let go, Mama frowned in confusion.

"Raveena, did you feel that?"

"Feel what?" I asked before the sensation overcame me too—two ghostly arms, wrapping warmly over my shoulders like a fuzzy blanket.

As warm as a heartfelt goodbye.

TWENTY-THREE

A Mother-Daughter Surprise

One Week Later

The school assembly was about to begin. Students brimmed with chatter and excitement. I crossed and uncrossed my legs, fidgeting as I awaited the news.

"And now, what you've all been waiting for," Mrs. Nkosi, our interim principal, announced from the gymnasium stage like a WWE wrestling show host. "I have received confirmation that the arts program has been given a higher budget, and with some emergency government funding, our school will have it up and running by next month!"

"Woo-hoo!" I high-fived my friends. Cheers erupted. I hadn't realized just how much the lack of arts programs at the school was affecting other kids, not just the Fierce Four. Even Mateo's eighth-grade buddy Jaiden clapped before hurriedly crossing his arms like he didn't want to be caught.

I threw my arms around my friends' shoulders. Assemblies were the best because you got to sit with your friends *and* miss class. But Mrs. Nkosi being the principal made things all the better.

"And that's not all!" Mrs. Nkosi beamed beneath her signature glasses. "You might have noticed some vandalism from the festival. Our winning business competitor decided to anonymously donate their funds to help repair the school. The rest of the money will be put into whatever the competitors hoped to receive, whether it was to support the arts program, get new vending machines, or update our jerseys. Now, let's get haunting!"

I loved our new school motto. Mostly because it *totally* fit the Spirit Service vibe.

"And now, for a special performance from two of Hollows' Peak Middle's finest arts students—Lillian Baxter and Raveena Gill!"

Lillian and I made our way to the front of the crowd and behind the curtained stage, where our instruments and music stands were waiting for us. Mrs. Nkosi asked us last week if we could put together a small performance in honor of the arts. I was buzzing with nerves and jitters—but the good kind, the ones that meant we were doing what we loved, and we cared about it more than anyone could know.

This is for you, Grandmama.

Time to perform.

Lillian began with a riveting sax solo before I joined in with my flute, harmonizing with her distinct smooth notes. We played a part of Grandmama's favorite piece, "Canon in D."

As we approached the end of the piece, it was time

for our surprise guest. I glanced backstage to where she was waiting, her bow in hand. She gave me a small wave.

Mama strolled onstage with her violin, moving the bow over the strings with profound confidence. Her skills were second to none and melded beautifully with our wind instruments. It was her idea to join us. To show us, and herself, that music had the power to heal.

Like Georgia's, my grief wasn't gone. But music was one of my sources of happiness, the thing that poked inside me and let out the light for everyone to see.

When we finished, the crowd roared. Wherever Grandmama was now, I was certain she was watching over me.

In the hallway, our classmates gave us tons of applause and compliments like *Nice job, Raveena!* and *Rad performance, Lillian!* Some kids even wanted me to sign their backpacks. It was like being a mini celebrity!

Except we weren't doing this for fame. We were doing it for the passion planted deep within us—and it was finally time for it to blossom.

I crossed paths with Mateo by my locker and gave him a nod. "Pretty cool what you did there, putting your team's winnings toward repairing the school."

"Me?" Mateo made a completely unconvincing *pshhhh* sound. "I have no clue what you're talking about, Gill."

"It's okay, Mateo. I know who you are deep down."

"Y-you do?" Mateo stuttered.

"Yeah," I answered, nonchalant. "A total clown. And a great roller skater."

"Har har. Thanks, though. I still owe you that lesson, don't I?"

I didn't know why that made me blush.

"Yeah, you do owe me," I said.

Mateo swallowed, glancing around. "So you guys actually helped spirits move on using a phantom phone?"

"Yep. I can show you the phone sometime. You know . . . after our lesson."

Now *Mateo* was blushing. "Uhh, Rudy, is that you? Gotta run!"

Mateo ducked his head and escaped. Some things never changed . . . or had they? A warm feeling played hide-and-seek in my stomach. I didn't exactly want to find it—just feel it out. Now that I'd finally dropped my resentment toward him, I had all the time in the world.

After school, I headed to El Grillo and settled down in the shed as Aiko watered the herbs. She wore a new maroon sweatshirt that read, RECOMMEND ME A GHOSTLY PODCAST, PLEASE! Lillian's argyle sweater-vest perfectly matched her forget-me-not blue rain boots. She was currently flipping through the *Guidebook for Guardians* as if we had a pop quiz on it tomorrow.

Blair was trying out a new hairstyle today—a cute crown of braids and a flowy floral dress with thick leggings. She said that fashion was one of her new ways of gaining confidence.

She placed the signature phantom phone out on the table, and everyone stopped what they were doing for another look.

Remember when she said we'd let go of this whole Spirit Service thing when the competition ended? Not happening. We'd all mutually decided to rotate the phone between us. This week Blair was in charge.

Despite knowing the damage the phone caused—to friendships, and even people's lives—we knew we were reversing that damage day by day. Being a Guardian wasn't just something you could walk away from.

Besides, what we'd gone through in the past two months was like a Guardian trial run. It was time to be *real* full-on Guardians now. Paola would be so proud.

"Guess what? We've got *ten* new bookings this month alone! We're crushing it!" Secretary Blair announced. Ever since the town saw how we helped the fire spirits move on, word of mouth spread like wildfire. Everyone wanted a chance to see the phantom phone—and speak to their cherished loved ones.

I was lucky to communicate with Grandmama. Even if saying goodbye to her wasn't the send-off I expected, this whole topsy-turvy journey—with the phone, with my friends—was totally worth it.

Lillian pulled out her notepad and calculator, showing us how much money we would be making. "The numbers don't lie," she agreed. Since the business competition was no more, we all decided to donate any funds we received back to the town. The community center was following suit with the school and starting free cooking lessons for kids. Blair had even started volunteering there on weekends.

"Spirit Service is *booming*," Aiko added heartily. All the girls turned to me expectantly.

Raveena Gill, Lillian Baxter, Blair Ricci, and Aiko Tanaka. We were more than the Fierce Four.

We were a fierce family.

I stood up on my chair, startling my friends.

Lillian leaned forward. "President Raveena has a speech to make!"

"I wanted you all to know how proud I am of you," I said. "And that sometimes I don't feel like I deserve the position of president. But I'm willing to do whatever it takes to make sure this business doesn't get in the way of what's most important: our friendship."

"And helping spirits," Aiko said, but I could tell she was batting back tears.

"Exactly. So, in the spirit of reopening our business to the public, and to our parents for the first time, who wants to do a little ribbon cutting?"

I pulled out my safety scissors and ribbon. The girls excitedly took both ends.

"Cheers to being besties," I said as I snipped the ribbon. I placed the scissors in my backpack before my friends and I put our crossed arms between us for our signature handshake.

"And . . . break!" I said.

"Time to *celebrate!*" Aiko clapped.

"Later," Lillian said, pointing at the shadows crowding outside the shed.

A knock came at our door, and the next client came waltzing through.

"Mr. Yoon?" I gasped. "Mrs. Yoon?"

"We saw what you girls did to help my father's old friend Georgia," Mr. Yoon said, his kind smile returning. I couldn't believe that not too long ago, my friends had been *zapped* and turned into Spirit Guardians in Yoon's Antiques!

"I look forward to returning as your music teacher," Mrs. Yoon said brightly. "Thank you for booking us at the last minute."

"My father told me stories about this phone, but never did I know it could stretch past the limits of my imagination," Mr. Yoon added. "We'd love to contact my father, Hanbin, if possible."

"Of course! Let's see what this mighty phone has in store for us." Aiko rubbed her hands together. Like magic, the phone rang and brightened, bathing us in an ethereal glow.

That never got old.

As one, we picked up the receiver.

"Thank you for calling Spirit Service!" I said, my voice as clear as a bell. "How can we help you move on?"

EPILOGUE

Six Months Later

All was not well in Hollows' Peak Cemetery, and it began with a cool early autumn evening.

Chrysanthemums and daisies grew from the soil, their ivory petals unfurling beneath the stirring thunderclouds. One might even think those flowers were dancing in the drizzle, swaying to the tune of the raindrops.

But upon closer inspection, they would find that the flowers weren't dancing.

They were dying.

Situated in front of the headstone where all things shriveled, broke, and diminished, the petals fell one by one until the ground was barren. Fog rolled past the headstone, finally parting when the full moon appeared overhead, shining a glistening light over the grave.

HERE LIES ELIJAH HOLLOW.

The soil stirred. The ground trembled. Miles away in a girl's home, a book creaked open of its own accord, flipping to a page with a warning one should always heed.

If a passerby listened closely, they could hear a low, rumbling chuckle, partly masked by the crackle of thunder.

A call had been made . . . and it would not go unanswered.

ACKNOWLEDGMENTS

First and foremost, thank you to our family for their unwavering support, including our parents, grandparents, brother, cousins, and our aunts and uncles!

We'd like to thank the Ontario Arts Council and Mississauga Arts Council for generously funding this project.

Thanks to our Spirit Squad: Pete Knapp and Stuti Telidevara at Park & Fine Literary and Media, who supported us in this middle grade endeavour and helped make it a reality; and Dainese Santos, who got these characters and their ~feelings~ from the start! Your excitement for this series has been incredible.

Thank you to the whole Simon & Schuster BFYR team, including everyone in editorial, marketing, sales, and publicity. Thank you to production editor Kimberly Capriola, copyeditor Penina Lopez, and proofreader Elizabeth Mims.

Thank you to Simon & Schuster Canada, including Mackenzie Croft and Cayley Pimentel, for always cheering us on!

Thank you to Liz Parkes for the most amazing cover! You brought all four girls to life in the best way. (Also—RUFFLES!!) Huge thank-you to Sarah Creech for the awesome cover and jacket design.

Thanks to every author who blurbed *Spirit Service*—we're so grateful that you took the time to shine a light on this book.

And last but certainly not least, thanks to our readers, from excited kids to incredibly supportive teachers and librarians. We can't wait for you all to join us on the next Spirit Service adventure.

ABOUT THE AUTHORS

Sarena and Sasha Nanua are twin sisters who love stories about friendship, ghosts, and all things magical. Born during Diwali ten minutes apart, they began writing books together at the age of nine. They are graduates of the English and professional writing programs at the University of Toronto and are also the authors of *Sisters of the Snake* and *Daughters of the Dawn*. You can visit them online at SarenaSashaBooks.com.